Duke of DISGUISE

LADIES *of* WORTH

PHILIPPA JANE KEYWORTH

Copyright © 2024 by Philippa Jane Keyworth

All rights reserved.

The characters and events portrayed in this book are fictitious. Any similarity to real persons, living or dead, is coincidental and not intended by the author.

No part of this book may be reproduced, or stored in a retrieval system, or transmitted in any form or by any means, electronic, mechanical, photocopying, recording, or otherwise, without express written permission of the publisher.

ISBN (eBook): 978-1-7397076-8-2

ISBN (Print): 978-1-7397076-7-5

ALSO BY
PHILIPPA JANE KEYWORTH

LADIES OF WORTH SERIES

Fool Me Twice

A Dangerous Deal

Lord of Worth

Duke of Disguise

REGENCY ROMANCES

The Widow's Redeemer

The Unexpected Earl

MULTI-AUTHOR SERIES

Finding Miss Giles

FANTASY

The Edict

CHAPTER ONE

Paris, France 1776

Avers moved through the candlelight of Madame Pertuis' salon, the warm glow catching on the silver of his suit's embroidery and the diamonds at his throat. Ostentatious rococo mouldings and gilt furniture, designed to awe visitors, did not attract a second glance from him. Conversation hummed throughout the rooms—snippets of French, Italian and English catching his ear.

The Hôtel du Champions and its famous hostess attracted everyone of consequence in Parisian Society. Avers had secured his invitation after barely a week in the French capital thanks to his friend Wakeford. Now he was here, mingling with those who wished to discuss the latest writings of Marie-Emilie Maryon de Montanclos, and of course those who did not come for philosophy at all, but rather to discover the latest *on dit*. For those who held a penchant for neither of these activities, several gaming tables were set up in an adjacent room, many already in use.

"Bonsoir, Your Grace. How fortunate we are to have you with us this evening."

Avers paused before his hostess. She had used his assumed title. Good. His fake identity was working. Leaning back on one leg and allowing the other, with its beautifully clocked stocking, to be displayed to full advantage, he met the gaze of his salonnière.

"Madame Pertuis, I am the fortunate one. I can only beg forgiveness for missing the meal. I was at a game that could not be stopped."

"Ah, the cards," replied the handsome woman, chiding him as she would a child. "All men are the same."

"Alas, so we are, and I thank you for your gracious mercy in allowing me to attend all the later. I had not expected such a warm reception here in Paris." Avers examined the beautifully embroidered cuffs of his sapphire-blue suit. "Clearly news of my exploits in Italy have yet to reach your fine ears."

They had an audience.

A coterie of ladies on a nearby collection of brocade sofas had ceased their discourse in favour of watching the new arrival speaking to their host. Avers could not have hoped for a better opportunity to lay out the part he was to play.

He bowed low over Madame Pertuis' hand and, rather than kissing the air above, dared to lay a brief kiss upon the back of her glove, before rising and allowing the most provoking smile to curve his lips.

"I heard you were a lover, Your Grace," Madame Pertuis said, an answering smile playing about her mouth.

Avers surveyed his hostess, her blue eyes making him realise the talk of Madame Pertuis' beauty was not exaggerated. She had been the rage of Paris in her time.

But he was not here to admire beauty. Nor was he here to be a lover as his hostess termed it. His recent foray into that domain had left its mark and those wounds ran deep. When Wakeford had asked for his help urgently in France, it had been a blessing. Avers had left London and *her* behind.

"But I should warn you," she carried on, the smile still present, "I have a jealous husband."

The women behind them, who had been shamelessly listening in, began to titter at their hostess' words. Avers inclined his head in submission.

"I should not, for a moment, wish to come between you."

"You will join us? Or a drink perhaps?" Madame Pertuis asked, raising a hand to beckon a waiting footman. The golden thread in her dress sparkled as she moved, the brilliance of her dress adding to the radiant candlelight glowing from every surface and fixture in the room.

"A burgundy, please," he answered, directing his gaze towards the footman who bowed and disappeared to procure the drink.

Avers' hostess led him over to a vacant chair within the cluster of women who had been observing them. The few gentlemen present, standing behind the ladies, looked somewhat peeved by his being given primary position.

"May I present His Grace, the Duke of Tremaine—"

"Good evening," Avers said, bowing to each lady in turn as Madame Pertuis spoke their names.

Introductions completed, his hostess inclined her head and told the gathering she must go and check on her other guests. Avers felt all eyes on him as he took his seat. There was a brief pause, and feeling some expectation upon him to lead a conversation, he was just taking a breath to begin when one of the ladies spoke.

"And what brings you to Paris?" The woman had been

introduced as the wife of a much older gentleman standing behind them. She was fair, pretty, and the heart-shaped patch at the corner of her mouth quirked upwards as she smiled coquettishly at Avers.

He readied his well-rehearsed answer and engaged his audience with a sweeping look. And so the falsehoods began.

Emilie Cadeaux feigned interest in the Marquis de Dartois' conversation. The gentleman—in his early thirties and a close friend of her main admirer—had been telling her about the latest salon at the Académie Royale.

In truth, she would rather be at home right now, not at Madame Pertuis' fashionable gathering. The Comte de Vergelles had requested her presence here tonight, and a woman who relied on the admiration and gifts of others did not disobey their wishes. Even if the Comte had yet to appear this evening.

Vergelles had sent his friend on ahead to entertain Emilie, but the poor man did no such thing. Not that she would ever tell the Marquis that. He was always so attentive.

"It was very tall," Dartois said, describing the sculpture he had seen earlier that day, "and wide." He stretched out his arms and one limb came a little too close to the bundle of white wispy hair curled up on Emilie's lap.

The creature unfurled, emitting a growl, and snapped so quickly at Dartois that it nearly got one of his fingers.

"Sacré bleu!" the Marquis exclaimed, snatching his hand away.

"Lutin, no!" Emilie scolded, stifling a laugh.

"Evil little imp!" Dartois nursed his slender fingers as if the small dog really had bitten them. "Why you are wont to keep such a cur as your companion, I shall never understand."

Emilie bristled. Lutin was indeed a cur—a little stray she had found outside the Théâtre des Tuileries begging for scraps as an abandoned puppy. The memory only incensed her further as she considered the person who had dumped the unwanted animal—defenceless—in the centre of Paris.

But she swallowed the feelings down. She had learned to do so many years ago. Men did not like outbursts of emotion from women. They did not know what to do with them and considered them a nuisance, an irritating by-product of an otherwise entertaining object.

She feigned a laugh, tickling Lutin under the chin, causing the little terrier-like dog to gaze up adoringly at his mistress. "Not you, nor Lucien," she said, referring to the Comte de Vergelles. "But this petit monsieur—he is my sweetest comfort and safest confidant, are you not mon petit hérisson?"

"I have yet to meet a hedgehog that bites," Dartois replied waspishly. "Now, where was I?" He launched back into his description of the sculpture and was just regaining his flow when Emilie caught sight of Lucien.

The noble, clad in silver silk, had an effusion of lace at his throat and diamonds twinkling from both there and the buckles on his gleaming shoes. Gliding through the rooms, he gave off some feeling of otherness, moving like a phantom among the living. That's what had so captured Emilie initially. He had seemed to exude some power over others. A power she could not account for, nor understand.

Many female eyes followed Vergelles' progress. Eyes that vied to be those of his future wife. Emilie was not in the running.

The title of wife would not be dangled before her. No. The Comte had offered her a different one, befitting her status as a commoner—that of mistress.

She had not realised what the Comte expected in return for his lavish gifts at the beginning of their acquaintance. He'd spelled it out for her soon enough and she had been on the verge of letting him down gently when her living at the theatre had gone up in smoke. Now, her position was precarious and unless some other security appeared, Emilie would be forced to consider accepting his offer.

But not yet.

"Bonsoir, ma cherie," the Comte murmured as he reached her side.

The French nobleman bowed over her hand, kissing the air above an emerald ring he had gifted her, hoping to speed her choice. Upon rising, his pale eyes ran over her appearance, and one dark brow arched.

"No matching earrings?"

Emilie's fingers tightened involuntarily around Lutin's collar.

"I have a fondness for my pearls." She raised a hand and traced a fingertip over the perfect white gem dangling from her right ear.

They were not the earrings that Lucien had gifted her to match the emerald ring.

"And I think they suit this gown better than the emeralds," she said lightly, as if it were a little thing, and turned away from his unyielding gaze. Readjusting the little red neckerchief on Lutin's neck, she focused on breathing, in and out, in and out. He would give in soon. She had to wait for his initial anger to subside, and then she would throw him one of her disarming smiles and hope that he would not hold it against her.

When she finally looked up at him and smiled, he said nothing. Nor did he return the happy action.

She was fast learning that the Comte had particular requirements when it came to the women he courted for the position of his paramour. Number one among them was obedience.

"Sebastien," Dartois began. "You found him well?"

Emilie thanked the Marquis for distracting the Comte's ire from her. She needed to keep the Comte on her side while she made her decision. If she said yes, she would be given financial security beyond what she ever could have imagined. If she said no... well, he could destroy her in Society.

The Comte had turned from the duo to observe the room. His eyes did not stop scanning as he withdrew a solid silver snuffbox from his pocket and flicked the lid open with his index finger. He proceeded to take a pinch in each nostril before deigning to answer his friend.

"Bien," Vergelles replied, eyes drifting from one female to another around the room. "He has been very busy, our Sebastien. I understand his latest employee has proven a good return on investment already."

Emilie noticed several of the young women blush under the Comte's gaze before hiding their whispers and giggles behind painted fans.

"Positive news," said Dartois, not in the least put off by the Comte's impolite lack of attention. "I expect that return on investment to be passed on to us when the time comes."

Emilie knew better than to join in with this conversation. She half-listened, fingers twiddling Lutin's wispy hair into spikes along his back—her little hedgehog.

"You will tell him I am visiting him soon?"

"I already did," the Comte replied, snapping the snuffbox shut. "Mademoiselle Cadeaux, are you of a mind to game or converse this evening?"

She was of a mind to do neither, but she knew better than to say so.

"Whatever my Lord desires."

A smile crept slowly across the Comte's face, not meeting the pale eyes that contrasted so shockingly with his coal-black brows. Others said he was handsome, but the sharp jaw and aquiline features were ones that Emilie tolerated, not admired. She accepted the Comte's attentions because she understood her place in the world and its inherent precariousness. She did so because she wished to survive.

CHAPTER TWO

Half an hour later, Emilie and the Comte were at play with two others. Loo was the game, one which Emilie knew the Comte did not care for, but he would rather play than join in what he termed, 'the pointless chatter of the would-be philosophers'.

While Madame Pertuis' salons were held to discuss the latest works of the great thinkers of the day, there were plenty whose limited understanding led to uninformed debate, filled with ignorant rantings and self-assured statements that stood on little foundation and large ego. The Comte considered himself above all this. He had no use for chatter about abstract ideas that seemingly had no bearing upon him. Only where philosophy became action did he take note, and that was slow in fermenting in the French populace.

Emilie knew better than the Comte, though she would never say so. Yes, here were the arrogant and the narrow-minded, but there were also those who considered the challenges of the day, or grappled with the preconceived notions Society held. Those discussions, when Emilie heard them, were electric.

Because she was not from the world of these people—the nobility and the elite. She saw parts of Society they were not privy to. The parts that these Societal ideas could shape and affect. But as the Comte's interest began and ended with his own affairs, she was not given the opportunity to listen to those around her. No. Instead, she was here at play with him and two unknown gentlemen.

"You play better than I," said one of the strangers.

Emilie had not seen him before. He was English, and though every now and then she heard him converse a little in passable French, he mainly spoke in his mother tongue. She noted that when she had been introduced to him as the Comte's companion, there had been the slightest hardening of his brown eyes and an almost imperceptible pursing of his lips.

"Merci," was the only reply the Comte offered, laying another card on the table.

Vergelles did not appreciate chit-chat while at play.

"Have you been in Paris long, Your Grace?" the second stranger, one of Emilie's own countrymen, asked.

"Nay—I have arrived only lately. A week on Wednesday. This is my first real venture into Society," replied the Englishman in his deep voice.

He carried a tone of... what was it? Emilie couldn't put her finger on the impression he was giving off. At first she thought it arrogance, that slow way of speaking, the drawl, but she was not sure from his relaxed pose and half-interest in the game. Perhaps he was one of the ton whose laissez-faire attitude was born from an excess of wealth. It would have no effect on the Englishman if he won or lost at the tables tonight.

"And your first engagement is to Madame Pertuis' salon? God must be smiling upon you if you secured an invitation so readily," the French stranger responded.

The Englishman smiled lazily, a note of mocking in his next words. "I am all gratefulness at such a happenstance."

His cavalier attitude grated on Emilie. She found herself taking an instant aversion to the man. Madame Pertuis may occasionally grate on Emilie, but she was a gracious hostess and to mock the fortune of an invitation to her gatherings was insulting.

"As we all are," Emilie said softly, laying a card and not looking up from her hand. Madame Pertuis had always treated Emilie as any other guest in spite of her low birth. She would not allow some upstart Englishman to deride her.

"I believe my name had much to do with it," the Englishman carried on, either feeling no barb in Emilie's carefully spoken words or choosing to ignore them. "It's good to know it still works."

"I was sorry to hear of your father's passing," the Frenchman replied. "The old Duke of Tremaine was a regular in Paris Society in his youth, I understand."

Emilie's heart twinged and she looked across at the Englishman to see any outward shows of grief.

She saw none. The gentleman in question, of medium height and broad shouldered, laying claim to heavily hooded brown eyes and a firm jaw, was dressed in the first stare of fashion. A little less flamboyant than the true dandies of Paris, but the cut of his jacket could not be described as anything less than exceptional, even if the wine colour was more muted than his sartorially daring French counterparts.

"Thank you for your condolences," the Englishman said, "though we were never close. And now I've alienated my uncle as well. I'm afraid I ran through a great deal of money on inheriting, and he's been forced to take the helm to right the ship. Or so he told me in his letter, and bid me, rather forcefully, come to Paris and desist from my wild activities. I'm afraid I'm quite out of sorts with my family."

Emilie managed a few more surreptitious glances at the English Duke without drawing Lucien's attention. He appeared to her completely unaffected by his father's recent death or his family troubles. In fact, she was fairly sure she observed the light of amusement in his eyes.

"I am told I'm ruining the family name. But now I shall be able to write to my uncle and tell him all is not lost." His expression amused—his audience rapt. "For I was invited to Madame Pertuis' salon in under a sennight of my arrival in Paris."

"Yes, but of course," said the Frenchman in complete sincerity.

Clearly Emilie's fellow countryman had not encountered English humour before.

"Your uncle will be pleased to hear it, no doubt?" the Frenchman added politely.

"One cannot expect a paternal figure to be pleased when gaming debts are hanging over them."

The Frenchman halted halfway through laying a card and directed a sharp-eyed gaze at the Duke of Tremaine.

"Oh, nothing to worry about, mon ami. The debts were paid and I've a tolerably deep pocket for now. No. It was the attempted elopement with an Italian beauty that really caused uncle the apoplexy. That and the fighting cocks."

"Fighting... cocks?" The Frenchman's attention on the game was all but lost. His mouth hung a little slack as he eyed the Englishman in bewilderment.

"It is not really the conversation to have in polite company," the Englishman said, not looking at Emilie, but rather gesturing at the other room where the group of ladies he'd been sitting with earlier still sat chattering away.

"Do not stop on my account," Emilie said, one brow raised in challenge at the Duke of Tremaine, before dropping her gaze quickly to her cards again. He may think of her what he wished, but she would challenge him when she could at the very least.

"I have not yet met a woman with a taste for blood sports, but if you insist," said the Duke, warming to his theme, and turning back to his audience of one. "There was a gaming set in Greece which I joined. Established a neat little cock pit just down from the Acropolis and had a good game going. Not the behaviour of a gentleman, according to my uncle, and less than helpful for the fortunes of the Tremaine estate when I had a losing streak." He sighed heavily. "I had to sell off all my birds."

"I am sure they were thankful for their escape," said Emilie, gaze flicking up at the Duke.

He held it a moment, a measuring look in his eyes, and then the lids dropped low again in that lazy way of his and he chuckled.

"I expect they were. Though," he mused, turning back to his cards, Emilie non-existent to him once again, "there was one cock, named Agamemnon—I swear he positively wanted to die."

Emilie drew breath to reply when the Comte cut in.

"Perhaps he too had experienced this dull play?"

The Duke of Tremaine's languid eyes drifted over to Vergelles. He licked his lips, as though he were tasting the acerbic tone of the Comte's words, and smiled affably.

"That could have been it."

Emilie felt the Comte tense beside her. It was unusual for others not to be cowed by his manner. The Englishman appeared to be totally unaffected.

"But the real question," said the Duke, his tone changing, its edge hardening, and a provoking look in his brown eyes, "is whether I have been dull enough to throw off your concentration from the game." He laid his final cards. "My win, I believe."

Emilie's fine brows rose. She glanced quickly over at the

hand lately played. Yes, the Duke of Tremaine had indeed won.

He had hoodwinked them all. The right-hand side of her mouth quirked upwards, and she felt a brief flash of admiration for the gentleman. Then, remembering the man beside her, she risked a glance at the Comte.

The French noble had not moved a muscle. His dark gaze on the Duke was unflinching. Coldness crept out from Emilie's chest and down her limbs. She recognised that look. Vergelles was angry and this self-confident Englishman had no idea who he was provoking.

"A clever plan," Emilie asserted in her most pacifying voice. "You must tell us how you managed to be so charming *and* play so well."

The Comte threw down his cards and rested a hand on her chairback, his fingers hanging down and brushing the top of her shoulder before resting there, the pressure increasing.

"So well," Vergelles echoed. He slid his hand down Emilie's arm, pressing her wrist in a command for her to be silent.

She shut her mouth obediently and leaned back from the table, removing herself from the conversation, and dropping her gaze to her lap.

"Too well for my companion and I—" the Comte began.

"You're not a sore loser, are you?" the Englishman drawled.

Emilie's breathing grew shallow. Her chest tightened. She had seen the Comte lose his temper over less in the past few months.

To her surprise, however, he let out a mirthless laugh.

"A word of advice, my little English lord," he said, his voice so cool, the air seemed to freeze around him. "We French are the creators of Polite Society, and it is your little island that has mimicked us. I suggest you practise some of our famed etiquette if you wish to enjoy your time here in Paris."

"Of course," the Duke said affably, completely unfazed by the Comte's coldness or his harsh set-down. "Until next time?" He held out a casual hand, a lazy smile on his handsome face.

Vergelles hesitated before placing a pale white hand, adorned with jewelled rings, in the Englishman's own.

"Bonsoir," he said, not answering the question and rising from his chair as he did so.

Knowing what was required of her, Emilie rose without bidding and echoed the Comte's farewell.

When they were a little way from the table, she heard Vergelles curse under his breath.

"Imbecile!"

All the tension returned, and Emilie did not breathe easily again until they took their leave of Madame Pertuis' salon and made their way to one of the Comte's regular gambling haunts on the other side of Paris.

Whoever that Englishman was, he was a fool, and he certainly had no idea who he was dealing with. She hoped, for his sake, they did not meet again.

CHAPTER THREE

"You made him mad at you?" asked Wakeford in the breakfast room of the Hôtel du Tremaine the next morning. "Not exactly what I asked you to do."

Until now, Wakeford and Avers had only met briefly since the latter's arrival in France, with Wakeford welcoming the faux Duke of Tremaine to the family Hôtel as any relation would have been obliged to do. Aside from the show they had put on for the servants, there had been little talk of the scheme they were participating in.

"He will not easily forget me," replied Avers, sipping his black coffee and eyeing the unappealing cold beef on his plate.

The chef, an old retainer of the Duke's family, was not what one could call a 'fashionable' French chef currently the rage in London and Paris. In fact, the nomenclature 'chef' was rather a generous one when applied to the Tremaines' servant.

"Because he dislikes you? Hardly the way to persuade him to confide in you."

"And you suppose a friendly Englishman he doesn't know, asking him about his involvement in stealing British government papers, would fare better?"

Wakeford blew his cheeks out and collapsed into one of the Chippendale chairs.

"Curse it man! I have to report to Viscount Stormont in Versailles and write to the Secretary of the Southern Department, Viscount Weymouth, in two days and what am I to say —you won against the man at loo?"

"And angered him—don't forget that part." Avers finished his coffee and placed his empty cup on the table, licking his lips and considering whether to pour another.

"Be serious, man!"

"I am, Robert." Avers' brows lowered, the funning tone in his voice disappeared. "I cannot form a relationship with the man in one evening. I need time."

"Time I do not have. Stormont is furious and my superiors in London are breathing down my neck. Ever since those letters went missing, I've been beside myself. It's not a good look for an envoy of the British ambassador to Paris to have papers stolen from under his nose." He rubbed the back of his neck, lines of worry etched into his forehead. "I swear I'm under surveillance just as much as my offices."

"You are *not* guilty," Avers said firmly.

"You might believe that—having known me since before I was breeched—but those in London have no reason to trust me apart from my word until we capture the perpetrators. Stormont is giving me time to discover who's responsible, but even he can't protect me forever. If I can't prove the leak is coming from elsewhere, I'll be recalled to England. I have a worrying suspicion that if that happens, whether I'm guilty or not, my neck will fit the noose."

Avers watched his friend, the rubbing of his neck now frenzied, and he suddenly understood the unconscious movement.

"It hasn't come to that yet," he said with more gentleness. "I am here now, at your request, and I am at your disposal. Let us start at the beginning. What led you to the Comte de Vergelles as the potential thief in the first place?"

"A man called Mescaux."

The redirection of Wakeford's sober thoughts did the trick. He emerged from his doom-laden imaginings and began firing off the facts.

"He was in the Comte's employ as a footman at the time of his arrest. My men caught him in Montmartre trying to sell copies of papers from my offices. We already knew of the leak when we found some of our information in the hands of the Spanish several weeks before, so we had an ear to the ground, and heard of the meeting through our contacts. Fortunately for us, we were able to have one of our men masquerade as a potential buyer, and Mescaux attempted to sell our own information back to us."

"But shouldn't that be enough?"

"Hardly," Wakeford replied, mouth drawn down in frustration. "The footman cannot be the brains of the operation. That was clear from his questioning. Wouldn't say a word at first. No explanation as to how he got hold of government secrets and why he was trying to sell them. He wouldn't even admit to understanding the particulars of the information, though he must have known their value to try and sell them.

"When we mentioned Vergelles he outright denied any current connection with the Comte. Mescaux said he'd been sacked weeks ago and that the papers had fallen out of a passing carriage when he'd been walking through the city.

"There were more holes in his story than a fine lace handkerchief. Even if he had pointed the finger at the Comte, I would have had trouble convincing my superiors to pursue him on the word of a lackey. Vergelles has powerful friends on both sides of the Channel. His shipping concerns make money for his investors and whether or not they're legitimate, the wealth is enough to keep eyes away from him."

At that moment, a servant appeared to clear Avers' plate. The two men fell silent, each considering his own thoughts. Once the servant was safely out of the room, Avers spoke again.

"But you are certain that it's him?"

"Without a doubt. Vergelles is at the centre. I can feel it in my gut, but I've been having a tough time gathering hard evidence. The normal ways of catching him aren't working. The French say they are finding nothing in their Cabinet Noir —but I suspect the Comte is too well connected for an honest answer from them, even if he is a traitor. It suits them if he is a fly irritating the body of England.

"We have set up our own faux Cabinet Noir in my offices to intercept the Comte's post and copy it out for later analysis before it is delivered to him. I doubt the letters have had less than two people read them before Vergelles sets eyes on them. Perhaps more. But they are filled with nothing of import. Hence my calling you out of desperation. I need someone to befriend the Comte and break into this circle of his."

Avers nodded, his gaze moving from his friend into the middle distance as he considered all that had been said. It was some moments before he spoke again.

"I'm not asking for more time because of any lack of effort or urgency on my part, Robert. I understand the seriousness of your situation. But you have given me the role of your estranged cousin to play, and you must allow me time to play it well if we are to catch the Comte."

Wakeford rubbed a hand over his brow and face, pulling his cheeks down in an unflattering way, and ended contemplatively rubbing his chin. He appeared to have aged a decade since Avers had seen him in London six months ago.

That had been before taking up this role of playing the new Duke of Tremaine, a useful ruse under which they might use the Duke's familial connections in France to infiltrate the Comte's spy ring.

At least, that was the hope.

Six months ago when they had last met in London, the fake Tremaine had been himself—Lord Avers, the third son of the Duke of Mountefield—with few political connections in France, and an obsession with a woman who had since proven herself false. With nothing keeping him in England, when Wakeford's mysterious plea for help arrived, Avers had jumped at the chance to escape to France for a change of scene.

"Dash it all, Avers! I know you're right. It's just a deuced awkward situation when my office is the source of the leak. You've no idea what hot water I'm in."

"I don't doubt it. But if we're to make this work, you'd better keep calling me by your cousin's name. You've no notion how nosy servants can be. Listening at keyholes is a favourite pastime, and given the delicacy of this situation, we cannot be too careful, even in your family's Hôtel. It's exactly how my all-knowing aunt, Lady Goring, gets half of London's gossip before it makes its way into the drawing rooms of Polite Society."

Avers walked over to the sideboard and held a decanter of amber liquid aloft. "Drink? Feels odd raiding another man's liquor—a breach of confidence," he mused, mostly to himself.

"My cousin wouldn't mind—more interested in his classical history books than a decent brandy," Wakeford replied, a glumness now in his tone.

"Hence the extension of his Grand Tour?"

"Yes. It's what drove the late Duke so mad. Couldn't understand the scholar he'd sired. Barely spoke to each other by the end. I don't think my cousin will ever return from those ancient places. He'd be happy living in a tent and dusting antiquities for the rest of his days."

"Convenient for us then—and do we really bear so much of a resemblance to each other, even after all these years?"

All three gentlemen had been at Harrow together. During that time, Avers had frequently been mistaken for Tremaine. Both were of moderate height and well-built, with brown eyes and the aquiline nose so associated with the aristocracy. Moreover, the two men shared those same hooded eyes.

"Yes. Though last time I saw Tremaine he'd grown a beard in veneration of Sophocles."

"I shall not be doing that." Avers ran a hand over his smooth chin. "That's where I draw the line."

"I know it's a madcap scheme," Wakeford said, no longer taking in his friend's words, but following his own worried line of thought. He took the proffered glass from Avers without pause and tossed it off with zeal. "I didn't know what else to do. That's why I sent my man to you with a letter. I knew you, of all my friends, would come quietly to Paris if I asked."

"The offer couldn't have come at a better time," Avers said affably, his tone at odds with his friend's mood.

"How can you be so dashed calm all the time?"

"Practice." Avers retook his chair and took a meditative sip of brandy.

In truth, he hadn't realised how much he'd needed to get out of London until Wakeford's servant had arrived with the letter. The distraction of this scheme was exactly what he needed. With his cousin Sophie lately married, and the complications surrounding her nuptials resolved, all that had been left for Avers in London were unpleasant memories.

He wouldn't have called coming to his friend Wakeford's aid in Paris 'running away' exactly, but the offer of such a diversion had been gratefully received.

Besides, Wakeford was a good friend. They'd grown up

together and the idea that he was at risk of being suspected a traitor would have been laughable if it hadn't been so serious.

"You really do look like Charlie," Wakeford said, eyes widening as they stared wonderingly over at his friend.

Avers came to himself and returned Wakeford's gaze. "Just as well I do in the circumstances."

"I'm afraid my cousin will be rather angry when he finds out the stories we're fabricating about him—as will my father when he hears."

"Yes. Agamemnon was a favourite falsehood of mine."

"Agamemnon!" Wakeford exclaimed, jerked somewhat out of his gloomy attitude.

"Don't concern yourself. The mythical King of Mycenae was just part of a cock fighting story I conjured to explain away some of my notoriety in Greece. The name seemed fitting, considering your cousin's interests."

Wakeford gave an appreciative nod. "I suppose it was his one vice—cock fighting. Clever of you to remember."

"The devil's in the detail," Avers replied.

"Anything else I should know about your meeting with the Comte?"

Avers recounted the whole of his interaction with Vergelles, not leaving anything out, to ensure, hereon, they were singing from the same hymn sheet.

"Do you think they swallowed the story?"

"Largely," Avers said. "The next meeting will tell me more. Have you knowledge of where I might *bump into* the Comte again?"

"Yes—that's the other reason I'm here. The Comte de Vergelles and his cronies meet at the Café Procope almost daily. It should be easy enough to find them there. Hopefully, you can charm the man this time."

Avers nodded, finishing his brandy and setting his glass down. He drew the tips of his fingers together meditatively.

While Wakeford was sure it was the Comte orchestrating the information leak from his offices, Avers was interested in all Vergelles' associates. Even the woman. The dark-haired lady reappeared in Avers' mind—her elfin features, her measuring gaze.

"What do you know about Mademoiselle Cadeaux?"

"The Comte's mistress?" Wakeford asked.

So, Avers had been correct in his assumption at the salon.

"An actress, as I understand it. Not brilliantly well-known. Until she met the Comte, I believe she was up and coming at the Théâtre des Tuileries."

Interesting. A woman who had walked the boards and managed to snare a Comte was no fool. Neither would she be completely in the dark as to her lover's activities. She may prove useful, either as a tap of information, or a weak link through which he might break into Vergelles' circle.

He would try flattery. It wouldn't be a falsehood—Mademoiselle Cadeaux had a prettiness about her—but disconcertingly, he had been unable to read her.

And Avers could usually read everyone. Yes, he would need to keep an eye on her.

"Settling in otherwise?" Wakeford asked, breaking into his line of thought.

"Very well," Avers drawled, a half-smile curving his lips. "I have never been afforded such command as the third son."

"Anything you need?"

"Hmm?" Avers dropped his steepled fingers, his hands hanging casually from the chair arms and a wolfish smile taking over his languid expression. "Yes—I should appreciate a fight with you."

CHAPTER FOUR

The following day Avers strolled towards the Jardin des Tuileries on his way to the Café Procope, with all the appearance of boredom. It would have been far more modish to call a chair, but he wished to clear his mind before he encountered the Comte. There was a role he must play, and he needed to get into the persona of the spendthrift, scapegrace Duke of Tremaine.

He struck out with a diamond hilted ebony cane, courtesy of the Tremaine vault, and a beaver hat set at a rakish angle on his powdered hair. He wore an embroidered suit of puce silk which was at once rich and uncaring thanks to the way he wore it open, his cloak thrown back to expose it.

He regretted the roquelaure. The sun had arrived over Paris after an uncertain start and the heavy cloak was too hot already. Still, he'd taken great care over his appearance today. His valet, the only servant with him from England, had been upset by his master's sudden bent for the gaudy. But Avers had ignored the older man's protestations and scandalised chiding. This costume suited the devil-may-care attitude of the Duke of Tremaine he had constructed.

He meandered through the mix of people on the streets, carriages and chairs passing down the centre of the road, street sellers and hawkers propping up its edges. There were few people of quality walking the thoroughfare, no doubt preferring to be dropped at their destinations, thus avoiding the dirty streets.

There were those of the middling sort passing by Avers, their clothes plainer, and expressions ones of purpose as they strode along. They would not be walking purposelessly through pretty gardens today or sitting aimlessly in cafés. No, they would be in the law courts, the merchants' guilds, moving the mechanisms of economy that allowed the country's nobility to live in leisure off the third estate—the peasants and professionals in French Society.

Still, today was different. Avers did have a purpose beyond amusement and he must focus if he wished to aid Wakeford.

"Eau de vie!" The street seller's cry—let out with sudden shrillness as he passed—caused Avers to jerk in his step and almost stumble into the path of an oncoming carriage.

He shot the hawker an unimpressed frown. The old woman stared expectantly at him from beneath a floppy white cap. Her bird-like features twitched, eyes darting, as she tried to determine whether the gentleman's initial start would give way to a sale.

She jerked a cup of drink towards him, the gesture showering a little of the water and brandy concoction on the knee of her rough woollen dress.

"Eau de vie!" she said again.

Avers suspected, had she not had a basket of jars with identical looking liquid perched precariously on her knees, she might have pressed her sale home by forcing the cup up into his face.

"Non, merci," he replied, touching the handle of his cane to the brim of his hat.

The streets were punctuated with pedlars, either those with stationary stalls like this woman, or water-bearers and kindling sellers going from house to house.

The woman, no doubt unused to being acknowledged, took this as encouragement. "Oui, monsieur. C'est bon eau de vie. It gives life," she said in broken English, clearly identifying Avers' accent.

She removed the tray of jars from her lap and came forward, offering the glass again. Avers stepped back, knocking into a water bearer behind him, causing the man's full buckets to slosh water out from under their lids and soak his stocking.

"Imbécile!" the angry young man cried.

"Pardon," Avers said, righting himself and smiling affably at the cross water bearer who clearly hadn't seen it was a gentleman of quality he was cursing. "For your troubles." Drawing a silver coin from his pocket, Avers dropped it into the man's waistcoat.

"And no more of your distractions," he commanded, turning back to the eau de vie seller and holding up a restraining hand.

The old woman threw her free arm up in the air, exasperated, and then without pause tossed off the now half-cup of eau du vie herself, causing Avers to laugh heartily as he turned on his way.

At the west entrance to the Jardin des Tuileries, Avers took the curving Fer à Cheval path towards the octagonal lake. Maintaining an easy pace as he followed the edge of the Bassin Octogonal, its fountain defying gravity and pattering across the broad waters, he meandered through the mix of people already promenading in the mid-morning sun.

Up ahead, towards the central path, were a series of street performers and sellers. There were more of the quality here. Riders passed by and open-topped carriages displayed their fashionably adorned aristocratic contents for Society to see.

Expensive silks milled about, extravagant millinery stood out in the crowd, and most noticeable of all, the loud, entitled voices of the nobility rang out, as if every passer-by might be interested in what they had to say.

While last night was a time to build his credibility within Society, today he was on the hunt for his prey, and no greetings and niceties were necessary. He picked up the pace a little, making it past swells in the crowd where they gathered around one performer or another. At that moment, Avers heard the sound of a woman arguing, the words cutting through the focus he had on his destination.

The confrontation was in rapid-fire French, and he might have lost attention quickly, had not the voice sounded familiar.

"You are a thief, sir," the woman snapped. "Last week they were half the price."

Avers slowed his pace subconsciously, and began scanning the crowd. He was almost certain he recognised that voice.

"I shall pay you no more than two sous." An indignant little bark punctuated this statement.

"I will not be moved," the truculent seller responded.

Avers caught sight of him. Stout and thunder-faced, he wore breeches, a linen jacket and a faded white shirt, tied with a jaunty red cravat at odds with its wearer's humour. In his hand was a small parcel, wrapped in brown paper and bound with string, and he was using it to gesture ferociously at the woman who accosted him.

A dark-haired woman with elfin features.

"Do not be such a stubborn, vieille chèvre," the woman replied, now in a weary tone, rolling her eyes with the words. "I have no time for your stupidity."

The man did indeed look like an old goat with his bandy legs and grizzled grey beard. The corner of Avers mouth twitched as he halted beside Mademoiselle Cadeaux. The dog growled as he spotted Avers' approach, following his advance with intent little eyes.

"Be quiet you impertinent brute," Avers commanded in an amused voice, reaching out his gloved hand to pull gently at one of the dog's ears.

"Mademoiselle Cadeaux?" he queried as the dark-haired woman's gaze dropped to her dog and saw the sudden adoration in the animal's face at being petted.

The shadow of surprise moved across her features before she turned back, drawing breath, seemingly intent on continuing her battle despite the interruption.

"Trouble?" Avers asked, a lazy smile unfurling on his lips. "The Duke of Tremaine—I believe we met at Madame Pertuis' salon three night's since."

His persistence drew Mademoiselle Cadeaux's eyes back towards him and in them he beheld undisguised suspicion. It was almost a full minute before she replied, and Avers almost felt intimidated. *Almost.*

"Bonjour, Your Grace," she said at last, inclining her head. "You will excuse me." She turned immediately back to the vendor who still held provokingly before her the brown parcel she desired.

"Are you finished being stupid? My Lutin will have his biscuits and you will have no more than two sous!"

"C'est impossible!" cried the man angrily. "The liver alone has doubled in price. I can let you have them for no less than four sous." Putting the parcel back in his cart, he made ready to move off.

At that point, Avers stepped forward. "Allow me," he said gallantly, taking out four copper coins and offering them to the man.

The vendor looked delighted, immediately taking on deferential tones and exchanging the parcel for the money, tugging his forelock at Avers and moving off. Though that was not before one final glare at the woman who had defied him.

Avers turned, holding out the parcel to Mademoiselle Cadeaux, but rather than finding a grateful expression upon the woman's face, she looked incensed.

How interesting.

The little white dog craned his neck from his mistress' embrace, sniffing the air near the parcel, and she instinctively moved her pet away.

"It is no trick," said Avers, gesturing for her to take the parcel.

It was his good fortune to come across the Comte's mistress by chance and be able to engage her so easily. The purchase of the dog biscuits was calculated. She would be forced by politeness to speak to him further. That was if she stopped looking daggers at him.

"I shall not pay you back for this," Mademoiselle Cadeaux said, taking the offered parcel and immediately brandishing it back at Avers.

This action caused the dog to try and leap from her arm to get the package between his teeth and she very nearly dropped the creature. "Lutin, stop it!"

"I wouldn't dream of accepting payment," he said, the calmness of his tone at odds with hers.

She eyed Avers and then said ungenerously, "You were robbed. That man is a thief. The biscuits are only worth half of what you paid."

"To aid a beautiful woman and her beast, I consider the biscuits worth at least four sous," he said smoothly.

He had not expected such a display of raw emotion from a well-practised mistress. And the anger was about spending money which he had no doubt was given her by the Comte. Intriguing.

So, was it not the money she was angry at, but rather his

assumption that she needed his help at all? Most women would be happy having a gentleman rescue them from such a situation. Worse, the compliment he had just paid her had not resulted in a smile.

No, she was frowning at him. If he had been susceptible to feminine beauty at this time in his life, he might have found the petulant, delicate face charming. But he was not. The last year had taught him just how false such charm could be. He was immune. That fact suited his cause, for he intended to gain Mademoiselle Cadeaux's good graces, and use her access to the Comte to smooth his journey into the French noble's confidences. Now, if only he could deal with that frown.

CHAPTER FIVE

The annoying Englishman did not appear to be leaving. Emilie continued to frown at him, and he continued to smile lazily at her, completely unaffected by her expression or her tone.

He was *insufferable*.

Paused as they were, in the midst of a stream of people following the central path through the gardens, Emilie found herself jostled more than once. Lutin began growling in her arms.

"Good day—" she began, determined to leave this interfering Englishman in her wake.

"It's getting rather crowded," the Duke cut in. "Perhaps I may escort you and your canine companion to one of the smaller paths for respite?" He offered her his arm.

Respite? Had she been so transparent in her frustration with the crowds? How vexing. This man had caught her unawares and she was allowing him to read her like a book. Her outburst a few moments ago had already made her feel foolish. Why must men behave as though she constantly needed managing?

Another person jostled her and Lutin barked. She soothed the little dog, cooing in his ear, and then looked back to the Duke of Tremaine's offered arm.

"Very well." If he was not going to leave, she may as well make use of his taller figure. He would be excellent at parting the crowds.

She slipped her hand, still holding the parcel, onto his arm, and to her surprise he took the biscuits from her.

"Allow me to carry them for you," he said, depositing the package in his pocket.

The kind gesture from the self-serving aristocrat surprised her. It would have been insignificant if not for two reasons. Firstly, the Duke had, up until now, appeared as selfish as any other well-born gentleman. Secondly, no one went out of their way to show kindness to a woman of Emilie's station.

They had almost reached the centre of the Jardin des Tuileries when the Duke turned them left. The crowds began to thin. On either side were formal gardens, shrubs and flowers arranged in lines and borders, and ahead a set of shallow steps leading up to an elevated path.

In spite of his small display of kindness, Emilie was formulating an excuse to take her leave of the Duke—with the hard-sought dog biscuits in her possession—when he spoke again.

"Might your brave hound like to stretch his short legs? As delectable as being in your arms must be, I can't help but think the beast should be set free."

Emilie resisted the urge to roll her eyes at his sycophancy and any warming she had felt towards him immediately cooled. "Now we are past that last entertainer, I shall put him down," she said. "Lutin cannot abide monkeys and he has had an altercation with that little black one before."

The Duke looked back to where she indicated. A young dark-haired man was laughing and joking with the crowds, a tiny monkey wearing a striped suit sitting upon his shoulders, pretending to pick fleas out of his hair and throw them at the crowd. Cries of surprise and laughter rang out.

"Ah, a simian tormentor." Tremaine nodded knowingly. "You know best, Mademoiselle."

She was at once pleased that he had deferred to her better judgement and suspicious that his tone was not in the least sincere.

She had received the distinct impression, when they first met, that he disapproved of her. It was to be expected from the more conservative in Society. However commonplace it was for a noble to have a mistress, there were those who disapproved, and she had assumed this Duke was one of them. An irony, considering his penchant for cock fights, elopements and gaming.

Yet here he was flattering her and not leaving her company. What did he want? Did he hope to steal her attentions away from the Comte de Vergelles who he had seen her with before? Or did he just take perverse pleasure in provoking others?

They reached the end of the path and ascended the few steps up onto the gravel walkway that ran along the edge of the Jardin des Tuileries. There were now very few others walking in the same direction. A group of ladies were some fifty yards ahead and another couple strolled a fair way behind. Observing these distances and considering it safe, Emilie removed her hand from the Duke's arm, and bent to place Lutin on the floor, allowing him to wander on his lead and sniff to his heart's content.

"Tell me," the English nobleman said, offering his arm again.

Emilie wished very much she could refuse, but it would be impolite not to take it. She could not quite read the Duke, and she could read people well—but he appeared as a series of contradictions that made her feel uneasy.

"How long have you been in Paris?"

The directness of his question put her on her guard. She said nothing for a few moments and then, as if she had not heard him, asked, "Are you in Paris long, Your Grace?" Was it cruel to hope he said no?

"As long as my uncle deems fit," he replied, amusement in his voice.

"Ah, the cock pit," Emilie said.

Every now and then she paused to let Lutin sniff some patch of ground or a fallen leaf.

"You listened," Tremaine said with mock-gratefulness. "And you—or are you determined to remain a mystery?"

That was unexpected. She had thought him likely to speak at length about himself and his exploits. The speed with which he turned the question back upon her caused her to answer without thinking.

"I was born in Paris."

"Ah, a Parisian through and through."

He had a way of speaking where he elongated words, drawling them out, as though he were bored, not just of the conversation, but of the language itself. It smacked of arrogance.

"I am surprised."

The words were dangled like bait, ready for her to snatch, and to her immense ire she found herself doing just that. "Oh?" At least her tone wasn't inviting.

"I detect a distinct lack of pride in your heritage. That is not normal for a Parisian, n'est pas?"

He was not being put off by her obvious aversion to his enquiries. It was common among the nobility—a complete lack of awareness of others. They cared about only what interested them, what served them. He was just like Lucien.

In the present moment, what interested the Duke was her. She was fast coming to the conclusion he was not interested in taking her attentions from the Comte—she was a plaything to him. A bored petulant English noble looking for a distraction in his imposed exile.

"You know much of the Parisians?" she asked, not giving anything further away. She would keep whatever cards she had close to her chest.

"Only a little. I'd been in Greece and Italy for several years before coming back to Society."

"Ah—Agamemnon," she muttered under her breath.

"Exactement!" the Duke exclaimed "You have a first-rate mind—does the Comte buy you books on ancient history?"

They were approaching a series of promenading parties coming in the opposite direction and she hoped this would disrupt his enquiries. But despite him attracting the attention of several ladies passing by, his gaze did not falter from the path ahead, and he continued the same line of conversation.

"Or perhaps you bargain for books yourself as well as dog biscuits?"

A smile tugged at the corner of her mouth, begging to be set free.

"I shall tell no one if you find the humour of an Englishman amusing. Your secret is safe with me."

Curse him! How was he so observant?

Another party passed them by and within it was a tall, slender lady, quite beautiful, wearing a cornflower-blue dress and matching coat. The woman noticed the Duke, whose height and classical features Emilie had to admit were handsome, and fluttered her eyelashes in his direction.

The Duke paid no attention.

"Along with the secret of disdaining your heritage, of course."

"I don't disdain my heritage," Emilie retorted.

The man did not know of what he spoke. The Duke of Tremaine had no knowledge outside of the shimmering salons of aristocratic Society. He was of the rank whose narrow existence birthed an ennui that could only be challenged by excess. The excesses of gambling and affairs of the heart, both of which she knew him guilty.

If he hadn't so provoked the Comte on their first meeting, Emilie would have expected Vergelles to single out the Duke later on. Tremaine was just the sort of man the Comte usually befriended to encourage business investments from. Fools with money.

"Oh, I have upset you—or was the upset caused by your being saved from that thieving market seller by an Englishman?" Then, with marginally less sarcasm, "I think in actuality, I intruded upon you, took over the situation in a failed attempt at gallantry, and have now forced my unwelcome company upon you with an inordinate number of questions."

"Oui," she said without a second thought.

The bluntness of her reply, which she had not meant to say out loud, caused her to clap a free hand over her mouth.

Now the Duke was laughing. "Candour—now *that* I can respect."

"Pardon!" she said, her barbed tone disappearing completely.

This nobleman was horrifyingly astute with an uncanny ability to read her mind. The only thing which combatted her mortification even a little, was the light of amusement she saw in his eyes when she glanced worriedly at him. Accompanying that gleam was the most disarming smile.

"Forgive me," she repeated in English, "I was just... surprised by you when you interrupted me speaking to the biscuit seller. I am used to my morning trips to the Jardin des Tuileries alone. It is my time with Lutin."

"Ah, say no more." The Duke's tone was gentle. "There is something sacred in the little routines of our lives, no? They provide sanity in an otherwise chaotic world."

The Englishman couldn't have spoken truer words. "That is exactly it," she said.

"In that case, all is forgiven," he said generously. "Before I lost interest in my studies, I once threw a shoe at my cousin when he interrupted me reading."

He recounted the memory in such a serious tone that Emilie did not immediately take in what he had said. When it finally registered, she was overwhelmed with a desire to laugh. She stifled it, an errant squeal escaping.

"Ah," said the Duke knowingly, "That is the way into your good graces, then—violent anecdotes. I shall take note."

"Absolument pas!" Emilie replied severely, stifling a rebellious laugh.

Whatever she thought of this Englishman, he was amusing.

By this time, they had followed the gravel path around the north side of the gardens, and then looped back to approach their starting point.

Lutin stopped sniffing. In fact, he stopped altogether, planting his fluffy bottom on a patch of grass, ears pricked up at his mistress, waiting expectantly. Emilie was not paying attention—thanks to the distracting English Duke—and jerked back when the lead pulled taut.

"Oh, mon dieu—toi petit diable!" she said, rebuking her furry companion, then remembering, she said, "Of course—you want your biscuit."

She turned to the Duke. "Please may I have them? It is another little routine—he always gets a biscuit halfway round the gardens."

"But of course—feed le petit diable." The English noble bowed deeply towards Lutin before rising and retrieving the biscuits from his pocket.

She had to stop herself from laughing. Taking the parcel, she undid the string and drew out one of the canine delights within, requesting her little dog beg for the biscuit before she handed it over.

"Do you often frequent Madame Pertuis' salons with the Comte?"

Emilie straightened—Lutin having wolfed down a whole biscuit by then—and batted her skirts back into submission before touching a hand to her hat to ensure it was still in place.

"Oui."

"She appears a popular lady in Paris," the Duke said. "She told me she has held no less than thirty salons this year alone."

"Mais oui," Emilie said, keeping her voice level despite her dislike of the woman rising to the surface. "Madame Pertuis enjoys being the host." She stopped short of what she really wanted to say.

"So she told me... *several* times."

Emilie glanced up at him to see what expression went with his words. There was the veriest gleam in his brown eyes.

"I have no doubt," she said, an answering curve on her full lips.

Madame Pertuis truly drew out the worst in Emilie. If there was one thing she couldn't stand, it was self-absorption. It was not that she herself proclaimed immunity from such an affliction, it was part of the human condition, but while some tried to curb the trait, Madame Pertuis appeared to nurture it.

"She also told me about her charitable efforts—estimable, indeed."

This time Emilie bit her tongue. She had no wish to be bitter, and the fact Madame Pertuis gave to the poor in order to talk about it did not negate the good her generosity did.

"I have never been so over faced by another's virtues, nor so well-informed about a new acquaintance, in the space of a single evening."

Emilie began to giggle.

"Ah, I see you are no more fool than I, then. I do not

believe I left her establishment with her knowing any more than the name I came with—whilst I can recite her philanthropic endeavours for the past year."

She finally gave into full-blown laughter.

"I am surprised the Comte de Vergelles does not find the same."

The Duke's sudden change in focus did not go unnoticed.

"How long have you and he been going to Madame Pertuis' soirées?"

"I cannot remember," Emilie said, the brief bridge of affability built between them severed by her vagueness.

The Duke either did not notice her sudden frostiness or chose to ignore it.

"And when you are not at the salon—what does Mademoiselle Cadeaux and her master like to do?"

Her master? The blunt description hit Emilie hard.

"Oh, please do not be offended," he said, in reply to her altered expression. "We may be frank—while I do not choose to partake in such activities myself, I understand the arrangement. Being the paid companion of a Comte must have its advantages. There is surely a world of amusement open to you."

He *understood* the arrangement. *Paid companion*. He took no pains to hide the fiscal nature of the situation he assumed was in place. He spoke with such certain cold detachment, and with such obvious distaste, that Emilie felt a sudden rebellious desire not to correct him.

He thought her already mistress to the Comte, not being courted by him for the role, and Tremaine assumed she was brazen enough to discuss it like a business transaction. She wished in that moment she had a thicker skin. She wished that the years of making her way in this difficult world, climbing up from the gutters of Paris to an independent and self-sufficient position, had numbed her to judgement from others. Alas, it had not.

"The theatre—Mademoiselle Saint-Val Cadette's plays," she responded, omitting the correction she could have given in that moment. Let him think what he wanted and judge her accordingly. What did his good opinion matter to her?

Any warmth she had felt towards this man in his amusing moments disintegrated. To the Comte she was an object for his pleasure—to this Duke, a fallen woman.

"Indeed? I have not seen her on the stage yet, but I hear great things."

"Well, you must while you're in Paris," Emilie replied, all serene politeness, the raw emotions he had provoked pushed deep below the surface.

"And where is the Comte today? He does not accompany you to purchase Lutin's biscuits?"

Finally, she saw it. The Duke of Tremaine was not interested in her, who he assumed was a common mistress, a woman who he clearly disdained. No, he was interested in who she was connected to. The Duke was interested in Lucien.

She should have known his seemingly kind and misguided gesture to purchase Lutin's biscuits had an ulterior motive.

"The Comte de Vergelles does not like animals. I believe he is in the Café Procope. I am to meet him shortly, so if you will excuse me, I shall take my leave. Thank you for the biscuits." She placed the remainder of the biscuits in their brown paper in her pocket and drew in Lutin's lead, beckoning the wispy little creature towards her. "Bonjour, Your Grace."

Emilie curtseyed and turned on her heel before he could reply.

CHAPTER SIX

Perhaps he had been too forceful, Avers mused as he watched Mademoiselle Cadeaux walking away. Her purposeful glide brought her petite figure swiftly to a set of shallow steps. With her little white dog trotting faithfully at her side, she descended them onto one of the paths that led to the main thoroughfare, and before long she was lost in the promenaders.

Avers stayed where he was. Unfortunately, he was heading to the same destination as Mademoiselle Cadeaux. He considered whether it was wise to go to the café given that it would appear very much like he was following her, but Wakeford was counting on him, and he needed to get there on time.

He would wait five minutes and then follow. While he waited, he might gather his thoughts, for although his mind was focused on the mission, the unplanned meeting with Mademoiselle Cadeaux had thrown up unexpectedly strong feelings.

She had not been what he had supposed. She had walked with poise, her chin high and her face ever forward, and she had spoken with confidence. Not like the mistresses Avers had come across before. No coquettishness towards him, no pining for her lover, no play-acting the courtesan.

Mademoiselle Cadeaux had even appeared offended when he had acknowledged her position as the Comte's mistress. What an irony—to be offended by the truth—for that is what she was: a mistress. A woman who traded her beauty and company for money and position.

The very idea of it made his stomach clench. She was just like Miss Curshaw— when she had broken his heart. A woman who used her wiles to benefit from a man's fortune. That was the fate of all who married. To be at the mercy of someone who cared nothing for the most valuable object they possessed—their heart.

No.

No, that was not always true. There were exceptions, such as Lord and Lady Worth who had recently married. Theirs had been a meeting of the minds. But that was the exception *not* the rule in Avers' experience.

Despite not knowing Mademoiselle Cadeaux from Eve, she had provoked such visceral emotions in him, that his usual finesse had been overridden. That made him cross, and when he had lost his temper, he had also lost his subtlety and discretion. He had wanted to call her out for what she was choosing to do—to use another for her own gain.

Avers pushed back once more at the bitter feelings and the strong emotions which came again and again like waves crashing over him. He needed to get a hold of himself. But Mademoiselle Cadeaux was like Miss Curshaw. She no doubt schemed for her position, spun falsehoods and promises until she caught the Comte in her web, discarding all lesser prizes.

And that's what Avers was—a lesser prize.

The third son of the Duke of Mountefield, with no hopes of succeeding to the Dukedom or the vast, if beleaguered, estates attached to the title. No, that would all go to William, the eldest son by the Duke's first marriage. Avers enjoyed only a modest income from a small property inherited from his mother—the Duke's second wife—along with the barony he laid claim to from his maternal line.

Yet, all those months ago Avers had been fool enough to believe material things were of no consequence where love was concerned. That love which was earnest and true would weather any difficulty in life and lack of fortune, even the onset of age and the loss of beauty. Wasn't that the hope? The desire?

Drawing himself out of these maudlin reveries he headed after Mademoiselle Cadeaux and towards the Café Procope.

Avers had come to Paris for a distraction—for something to do while his heart healed— and he intended to fulfil his mission.

CHAPTER SEVEN

The Café Procope was on the rue Mazarin south of the Seine. Its dark blue door was propped open, the air not cold enough to ensure it was kept closed, and a sign announcing the establishment swinging above.

Avers nodded to one of the staff upon entering and was immediately enveloped in the smoke of a dozen pipes. The air hung blue and thick with it, the dark richly coloured interiors making it seem hazier. Out of this atmosphere appeared men sat at tables, drinks in hand, conversation flowing freely and animatedly, the place simmering with energy.

Moving to the side as a servant carrying a tray of delicious smelling food came past, Avers scanned the café dwellers to find his quarry. There were young wits speaking out loudly, setting themselves up as the arbiters of their group's discussions, those who railed against the self-appointed originals, and others who sat back to absorb all that was said. Among the youths were those approaching middle age, and the solemn elderly patron. There was the thinker, the politician and the artisan, shoulder-to-shoulder partaking of victuals and philosophy in equal measure.

Avers spied the Comte de Vergelles and the Marquis de Dartois sat at the far end of the establishment with two gentlemen he did not recognise. Several glasses in various states of consumption and a scattering of empty dishes were strewn across the covers as well as a large plate of sweetmeats in the centre.

The incongruity of this scene of grown men—in solemn conversation—eating candied nuts like a group of schoolroom misses, was somewhat amusing. Avers' lips twitched, but he did not let them curve into more than what constituted a haughty smile as he observed the café's patrons.

Striking out towards an empty table only two down from the Comte's party, Avers meandered purposefully close to where they sat, noting that there was no sign of Mademoiselle Cadeaux.

In all fairness, this was a male domain, though mistresses often transgressed those unspoken boundaries. Avers wondered if she'd lied to escape his company. It was just as well. Mademoiselle Cadeaux would have proved a distraction, and he could afford none. He had only just made it to the café in time for their plan.

Just as Avers thought he may have to be the one who hailed the Comte's party, Dartois saluted him with a wine glass and called out, "The victor at the tables!"

Avers did not immediately turn towards the exclamation. He allowed a few seconds, then swivelled slowly, one brow raised in query and that haughty smile still on his lips.

"Good morning to you," Avers drawled, detouring from his route and coming to stand by their table, ebony cane planted as he made them a pretty bow.

Dartois returned the haughty smile of the faux Duke with a self-satisfied one of his own. The Marquis had a relaxed confidence that sat in opposition to the cold frostiness of his companion the Comte.

"And a fair morning at that—I have just spent a delightful time in the Jardin des Tuileries."

If the Comte knew where his mistress had been this morning, and connected that with Avers' words, he did not show it.

"You are in fine spirits—the French air, it agrees with you," said Dartois.

"That, and my newly deepened pockets." Avers risked a wink at the Comte, whose blazing eyes could have struck the strongest man down.

Dartois laughed. "He is a fine one, this English Duke." The Marquis rose and slapped a hand on Avers' shoulder. "I like him."

"More than your friend," Avers said, eyes rolling slowly over to the Comte, and fixing him with a languid stare, a half-smile playing on his lips. "But I must thank you—sincerely—Vergelles, for I stood in great need of blunt. Losing to an English upstart like me is not easy. I am the most uncharitable winner."

"Your self-awareness is at least one virtue," replied the Comte acerbically.

Avers inclined his head in thanks. Silence fell for a few moments, and he wondered if he'd need to force an invitation to join them.

"But not so virtuous in your relations with your family, I hear," said Dartois, a fair brow rising in question, that confident smile ever-present. "First your uncle in England, and now I gather you're warring with your cousin here."

Excellent. The rumour-mill had done its work.

"Family!" Avers sighed, as if that exclamation, along with the hands and eyes he cast up at the ceiling, explained the whole. "Alas, I'm not the Duke they wanted. According to my uncle, I've damaged my estate to the point of ruin, and I've had to leave all my affairs to him to sort out. First it was the travel and then the gambling. I'm on pin money until my uncle says otherwise. I'm looking to be empty pocketed before the month's end."

"Ah, we cannot have that," Dartois said, pulling out a chair and gesturing for him to sit.

Vergelles shifted, staring hard at the newcomer, and not echoing his companion's invitation.

"I fear you may find our conversation boring," the Comte said coldly, "after the exploits you enjoyed in Italy."

"I am sure I can tolerate it." Avers rested his cane against his chair and gestured for the server's attention. "What do you suggest to drink?"

"It depends on your English palate—do you appreciate wine?"

He knew the Comte was goading him, but instead of giving the French noble the response he wanted, Avers smiled lazily at him. "I've been known to drink it."

"He is English, Simeon," the Comte said to the waiter, as if explaining that Avers was some kind of leper. "Something easy for him to drink, n'est pas?"

"Oui, my Lord," the servant replied, bowing twice before scurrying away.

Lucien tapped a finger on a mother-of-pearl snuff box he had placed on the table before him. "We were discussing the state of Paris' water supply," he said after a few moments. "They are building new fountains all over the city to cater for the populace."

"Not the easiest way to water an entire city," Avers said.

His valet had complained about it when drawing his master a bath two nights ago. The water bearers couldn't keep up with demand despite coming and going from the residence most of the day.

But was this *really* the subject of their conversation?

"I hear London has wooden pipes serving the city now," Dartois said. "Right into the houses."

Apparently this dull topic *was* what they were discussing. Avers was doomed to have a conversation about water supplies... and the Marquis had a light in his eyes which implied he was actually interested.

"An ongoing endeavour from my understanding," Avers said.

Perhaps this was the Comte's way of driving him off. Bore him until he gave in and left in pursuit of more interesting company.

"You complain of inefficiency and yet in England you cannot choose the water you drink if it's being sent to you through pipes," said the Comte. "Here in Paris we can instruct water bearers to procure water from the sweetest wells of the city."

Dartois chuckled. "I think we have bored His Grace long enough with the water supplies of Paris."

Surprisingly the Comte heeded his friend and fell silent once again.

"What will Your Grace do while you are here in Paris—are you for the gaming tables or do you plan to embroil yourself in cock fighting again?"

This was the perfect opportunity. "Neither," Avers replied.

At that moment the server arrived with his drink and he paused to take a sip before continuing. "My uncle has arranged a post with my cousin's office that forms a branch of the Southern Department here in Paris."

The Comte was still tapping on his snuff box and the other two men, who had not been introduced, maintained silent observance. This was the moment. The trap was baited, and it was time to see if Avers' prey would take it.

DUKE OF DISGUISE

"The Southern Department?" Dartois said, his tone implying only moderate interest. "Your Crown enjoys their little outposts in our city. We're teeming with ambassadors and dignitaries from England. You'll be one more to add to the throng."

After seeing the Comte playing with his unopened snuff box, Avers drew his own from his pocket and proceeded to take a pinch. "How very disappointing. I rather like to think of myself as an original."

Vergelles stopped tapping and when Avers had finished taking the tobacco, he found himself under a hard stare, almost as if the Comte were annoyed to be copied.

"A cock fighting English Duke in the Southern Department—is that not original enough for you?" the Comte asked, his tone just the wrong side of sharp.

"Lucien is right. It does not seem the kind of work that would suit you at all, Your Grace. Are you expecting to stay long at the Southern Department?" asked Dartois.

Avers shrugged. "Lord knows! I think it shall be exceedingly dull, but it is a condition of my stay in Paris. My uncle believes I need to be occupied—to be shown by my dullard of a cousin how to settle, to take on responsibility, before I can be trusted with the control of my estates. Never had much of a mind to be responsible, you know. It's always seemed much more the thing for other people to do. I'm made for amusement."

"So your cousin is not pleased that you are joining him here?" asked Dartois.

The Marquis was certainly far easier to engage than the Comte, but it was not his trust Avers was here to gain.

"Robert has never been pleased with my presence. He's the studious sort—always has been—can't understand how I lost interest in my studies and fell into more pleasurable

49

pursuits. He always wishes to be occupied in some correspondence, or figures or discussions. I imagine all I shall be to him here is a hindrance. I'm more like to get under his feet than be an aid."

Dartois chuckled. "Yes, I know your cousin to be a serious man."

Avers finished his drink. "I'm surprised you know of him at all—dull dog that he is. I took it he was little in Paris Society."

"Ah." Dartois waved a hand at nothing in particular. "Paris talks."

Avers only wished the Comte would talk.

A moment later, Vergelles broke his silence. "Will your work at the Southern Department keep you in Paris for some time?"

"Devil take it—I hope not! Uncle's allowance is dashed small. Barely enough for a man to live on, let alone game and entertain oneself."

"Tremaine!"

The sharp salute came from the front of the establishment. Wakeford stood there, chest heaving, cheeks flushed. Avers could almost believe his anger was real.

The newcomer strode over to their table, executed a punctilious bow to the rest of the group—begging their pardon—before turning blazing eyes on his faux cousin.

"Charles," he hissed very much above a whisper. "You were supposed to meet me three hours ago."

"Was I?" Avers drawled back, not attempting to lower his voice.

"You know very well you were. I had to hunt you down like some absconded servant."

"How very dramatic of you," Avers said, his voice even, unaffected by his fictional cousin's mood. "You ought to speak to the Comédie-Française to see if they will engage you."

DUKE OF DISGUISE

Wakeford gave an angry scoff at the insulting suggestion.

"If you will be so melodramatic, you can hardly blame me for encouraging you to become an actor. Besides, what's all the fuss about? I would have made it to your offices sooner or later."

"You know very well," said Wakeford through gritted teeth, "that we had arranged ten o'clock, to suit your sensibilities about mornings."

"They are abominable." Avers examined one of his polished fingernails, eyes flicking up provokingly at his faux cousin. "Was it really today we were to meet?"

"You're insufferable!"

"So I've been told. Come now, cousin. Let's talk over there, and leave my friends in peace."

Wakeford kept muttering and hissing, but allowed Avers to guide him to the far side of the café. Ensuring they could still be seen by Vergelles and his companions, but far enough away to be out of earshot, Avers turned a grin upon his friend.

"Excellent timing—and that temper Wakeford—I half-believed you were serious."

"I had only to recall our last tennis match and the dirty way you played."

As Wakeford faced the Comte's table, while Avers sat opposite him, he kept up his furrowed brow and cross expression.

Avers raised his hands in supplication. "There was nothing illegal about my play, except your propensity to move with criminal slowness across the court."

"If I could hit the ball like you—"

"Ah, but therein lies the rub."

Wakeford paused, looked up at the ceiling in faux exasperation and shook his head.

"Are we to be believed?" Avers asked, when his friend's gaze was level with his own again.

"They watch with interest," Wakeford said, looking about the room frustratedly as though he would rather be anywhere than having this conversation with the false Duke of Tremaine. "I think, perhaps, that is enough."

"Good. Then it is time for this argument to end." Avers straightened the cuffs of his jacket, throwing his shoulders back and his chest out.

"Will you come with me now then? Leave them guessing."

"Not at all—I must show myself willing to reject authority. Grow exasperated with me and leave with aplomb."

Wakeford sighed, and this gesture was real. He had never been one for causing a scene. At school, he had been a quiet, studious character, and though he had grown in social graces, he was by no means a lover of public attention.

"This had better work," he muttered, hands now on his hips.

"If it doesn't—though I am confident it shall—then I draw the line at fisticuffs. If it comes to violence against my friends, then I am afraid you will have to find another way into this spy ring."

"I might perform violence against you if you don't stop talking," Wakeford said peevishly. "You're really in your element in this character, aren't you?"

Once again, Avers examined his nails. "It is rather amusing."

Wakeford grimaced, then suddenly throwing his hands up in the air, he spun on his heel and stormed out of the Café Procope.

Avers did not immediately scurry back to his table. Instead, he pulled his snuffbox from his pocket, flicked open the lid with one practised finger, and inhaled a pinch, staring after his vanished cousin, shaking his head. When he had made quite the show of this disconsolate attitude, he snapped the container shut, sighed, and meandered his way back to the

Comte's table, sitting down and placing the gold snuffbox before him.

"I've been admiring your box," Avers said, pointing a long finger at Vergelles' snuffbox, which still rested beneath his tapping finger. "Mother-of-pearl, is it?"

"Oui," said the nobleman, his eyes examining and a faint pucker on his pale brow. "Merci for your compliment."

"And do you blend your own? Can't buy the ready-mixed stuff myself. They never get it right."

"You are very calm considering that little fracas with your cousin," said the Comte, raising a brow and looking meaningfully over at the door of the establishment.

"Oh Robert? He's just in a pucker because it was supposed to be my first day at his offices and I *absconded* as he so crudely put it. But there is always tomorrow, and so I told him, but he did not take it well."

"So we saw," the Comte replied, his tone cold and his top lip curling scornfully.

"Give me an investment with high returns—or a rich noble to fleece at the tables—and I shall be there on time. But some dreary political office where I shuffle papers and have important conversations with important people? No, I thank you. I wish my cousin would keep his grandiose notions of public service to himself, and leave me to my debauchery."

Dartois laughed.

"You will have to go at some point, though?" asked the Comte.

"Oh, yes—I suppose so," Avers replied. "But not today."

"Today we can drink." Dartois raised his glass. "And if we hear of any lucrative investments or nobles to fleece, you shall be the first to know."

A look passed between Vergelles and Dartois that was not lost on Avers, though he could not manage to decipher it.

Just at that moment, a server came to the table, bearing a

pewter tray upon which rested a note. The servant tapped the Comte's elbow nervously, almost moving out of the way, as if in anticipation of being struck, and offered the note as some kind of offering.

The Comte barely acknowledged the individual, taking the note without thanks, and flicked it open, quickly scanning the contents.

"Mademoiselle Cadeaux awaits me outside." He rose and the rest of the table followed suit. Inclining his head to his friends first, he then turned to Avers. "I wish you luck in your future endeavours," he murmured and then, turning sharply, he was gone.

Avers felt an awful sinking feeling at the Comte's words. There was no further invitation of engagement or acquaintance in them. He had a horrible feeling that his aim for today —to establish a rapport with the Comte, even if it was simply one of a transactional nature—had failed. There had been nothing short of asking the noble directly if he were involved in espionage that Avers could have done. The man was a cold fish and perhaps all his and Wakeford's efforts were in vain.

"Don't mind the Comte." Dartois' voice cut through Avers' thoughts. The Frenchman stood beside him, watching after the Comte, and he slapped a hand on Avers' shoulder. "He does not—how do you English say it? *Warm to people.*"

"You mean he don't like me?" Avers put an affected hand to his chest and wore a look of mock affront. "There has never been any accounting for taste. Besides, it's no skin off my nose, he may dislike me as much as he pleases."

Dartois laughed, slapping Avers across the back again.

"I like you, Monsieur le Duc. You have the wit of a Parisian. I am sure we shall meet again."

Avers bowed in acknowledgement of the compliment.

"The Comte is a man of business. If I hear of any dealings that might profit you, I shall let you know." Dartois put his hat on and touched the brim to Avers before bowing and taking his leave shortly after.

The two taciturn men followed and Avers watched them go with the faintest flicker of hope.

Perhaps his ruse would work after all.

CHAPTER EIGHT

The Théâtre des Tuileries was teeming with the best of Parisian Society on Thursday evening when Avers attended to see Mademoiselle Saint-Val Cadette in her latest play. While his interest in the actress had been piqued by Mademoiselle Cadeaux's mention of the famed tragedienne, the performance was not his principal reason for attending tonight.

No, his reason was twofold.

Firstly, he had been summoned by Wakeford who had sent him a missive earlier today begging to meet urgently. The theatre had been deemed the least conspicuous place to meet given that the Tremaine family rented a box there for the season. The feuding cousins might, therefore, quite believably attend by embarrassing coincidence on the same night.

Secondly, Mademoiselle Cadeaux had mentioned that she and the Comte regularly attended Mademoiselle Saint-Val Cadette's plays. Being that this evening was the debut of the actress' latest Greek tragedy, Avers had a fair hope that Vergelles and his companion would be in attendance tonight. Given that his previous attempt to engage the Comte had failed, a casual meeting would be fortuitous, and might afford Avers another opportunity.

Arriving a short time before the play started, Avers was shown by a punctilious little man in an affectatious wig to the Tremaine box, just as the crowds quieted in anticipation of the play beginning.

"I had almost given up on you."

"Apologies," Avers murmured, slipping into the seat beside Wakeford. Already he could hear the strain in his friend's voice. "I thought it best to avoid attention where possible."

The other man didn't respond. Avers noticed a decanter and two glasses, already filled with wine, were jiggling against each other on a side table. After a moment, he traced the cause to Wakeford, who's left leg bobbed up and down furiously. The man's hands were twitching too, clasping, unclasping, resting in his lap, on his leg and then on the arm of his seat.

A crease appeared in the centre of Avers' brow. "You are the bearer of ill tidings, I assume."

Wakeford's frantic movements abated, as if coming back to the present from whatever awful musings had been consuming his mind, and he jerked his head around to give Avers a quick look before turning back to the stage without saying anything.

Below the box, two actors had appeared on the boards. The woman Avers took to be Mademoiselle Saint-Val Cadette. She was a beauty, and with a mournful attitude and tone she began a monologue before a scenery of shipwreck and waves.

As she finished speaking, as if by magic, the sea was rolled away, replaced by newly rising Grecian hills. Avers might have admired the cleverness of this change, from the theatre nicknamed the *Salles des Machines* thanks to its ingenious stage machinery, had not Wakeford's demeanour been one of acute anxiety.

"The blackguards have stolen papers from my offices," his friend rasped in a voice of despair. "They haven't just got to the information and copied it out this time—they've taken the papers themselves. The filthy curs have dropped me well and truly in it. My superiors are threatening to have my head," he added through clenched teeth. "The papers are sensitive in the extreme—military in nature."

Avers' brow rose in shock. He had been at Wakeford's offices that morning to play his part as his reluctant cousin drafted in to work. The place had appeared to be locked up tighter than Newgate prison.

"How did they manage it?" he asked.

Wakeford shrugged despairingly, his profile one of defeat. "I don't know. I simply can't fathom it," he whispered.

Avers asked, searching for a clue in his friend's story, "Anything come through to your black room yet?"

"Nothing—but it didn't last time—the wily dogs. I'm cursed if I know how they're passing information on. No letters that the Comte receives are left unchecked by our men. If we can't retrieve the papers, we suspect they'll try and sell the information to the French—or worse, to our rebels in the Americas."

Wakeford's words fell like a lead weight on Avers' chest. This now went beyond an information leak of petty papers and government missives.

"Do you suppose they're using a cypher?" he asked, resisting the urge to reach out and stop his friend's leg from its incessant ascent and descent.

"I'd easily believe there's a cypher we're not recognising, but I tell you there isn't. I've had my best codebreakers on it. They can find no discernible pattern in any of the correspondence. And the Comte's letters come from no one of any merit, just bills from bootmakers and butchers or the dullest friends and relatives. That's why we're convinced they're finding some other way to communicate. We hear nothing of the secrets leaked from my offices until they turn up in the wrong hands. They're foiling us somehow."

Avers kept his eyes on the play as he listened intently to his friend's rapid words. Wakeford's final sentence dripped with exasperation.

"And this time they have stolen the actual papers from your offices?" Avers said, going back to the beginning of their conversation. There must be something in the story they were missing—something that would enlighten them.

"Exactly that—brazen fellows. We have the place locked up and no one was seen entering or leaving the building at the time. My secretary was due to be out all day at a meeting with Stormont in Versailles, but he came back early. It was him who found my desk broken open and the papers gone."

"And nothing was seen by your men?"

"Nothing."

"And your staff—are they trustworthy?"

"Every man of them."

"Servants?"

"Only my own and they're thoroughly searched before leaving—have been ever since the first incident, much to their consternation."

"And these documents are different from those copied before?"

"Yes—those were just documents about proposed levies."

"And these?"

"They're on General Howe's recommendations for British troop manoeuvres and positionings in the colonies. The French are determined to undermine us there after their losses."

"Worth a lot to the right bidder if battle strategy is involved."

Wakeford shook his head. "Hardly. They'll be out of date

by the time the information makes it across the Atlantic—it's the numbers on personnel and provisions in our forts that are the issue. My office has been asked to look at excise duties, potential losses in the conflict, and how we might squeeze the French and colonists in English markets. If those details get into the wrong hands our forces will be fighting an enemy who can identify where to attack us."

He wrung his hands. "I tell you, Avers, this time my superiors won't be patient. This is the third leak in as many months and by far the most sensitive. I'm finished."

After eyeing Wakeford's jittery movements a moment longer, Avers reached over and placed his hand on his friend's arm, pressing it firmly.

"We'll sort this mess out, Robert—you have my word," he said encouragingly. "I have it in hand. Meeting here tonight was not a random suggestion on my part." He leant forward to better see the individuals he had just caught sight of in another box.

The Comte de Vergelles and his mistress had appeared several boxes over at some point during the first half of the play. Avers wondered if Mademoiselle Cadeaux had intended to be here for the entirety of her favourite actress's play and her master had made her late. No doubt she gave up her power to dictate her hours for his wealth and it was a trade-off agreeable to her.

The candles surrounding their box, placed carefully to illuminate the ornate gilding of the carved balconette, reflected off their golden sconces and cast the couple in an equally warm glow. It was a light in which the jewels on Mademoiselle Cadeaux's neck were set to sparkle. Another benefit of her relationship with the Comte, no doubt.

"The scoundrel!" Wakeford cursed under his breath, half-rising from the chair.

Afraid his friend would do something rash, Avers' hand flew out and grasped his arm in a firm hold.

Arrested mid-movement, Wakeford fell back into his seat with a frustrated thump. "The brass of the man to be swanning about here after such a thing."

"Where else would he be?" asked Avers pragmatically. "Can't exactly announce he won't be attending social engagements due to his stealing of confidential papers to sell."

This blunt justification seemed to bring Wakeford back from the brink of his irrational anger, the man's shoulders relaxing beneath his silk jacket.

"Still deuced enraging."

"I couldn't agree more," Avers responded calmly.

"And you also agree he's the one pulling all the strings of this puppetry?"

"I find him difficult to read. A man who is so concealed in conversation is a deep pool indeed. And there is a hardness about him." Avers paused momentarily, considering the man in his mind. "Vergelles has the means, certainly, so with the facts on hand that you have given me, there is nothing that dissuades me from your opinion that he is in control. And if he is, and the man of business he's been painted as, then he will not pass up the opportunity I have presented him with. It is too tantalising to ignore however much he may detest me."

"His mistress looks beautiful tonight," said Wakeford, following his friend's gaze and offering up the comment out of nervous energy rather than any real appreciation.

"Hmm." Avers had chosen not to fully acknowledge Mademoiselle Cadeaux's charms before now. They were of no import in the current situation, and besides, getting swept away with such things could have painful consequences—not something he desired.

Still, when Avers moved his gaze from the Comte to his

mistress, he had to own that Wakeford had a point. Mademoiselle Cadeaux was dressed in green silk, bows and trimmings running up the open front and around the elbows of her sleeves, and the stomacher artfully adorned with silken flowers as though some woodland nymph had overseen the dressing of her this evening.

This most natural of colours contrasted with the pale smoothness of the skin of her shoulders and neck. She gently wafted a fan over herself to keep the heat of the theatre at bay, and between waves, temporary glimpses of her pale decolletage and the emerald and diamond jewels adorning it were seen. A coil of lightly powdered hair curled around her neck and ended near the jewels she wore. It had been allowed freedom from the high coiffure her hair had been styled in. Avers' gaze moved down a fraction and he saw those dark eyes of hers keenly observing the performers on the stage.

"She has a shabby white dog," Wakeford said. "Some stray from the streets of the city she refused to leave there—always causing a furore at parties and the like, stealing food and running amok."

The little devil was a stray? True, he hadn't looked like the normal lapdog of a lady. The little wire-haired canine had reminded Avers far more of the sort you'd find around a stableyard. Had Mademoiselle Cadeaux really rescued the little creature from the streets of Paris? Something in Avers' chest twinged.

"Not that she's free, mind—everyone in Society knows not to go near her—the Comte's got a devilish temper," said Wakeford. "But while you're here, why don't you try and forget that Curshaw chit? She's taking London by storm with her new husband from what I hear, but that leaves Paris to you." His voice suddenly turned sombre again. "After you've helped me find my papers, of course."

But Avers was no longer listening. He couldn't get past Wakeford's previous words, 'new husband'. He smarted from the sudden pain and found himself short of breath. The term should not have hit him as hard as it did. He'd known Miss Curshaw had wed some time ago. It wasn't a surprise. Yet it struck him like a blow to the gut. For some reason it was even worse that Wakeford had said it so casually. A fact thrown out as if it did not carry with it the ability to wound.

Avers shifted, uncrossing and recrossing his legs deliberately, and rolling his shoulders back. It wasn't as if he wanted the Curshaw girl anymore. When her true character had been revealed for the shallow and materially focused one it was— not to mention the way she had deceived Avers into thinking she really cared—he had found himself entirely put off. Yet, the betrayal did not smart any less. In fact, her total lack of feeling towards him twisted the knife a little further.

He had freely given his heart and received one in return. Or so he thought. Whether he had her heart for a short time, or whether he never had it at all, he would never know. Yet, even if it was illusion alone, believing he had her love meant that when she had so easily taken it away, when all her previous promises were reneged on, when she had shown an entire lack of feeling in response to his wholly deep love, he had broken.

That break had been so deep, so achingly painful, and so silently borne. Recovery did not seem an option. Survival, yes, but what he would be when he healed—*if* he healed—would be far removed from the man he was before.

Avers could not see how he could be the same when promises had been broken and love taken. And while a yearning for companionship existed, it was now tempered with a cynicism which would keep him safe.

Safe and alone.

The two gentlemen remained silent for the rest of the play —Avers lost in his thoughts and Wakeford, he supposed, absorbed by his fears.

Though Avers paid scant attention to what was transpiring on the stage, he could see that Mademoiselle Saint-Val Cadette's fame was justly deserved. She played a tragedienne with so much raw emotion that even he felt moved by her melancholy speeches. He followed it well enough, despite a wandering mind, as he knew the Greek tragedy from school.

As the final scene played out, he caught sight of Mademoiselle Cadeaux rising and leaving the Comte's box.

Avers rose, mind back on the task in hand, and squeezed his friend's shoulder. "I will bid you adieu, Wakeford. My quarry has taken flight."

Before the final lines were uttered on the stage, he disappeared silently out the back of the box, gone to hunt his prey.

CHAPTER NINE

When Avers descended the stairs into the foyer of the theatre, Mademoiselle Cadeaux was nowhere to be found.

It was the only public entrance to the building, and he'd made his way quickly there on leaving Wakeford, yet there was no sign of her. He waited a few minutes, expecting her to appear at any moment, but when she did not, fear rose in his chest. Had he missed her?

Frustration and guilt at failing his friend once again mingled with the fear. He couldn't feign a slow exit any longer without appearing odd. Avoiding the stares of several curious servants, he left the theatre, exiting at the same time as a few older patrons who were leaving early to avoid the crush.

The cool night air hit Avers' cheeks sharply. Whatever clouds had hung over Paris in the day had rolled back to reveal a chorus of bright shining stars and a waning moon.

Lining the streets were various carriages awaiting their owners, and several chairman leaning against their conveyances hoping for patronage when the play let out. Flambeaux lined the road directly outside the theatre doors. By the light of them, the Tremaine driver must have seen him appear, for he whipped up his horses from standing some fifty yards down the road and approached.

Avers walked a little way towards the advancing carriage, leaving the entrance to the theatre behind, the walls of the Tuileries Palace rising up beside him.

"Good evening, Your Grace," the driver said, drawing the horses to a halt and tipping his hat. "I hope the play was enjoyable?"

"Indeed, Hendricks, though I confess—" Avers was intending to offer a falsehood to explain his early departure from the play when movement in the corner of his eye arrested his attention.

The groom, who had leapt down from the back of the Tremaine carriage, was letting down the steps. But rather than ascending them, Avers turned to observe a small door in the impressive facade of the Palace open, and a small figure slip out.

No doubt some stagehand, or perhaps a bit player, was leaving for the night. Avers was just about to turn back to his driver when he recognised the individual leaving the theatre.

Mademoiselle Cadeaux.

Avers froze, praying she would not look his way, and God answered. The Frenchwoman turned in the opposite direction, pulling the hood of her cloak up, and walking with quick steps away from the well-lit theatre.

"I confess," Avers continued, keeping his eyes fixed on the retreating figure of Mademoiselle Cadeaux while he finished addressing his driver, "I feel the need for fresh air and stretching my legs. It's such a clear night, I'll walk back to the Hôtel."

"Are you sure, Your Grace? 'Tis three miles at least and these Parisians are—"

"I'm sure," Avers said before his servant could scaremonger him. "Off home with you."

Wherever Mademoiselle Cadeaux ventured alone, surely Avers would be safe to follow?

Stepping back to allow the groom to fold back up the steps, he nodded briefly to the driver in farewell. "If I'm not home by dawn you may send out a search party."

The driver did not find his master's dry words amusing, muttering something under his breath and shaking his head, but Avers was already turning on his heel and striking out after Mademoiselle Cadeaux.

Though Avers' legs were long and his stride fast, catching up with the woman was surprisingly difficult. For someone so petite, she moved exceedingly quick, and made swift work of the rue de Rivoli.

Glancing back over his shoulder, Avers saw no one else walking in this direction. So she was indeed alone—no companion, no protection.

For a woman to be walking the streets alone at night was unheard of. Where could she be going?

Perhaps she was walking to her own lodgings. But wouldn't she have left the theatre in the Comte's company if so? Or at least called a chair?

Or was her purpose something more sinister? Was Vergelles using her to meet his contact? With so much at stake for Wakeford, Avers had to find out.

At first Mademoiselle Cadeaux followed the main thoroughfare, passing carriages and carts, the life of the city not having ceased with sunset. Not once did she glance sideways. Was she purposefully avoiding attention or were these familiar sights to her?

Avers kept his distance. Fortunately, her rapid steps meant he had no fear of overtaking her. But still, without the distraction of crowds if she looked back she might recognise him.

Thankfully his valet had pressed the heavy roquelaure cloak upon him this evening, expressing his fear that the drop in temperature might otherwise trouble his master. It would do much to obscure Avers' fine clothes and figure should Mademoiselle Cadeaux turn around. And his valet had been right—he usually was about the weather—for the clear night had brought with it a biting breeze and it nipped at Avers' cheeks and gloved hands.

After a quarter of an hour on the same path, his quarry turned south towards the river. Before long the centre of the city revealed itself. The Seine's wide waters stretched out ahead, reflecting the stars above and the lantern lights along its banks. Barges of cargo to feed, clothe and entertain the city dwellers flowed incessantly back and forth along the river even at this time of night, struggling to keep up with the burgeoning metropolis.

Up ahead the small figure of Mademoiselle Cadeaux wove in and out of the few other individuals still on the streets, cloaked head down, avoiding comment or contact.

Avers still had no idea where she was going. Wakeford had told him that the Comte, along with the majority of Polite Society, resided in Faubourg Saint-Germain. That was south of the river—which had appeared to be the direction they were taking—but now she had turned east. She was not going to the Comte's residence, nor her own which Avers supposed would be near her benefactor.

The Pont Neuf rose out of the landscape ahead with its wide arches springing across the waters of the Seine. As they approached, Avers heard the street sellers who had set up shop on either side of the wide bridge's road, trying to get their last few sales of the night before packing up.

Pulling his hat down as low as he could on his brow, and his collar up high above his chin, he hid his face and fine clothes from others. While the diamond in his lace cravat was safely hidden, his shoe buckles were exposed—he only hoped they did not draw attention by catching the light of the lanterns dotted here and there along the path.

The sight of his own kind was now a dim memory. They had disappeared almost as soon as he'd left the theatre and now those that were out were of the middling and lower sort. Avers walked as far from the sellers' booths as he could without entering the middle of the road and risking collision with a carriage.

Gaining the end of the bridge without notice, he stepped onto the Île de la Cité, the ancient island that rose up in the middle of the Seine, and home to Notre-Dame, Louis IX's Saint-Chapelle, the Parlement of Paris and the Conciergerie.

The small island also housed a great deal of the Parisian poor and was no place for a woman to be walking alone at night.

His suspicions heightened. Was she meeting someone? Perhaps about the stolen papers? Why else would she risk her safety in such a fashion if not for some pressing reason?

After only a few moments walking the main street that encircled the north of the island, Mademoiselle Cadeaux turned towards its centre, slipping into a narrow street intersecting the central buildings. Avers followed and all at once the atmosphere changed.

Gone was the grand architecture of the recent century and the cool river air with it. Small, uneven residential dwellings crowded in around him, the clear sky reduced to a small strip overhead, and the smell of humanity living in close quarters rising up.

Only a few lone torches flickered here and there, the darkness creeping in and threatening in its intensity. What light there was cast by the flames came and went. Unreliable. Unnerving.

Underfoot, Avers could feel something slimy, his feet slipping on the uneven cobbles, and the smell became acrid. The only saving grace in this place was the sweet scent of wood smoke, though it warred with the stronger, nastier smells, and never truly won out.

What on earth was Mademoiselle Cadeaux doing in such a place? And if she was involved with the missing papers, was she acting on instructions from the Comte, or on her own accord?

The sound of something crashing nearby made Avers jump. He remembered with regret the duelling pistols he'd left in the Hôtel du Tremaine. That had been a mistake.

When nothing more calamitous happened, Avers put it down to a clumsy housewife. Quiet resumed in the alley and he continued on, wondering if the reason Wakeford hadn't found the man responsible for stealing secrets from his offices, was because he wasn't looking for a man at all.

Up ahead Mademoiselle Cadeaux stopped. Avers ducked into a doorway on the same side of the street, as far away as he could get from the nearest torch, and watched as the woman he'd been following knocked on one of the doors in the warped walls.

After a time, it was opened by someone Avers assumed to be an old man judging by his voice. A moment later a second door opened on the opposite side of the street and Avers heard a woman call out softly. The old man replied in the affirmative.

There was the sound of items being moved around inside the woman's house, then a light filtered into the dark alley, as she reappeared holding an oil lamp. She had a shawl that she held tightly wrapped around thin shoulders and Avers took her to be little more than eighteen. She smiled warmly at her visitor, a tooth missing in the left-hand side of her mouth, and Avers heard her greet Mademoiselle Cadeaux by name.

A quiet conversation in murmured French took place

between the trio and then Mademoiselle Cadeaux handed a small bag to the young woman.

"Merci, merci, you are so kind," she said, tapping her forehead and curtseying several times.

Mademoiselle Cadeaux murmured something in return and then the young woman began walking slowly in Avers' direction.

He pressed himself back against the doorway in which he sheltered, every fibre in his being tense, not even daring to breathe. Just a moment before he thought she would come upon him, she stopped at another door and knocked.

He could see her clearly now, and reckoned her to be even younger than his first assumption, perhaps no more than fifteen.

The door upon which she'd knocked was opened a crack and then, on seeing her, the inhabitant opened it a little wider.

"Bonsoir, Jeanne. Mademoiselle Cadeaux has come as she promised," said the young woman. "She has gifts for us. Magnificent gifts."

The second woman emitted a half-cry of joy and came forward to embrace the first, her voice breaking, speaking so rapidly Avers couldn't follow. Together, they headed back towards Mademoiselle Cadeaux and the elderly gentleman, who still stood talking.

Avers let out a sigh of relief. He'd almost been caught. Now was his chance to slip away, and while he wanted to stay to see what else unfolded, he couldn't risk it. Taking the opportunity, while the four individuals greeted one another, he kept to the wall as he hurried out of the alleyway and onto the main road encircling the Île de la Cité.

As soon as he left the narrow street, the air grew sweeter and the light from the heavens seemed able to penetrate the darkness once again. He walked a little way along the road and then stopped and turned to watch the entrance to the alley.

What had he just witnessed?

That was no meeting to sell secret information. While Mademoiselle Cadeaux's involvement could explain why none of the Comte's correspondence contained incriminating information, because she could be communicating on his behalf, it did not explain this night-time escapade.

Whatever these 'gifts' were that she was handing out, it couldn't be secrets from the British government. Such a thing would mean nothing to these people who were more concerned where their next meal would come from than the running of the country.

Could she be enlisting them for some plot of the Comte's connected with the recently stolen papers?

Avers could not figure out the truth, but what he did know was that this little skirmish had presented more questions than answers. Was Mademoiselle Cadeaux an unwitting pawn of the Comte's? Or was she in fact, the queen herself?

CHAPTER TEN

When Mademoiselle Cadeaux finally emerged from the dark alleyway on the Île de la Cité, Avers was waiting. She made her way south over the river and then turned west before procuring a chair. Avers followed suit, keeping his distance, until Mademoiselle Cadeaux reached Faubourg Saint-Germain and approached one of the hôtels.

It had seemed the gentlemanly thing to do—to see her home. She might have a penchant for wandering alone through the Parisian streets at night and be a suspect in the case of the missing papers, but that was no reason to leave her to the mercies of Paris' vagrants.

Avers wondered if the residence, an older looking hôtel built in the reign of Louis XIV, was one paid for by the Comte or the noble's own. Collaring a link boy who was walking past and offering him a coin, Avers found out it was indeed Vergelles' Hôtel. So, the woman was returning to her master after her night-time excursion. Interesting.

No doubt she had her own apartments too, paid for by the Comte. When Avers had mentioned the financial benefits of her arrangement with the French noble, he had been met with a cool reception. He'd thought the reaction borne from shame, and he brushed off any guilt at causing her discomfort. He had just been pointing out the truth.

Across the way, a servant finally answered the door and let Mademoiselle Cadeaux in. Once she was safely inside, Avers headed for home.

He walked. He needed to think.

Rather than discovering answers on his reconnaissance mission this evening he had found more questions. So, by the time he made it back to the Hôtel du Tremaine he had resolved to return to the Île de la Cité the following day to discover exactly what Mademoiselle Cadeaux had been doing there.

Returning to the narrow streets of the island early the next morning, Avers rapped on the doors of the dwellings Mademoiselle Cadeaux had visited. The first door returned no answer, but the second two revealed bleary-eyed inhabitants who eyed him with suspicion. The woman who had been addressed as Jeanne, and the old man—gave him nothing. Even the bribe of a few coins had no effect on them.

"Non," they said adamantly. "I don't know who this Mademoiselle Cadeaux is."

Apparently they had no recollection of the woman who had met them late last night. They claimed not to know who she was at all. Even when Avers had described Mademoiselle Cadeaux and the specifics of her visit last night, they had refused to identify her.

Finally, he tried the first door again. Just as he was about to turn away, it was answered, and the young woman Mademoiselle Cadeaux had initially spoken to last night appeared.

She was even younger than he had realised last night. No more than fourteen, with bright green eyes and a slender figure. No, he was wrong—she was thin. And now he could see her clearly, he realised as she opened the door and came forward, that she was limping. Her left foot dragged, no movement in it, hence her slow response to his knock.

"Bonjour, mademoiselle." Avers bowed towards her, giving his friendliest smile. "I have come on behalf of Mademoiselle Cadeaux to ensure her gifts were all that was expected last night."

"Mademoiselle Cadeaux!" the young girl breathed in reverential tones. "Oh yes, she has been most generous." The girl's face beamed with joyful innocence. "Both Mademoiselle and the other actresses. She said Mademoiselle Saint-Val Cadette had given her admirers' gifts as well and the lady has many! I will go and get bread this morning for myself and Réne." The young girl pointed over Avers' shoulder and he turned to see the old man who had been mute to him a short while ago, watching him warily from his doorway.

"I am just waiting for my aching to subside and then I will go." She gestured to her lame leg, but to Avers' surprise, continued to grin joyfully.

"An excellent idea," Avers replied, smiling back at her.

Mere yards from this alley the Concierge could be found, dispensing justice and housing royal prisoners. The irony was not lost on Avers. These people had been served a far harsher judgement in life than the political prisoners nearby.

Suddenly, the hurt of his heartbreak, though no less painful, shifted to a different place in his mind and the new perspective made it somewhat more bearable.

"They are very kind ladies," Avers said, pondering on the *admirers' gifts*, and hoping it might provoke a little more explanation. Already though, he was realising the purpose of Mademoiselle Cadeaux's visit here last night was the furthest thing removed from selling secret papers.

"They are, oh, they are," the girl said in the same breathy, awed tones. "Mademoiselle Cadeaux has insisted on coming to us once a sennight to give us the money the actresses receive from their admirers since last December. That is when the grain shortage happened, and we could not affor—"

"Béatrice!"

Avers jumped. The old man had appeared at his elbow.

He spoke in rapid-fire French to the girl and Avers failed to follow. But the result was written in her expression—she suddenly looked at Avers with fear.

"Are you... " She trailed off, then the old man spoke under his breath and Avers caught the title, *Comte*.

Stepping back to show he meant no harm, as the old man and Béatrice huddled together in the doorway, Avers inclined his head saying, "I am *not* the Comte de Vergelles."

The old man still looked suspicious. An interesting reaction.

"You have found me out though," Avers said ruefully to the old man, deciding some version of the truth would be best to try and prevent these people speaking to Mademoiselle Cadeaux of his visit. "I have recently made the acquaintance of Mademoiselle Cadeaux and I find myself... admiring her. When I saw her leave the theatre last night alone I worried and so I followed her here to ensure she was safe. I am afraid that when I did so my curiosity was piqued and so I decided to come back and find out why she had visited."

"Friends," the old man grunted.

Avers paused. Who was the old man talking about—his relationship with the Comte's mistress?

"Mademoiselle Cadeaux has not forgotten us."

Avers looked about himself with fresh eyes and a dawning realisation. Had Mademoiselle Cadeaux once lived here, in this dark and dirty alleyway, on the underbelly of Paris?

"Of course. She is a remarkable woman," Avers said. "And may I also give you a gift?" He reached inside his cloak and withdrew a purse full of coins, holding them out.

The sight of this girl—her bare and dirty home behind her, the worn clothes she wore and the lack of flesh in her cheeks—pulled at Avers' heart. He was rarely confronted with such blatant poverty. Even his servants were better dressed and fed than this old man and girl. What kind of future awaited them?

"Non." The old man put a protective arm around the girl and raised his hand.

"But I may buy flowers with this," Béatrice protested. "Please, Réne."

"Flowers?" Avers queried.

"I sell flowers on the Pont Neuf," said the girl brightly, "but I cannot always afford to buy them. Mademoiselle's gift will pay for bread, Réne, but with this gift, I could go to Les Halles for flowers from Provence."

"Then take it." Avers pushed it into her hands, ignoring Réne's obvious distrust. "I am not the Comte—can you not hear my English accent?" he asked in a tone to provoke amusement.

Béatrice grinned at him, clutching the coin purse to her chest, and even Réne relented a little.

"That man is evil," he muttered.

"Oh?" Avers asked.

"Mademoiselle Cadeaux would do well not to go near him. We hear things. We know to keep away from him."

These ominous words were the last Réne uttered. Despite Avers urging and coaxing him, hoping to find out more, the old man fell silent again.

"Well, I shall take up no more of your time, for you will be wanting to get to your flower market." Avers bowed as low as he would to any Countess or Duchess. "I thank you both for your time."

"No—thank you—and Mademoiselle Cadeaux," the girl said with sudden fervour, taking up Avers' hands to pull him to standing and pressing her fine, bony fingers around his own. "Please tell her how grateful we are."

Avers said nothing. He had no intention of passing on the message, and he could not bring himself to lie. Instead, he smiled at the girl, inclined his head towards Réne, who gave a brief nod back, and turned to leave. He exited the alley and the squalor in which the vast majority of Paris lived and returned to the city of his own kind.

What had he learned? That Mademoiselle Cadeaux had not come here to work on behalf of the Comte. From these people's reactions, it seemed they would have nothing to do with the French noble. She had in fact come for charitable efforts, to a people she had an affinity with because she, like them, had once been living hand-to-mouth in the back streets of the French capital.

Avers felt a strange sort of sheepishness at having intruded on a secret part of this woman's life. He had unwittingly done so and discovered a facet of her character previously hidden. From the secretive way she came to the Île de la Cité, it was not something she wanted advertised—the complete opposite of the bragging Madame Pertuis.

Avers had found out one very important piece of information. Mademoiselle Cadeaux was not who he'd thought she was. Not at all.

CHAPTER ELEVEN

On his return to the Hôtel du Tremaine, Avers found a missive from Wakeford. The men watching the Comte's movements had reported that whilst Vergelles was still at home, his mistress and the Marquis de Dartois were abroad.

Avers considered this information. Mademoiselle Cadeaux and Dartois were not his target and yet... it would surely be auspicious to cross paths with them and further his acquaintance. Yes, he should seek them out, to further his mission to find the missing papers. It had nothing to do with a brand-new desire to understand the woman who was proving an enigma.

Skipping breakfast, much to the Tremaine chef's chagrin, Avers struck out for the Champs-Élysées where his quarries had last been spotted. Perhaps, thought Avers as he tried to forget the distracting image of a dark-haired woman walking through the streets of Paris at night, he could secure an invitation to the Comte's residence from one of them. If the Comte would not confide in Avers willingly, the next best thing would be to gain access to his house and try to find the missing papers himself.

Dartois would likely be pleased to see him and might easily invite him to another social engagement. But he did not reside with the Comte and likely held less sway than the nobleman's mistress. It would be Mademoiselle Cadeaux who would hold the key to the Comte's door, and Avers was fairly sure she did not like him. He needed to overcome her aversion.

Once he reached the main thoroughfare it did not take him long to spot the couple among the throng, thanks to a series of sharp barks and a stream of angry French.

Rather than approach them directly, Avers ascertained where they were heading and found a place along their route where he might intersect them. The spot he chose was beside a street performer dazzling the crowds with acrobatic feats. The short, wiry man had a jolly little face and had already flipped backwards, landing on a box, and raising his arms to rapturous applause.

Avers followed suit and, tucking his cane under his arm, clapped heartily before tossing a few coins into the performer's hat on the floor. He kept his eyes on the acrobat-come-contortionist who was now bending backwards in the most unnatural way, and resisted the urge to look to the right where Mademoiselle Cadeaux and Dartois were standing.

While still bent double, the performer took a coin offered by a young girl, and the crowd laughed and crowed with delight. Avers joined in. Loudly.

"It *is* him." The male voice came from his right.

"Oui, and I am sure he does not wish for his enjoyment to be disturbed."

"Nonsense, Mademoiselle, you are too full of sensibility. We shall greet him and there are no monkeys by this performer who your little devil can try to dispatch."

Avers kept his eyes on the acrobat, concentrating on

keeping his body relaxed as he lounged back on one leg. He laughed again at the antics of the performer.

Dartois hailed him. "Your Grace."

Avers broke off laughing and scanned the crowd, surprised pleasure lighting his eyes as they fell upon the genial looking Dartois, and an aloof looking Mademoiselle Cadeaux.

Aloof—was that the look? He couldn't quite make it out. She had fixed a polite smile onto her countenance, but it held no warmth, and she looked less than inclined to strike up a conversation with the English Duke.

This was not a good start.

"Mademoiselle Cadeaux," Avers said, making a leg and bowing. "Dartois. What a pleasure to see you this fine day. Have you watched this man?" He turned immediately from them and gestured with his cane at the performer. "Never seen the like. I've half a mind to employ him just for entertainment at supper."

It was a good feint. His coming across the pair in the large city of Paris was convenient to say the least. He hoped faking an interest in something other than his object would set them at ease.

"How luck smiles her radiant face upon us to be fortuitous enough to bump into you twice in one week, Your Grace," Dartois said very prettily. "I have half a mind to think it fate."

"Then fate is a kind mistress to me today," Avers replied in a similarly hyperbolic style. "It seems Your Grace gets around Paris at a rate of knots," the Marquis continued. "Was it not you I saw at the Salles des Machines last night?"

Avers tensed. He had not seen Dartois at the theatre, but then again, once he had identified the Comte and his mistress, he'd had eyes for no one else.

"Oh yes, I followed a recommendation from Mademoiselle Cadeaux." Avers inclined his head towards the petite woman. "Unfortunate that the family box was inhabited when I arrived."

He had to reason away his meeting Wakeford and to play on the lie that it was happenstance seemed the only way to go.

"Ah! You have been recommending your theatrical friends to the Duke, then?" Dartois asked Mademoiselle Cadeaux. "A pity you were not there at the end, Mademoiselle, or you could have introduced His Grace to the famed Saint-Val Cadette."

"Oui," she answered, not returning Dartois' gaze, hers remaining fixed on the acrobat. "But I returned home early—the headache."

Avers allowed no change to come over his expression at the falsehood.

"Alas, I also had the headache," he said smoothly. "So I left early, though not before I could see the reason for Saint-Val Cadette's fame."

At this admission Mademoiselle Cadeaux turned to observe him, her dark eyes piercing, the look measuring.

"It's the result of my cousin's sermons," Avers said, pursuing the topic of his headache and using it to further embroider his false lineage. "I shall forever be an errant parishioner in his familial church."

"And where are you off to this morning?" Dartois asked. "Might you venture to the Île de la Cité to see some of our medieval architecture and sate that historical bent you have—or are you on your cousin's business?"

The mention of the Parisian island caused another sharp look from Mademoiselle Cadeaux. It was a coincidence, no doubt, Avers' alter-ego was known for his historical interests.

"A fine suggestion," Avers replied. "I have been told the chapel was one of the wonders of medieval Paris, so I must make time to pay it a visit—I still have some interest in antiquities—but for now I am in search of a spot of gaming. If I do not find something to line my pockets soon, I fear I shall expire from ennui before the week is out."

Was that a wrinkle on Mademoiselle Cadeaux's nose? Excellent. She was back to despising him, and that was better than fearing him discovering her philanthropic endeavours. If he was viewed as a threat, he may attract undue attention. He must appear the lazy, debauched Duke of Tremaine to make his way into the Comte's confidences.

"And you?" Avers replied in an easy drawl. "May I return the interrogation?" One brow rose slowly up in question.

"Nothing that will alleviate your ennui," Mademoiselle Cadeaux said, a little too quickly.

He had hit a nerve then, with the mention of his leaving the theatre early and Dartois speaking of the island in the Seine. She wished to be rid of him.

"Oh, don't mind Mademoiselle Cadeaux—the Comte is busy this morning and she is feeling neglected. I am sure we might entertain you for a little while."

"Don't be ridiculous, Dartois. I have no such feelings."

"And," the Marquis said with emphasis, ignoring her interjection, "her little devil of a dog just bit a monkey for which she was forced to pay the owner three sous." His handsome face broke into a smile, and when she glared back at him, he began to laugh.

"He is not a devil," Mademoiselle Cadeaux snapped. "He did not draw blood. He only wished to play and the owner was entirely too sensitive. His monkey threw a piece of fruit at Lutin. How else would he react but to try and catch it in his mouth?"

"Le petit diable," Avers murmured, crouching down and reaching towards the canine in question.

Dartois chuckled and gave a wry smile. "You risk your limbs."

"No, don't—" Mademoiselle Cadeaux protested.

Avers ignored both, and Lutin, in response to the human offering him succour, trotted merrily forwards and presented his ears to be scratched.

Mademoiselle Cadeaux cursed under her breath. When Avers looked up in response, she pursed her lips, and abruptly turned to face Dartois.

"You see, my Lord," she said. "I told you before, my Lutin is a good Lutin, not a bad one."

"A bad one?" Avers said, ceasing the ear-scratches, to the chagrin of Lutin, and rising to join the humans again. "Surely not—merely spirited."

"Yes, that's—" Mademoiselle Cadeaux broke off when she realised she was agreeing with him, then carried on a little less forcefully. "That's what I keep trying to explain to Dartois, but he will not listen."

"The evil imp can sense that there is room for only one devil in charge and when I am around, it is me," Dartois said, bowing mockingly and then sniffing at the little dog in question.

"A devil, eh?" said Avers.

Dartois shrugged. "So some have said."

He grinned in that disarming way of his and Avers believed him the last man who could ever be compared to such a creature.

"Now, to answer your question, I am instructed to entertain Mademoiselle Cadeaux until the Comte is finished with his business."

"The Comte de Vergelles is a busy man."

"When opportunity arises. And there are opportunities aplenty at present."

Avers was just wondering whether to push his luck and offer an obvious overture, when Dartois spoke again.

"You've mentioned your interest in business opportunities —perhaps the Comte's interests may align with yours. Why don't you come to the Café Procope a week Thursday? I know he'll be meeting with several of his associates then and may have something to tempt you."

"Dartois," Mademoiselle Cadeaux interjected, "I am sure His Grace would rather find a gaming table than a business opportunity while he is here in Paris."

Interesting. Had she really bought into Avers' persona of a wastrel aristocrat, or was she trying to keep him away from her master?

"I'm interested in both," he said, hedging his bets. "Amusement is a necessity, but so is lining one's pockets, and if business is the means, then so be it."

"There, you see? His Grace *is* interested, and he will come a week on Thursday." Dartois took Mademoiselle Cadeaux's hand onto his arm again and began to move off. "Adieu, Your Grace. Until next time."

Avers tipped his hat to the couple. A most productive morning. He had ruled out any connection between Mademoiselle Cadeaux's late night visits to the Île de la Cité and the stolen papers, and been offered a way into the Comte's circle by Dartois.

He was just about to move off when a commotion broke out to his left and he turned to see the wispy-haired Lutin trotting towards him, his red leather lead trailing on the floor behind.

"Lutin, no! You little devil!" Mademoiselle Cadeaux's cry sounded above the crowds that separated her from her pet.

Making a rapid decision, Avers stepped to the right as Lutin ran past him, his foot descending squarely on the trailing lead, and the dog jerked to anABuceremonious stop. His quarry caught, Avers bent down in a leisurely fashion to take up the lead firmly in his hand.

As he did so, the dog made use of the sudden slack, and darted towards his target—a biscuit lying on the floor to the left of Avers' feet where Mademoiselle Cadeaux had lately been standing.

His mistress caught up with him just as Lutin crunched the biscuit and swallowed it nearly whole. "Pardon, Your Grace. I must have dropped the treat by accident. The little terror took his first opportunity to escape."

"Not at all." Avers inclined his head and handed the lead over to her. "I'm glad I could be of assistance."

"It is not the first time you have aided me with my petit diable, and for that I am thankful."

Avers was taken aback by the sincerity in her voice. Was this the same woman who had rebuffed him more than once?

"He does not see, like I do, the dangers all around him," she continued. "It would be the same if you did not realise the world is much bigger and nastier than you first thought. That you might be taken... taken advantage of..."

Mademoiselle Cadeaux trailed off and it was obvious to Avers she was not talking about the mischievous Lutin at all.

She held his gaze rather than avoided it, and Avers realised just how dark and deep those eyes of hers were. A man could get lost in them. He wasn't sure he understood the woman who stood before him at all. He had thought he did—that she was a hard-nosed mistress—but she had travelled alone through dangerous streets to give to the poor and now she was... warning him.

Dartois was approaching behind her and when she saw Avers' gaze flick over her shoulder, she gathered up Lutin's lead and made to leave.

"Bonjour," she said, turning on her heel, and meeting her escort while he was still a way off.

Avers stared after her, only breaking his reverie to return Dartois' wave before the couple went on their way. Mademoiselle Cadeaux's words echoed in his mind,

The world is much bigger and nastier than you first thought. That you might be taken advantage of...

As he dwelt on her words, Avers deduced two things. One was that Mademoiselle Cadeaux had not dropped that biscuit by accident. The other, that she had been warning him.

But of what? And why would she do such a thing?

Her attempt to deter him was in vain. All she had done was confirm that Avers was pursuing the right lead with the Comte. She truly believed he was some gullible nobleman of whom the Comte and his allies might take advantage. And so he would be.

Avers would allow the snare to close in around him until it looked as though they had caught themselves a plump bit of game, and then he and Wakeford would turn the tables, and the Comte would become the prey. The game was afoot.

CHAPTER TWELVE

Emilie was watching Lucien polish the engraved silver barrel of a duelling pistol. She had been sat on the other side of his desk for nearly an hour with hardly a word from the Comte. But she was not here for conversation.

She was required to be here in payment for her walking Lutin that morning. It did not matter that the Comte had been otherwise engaged, only that she had not been ready and waiting for his summons when he sent for her. Her plans, her needs, her desires—they did not figure in Vergelles' mind, let alone his schemes.

As far as he was concerned, he paid for her undivided attention, and she had not given it. Therefore, she would pay the time back now, sitting here with him, responding when spoken to, and aside from that, maintaining silence, watching him attend to his deadly instruments.

She wondered, briefly, if he was doing this activity in front of her on purpose. The guns had looked freshly cleaned and oiled when he'd taken them out of their case. But the way he caressed those pistols, and the heavy stares he threw her way between polishes, were as good as telling her that within his hand resided the power—not hers.

Her mind flitted to Lutin who she'd left at her residence. The Comte did not allow the stray into his Hôtel, and she felt the loss of her petite companion acutely.

"Am I boring you?"

Vergelles' tone had a distinct edge to it and Emilie realised she'd glanced at the door during her ruminations on Lutin.

"Oh, non," she said in her best soothing voice. "I was merely wondering when Dartois would arrive. You are expecting him, are you not?"

She thought she'd done well to cover her slip up, but when she threw Lucien a winning smile, she saw no return on his lips or in his eyes.

He merely stared back at her for half a minute before he resumed polishing his second pistol.

"They are a pretty pair—are they by Le Page?" Emilie asked in the hopes of distracting him.

The Comte ignored her words, continuing his own line of thought. "I have not become bored, though I have waited these last several weeks for your answer—not a trifling half-hour while you polished a pistol."

The barbed words were aimed to draw blood, but Emilie did not flinch. She smiled again, her lips curving up more to the right and her best attempt at a twinkle in her eyes.

"Will you not allow the weaker sex their contrariness?" She reached forward to where his left hand rested on the desk, polishing cloth in his grasp, and traced a single finger over the back of it, pouting her lips. "I am not of strong mind like you, and I wish to be allowed to grow used to the idea of being... only yours."

"You are no one else's."

"Of course not."

Emilie was no one's. No man's. No family's. There was no

one in the world to whom she was a priority. Even to this Comte she was not a priority. She was a prize.

"You would do well to remember it. Your friend Mademoiselle Saint-Val Cadette would be the better for it as well."

Emilie stiffened.

"I thought that would get your attention."

She played for time. "What has the famed actress to do with me?"

"I have it on good authority from Monsieur Claude that she is a close friend of yours. Surely you do not wish for her career to be cut short—just as I ensured yours was?"

An icy wave of shock swept through Emilie's body. She had known her days walking the boards were numbered, and when they had ended abruptly a short time ago, she had accepted her fate.

Now though, she realised the Comte's hand had been in it.

"Perhaps you will consider my offer more seriously now."

Emilie resisted the urge to lunge across the table and strike him.

The idea of becoming any man's mistress repelled her. When the Comte de Vergelles had started showering her with gifts, she had never had any intention of acquiescing to his proposal.

But neither was she foolish enough to spurn the attentions of so powerful a man.

She had thought her delay in agreeing to his offer had gone unnoticed.

She was wrong.

In his impatience he'd engineered her dismissal, removing the stability of her theatre wages and forcing her to rely on his handouts to pay for her apartments and food. Now that he realised that coercion was not proving enough, he was threatening her friends.

What a fool she was.

"Ah, do I interrupt a lovers' tête-à-tête?" Dartois said from the doorway, making a leg and bestowing a dazzling smile on the room's two occupants.

"No," the Comte replied, and Emilie realised how very accurate that answer was.

"Good." Dartois entered the room and moved to the sideboard to pour drinks.

The tension in Emilie's frame increased as the Comte's revelations whirled in her mind.

"Not for Mademoiselle Cadeaux." The Comte raised a hand to stop Dartois pouring a third glass. "She will excuse us while we discuss business."

Inwardly breathing a sigh of relief, Emilie rose at the summary dismissal. "Of course."

"Always a shame to be deprived of your company, fair Mademoiselle. Did you tell Monsieur le Comte of our encounter with our new English friend on the Champs-Élysées?"

Her tension grew unbearable. She had no doubt Vergelles' possessiveness earlier would be exacerbated by news of her encounter with the English Duke.

"I've invited him to the Café Procope on Thursday week, Lucien. I trust you'll be amenable to our enlarged party?"

The Comte ignored Dartois' question, hard eyes darting to Emilie. "He takes an interest in you?"

"Her little scoundrel of a dog does," Dartois answered, seemingly oblivious to the tension rolling off his friend and directed at her. "He has no loyalty, running off to make friends with an Englishman while he tries to maim me—ought I to be offended, Mademoiselle?"

Emilie shrugged, looking as nonchalantly as she could into Dartois' eyes, which gleamed back at her.

"He would be better returning to his own country," hissed the Comte.

And leaving Emilie well alone—that was what he meant.

If the arrogant Duke paid attention to her warnings, she expected the Comte would receive his desire.

"I will leave you gentlemen to your discussions."

"Bien." The Comte's eyes were back on the pistols in his hand and the polishing cloth working across the barrel again.

She curtseyed to Dartois, who dropped a kiss on the back of her hand, and left the room.

As soon as she was in the hall she leant against the wall beside the door, finally feeling able to breathe again. After a moment, she looked around for a footman to fetch her cloak and hat and was about to move to the bell rope when a snatch of conversation caught her attention from the door she'd failed to properly close.

"Tremaine has agreed to attend the Café next week…"

She pressed back tightly against the wall, cocking her head to listen.

"Is his access worth the risk?"

"It isn't just access," Dartois said, his accents far more languid and playful than his counterpart. "His need for capital is a little… too easy—but that does not preclude the errant Duke from being useful to us."

"Useful? The man's a fool."

"Fools have their uses." Dartois yawned loudly, and Emilie wondered exactly what affect this action had on the Comte. She could imagine the look of displeasure.

"Very well."

That was surprising. She hadn't heard the Comte give up so easily before… or ever.

"We can always do with more friends, don't you think?" Dartois asked. "Though, even friends must be tested to find if they are worthy of our trust."

At that moment a door down the hall opened and Emilie almost yelped in surprise. She flattened her back to the wall, narrowly missing a sconce. The servant was carrying a basket of coal, preparing the fires for the evening, and headed across the hall to the drawing room.

Emilie didn't move a muscle.

The servant entered the drawing room and shut the door behind them, unaware that they had been observed.

She thanked God.

Glancing at the study door beside her, she considered her options. Should she quit the Comte's residence now or risk a little longer?

She had warned the Duke of Tremaine off the Comte's acquaintance. She didn't owe him anything more. She hadn't even owed him that. But she had seen the Comte's temper and had heard the rumours that his wealth stemmed from illicit sources. It was not her business. The Comte had made that clear. A woman, for him, was for pleasure. Not brain, nor sense, nor companionship.

So Emilie never asked Lucien about the origin of his wealth. But his fortune was vast enough for him to have risen from the middling ranks of society upwards until he could purchase a title and establish himself in the French ton.

Outwardly he appeared to have taken advantage of the trade between his home country and England, playing the levies of the English government for his gain, but he'd seen far more success than others. It so far exceeded them that questions had been asked and continued to swirl around the Comte de Vergelles.

The last man who'd been foolish enough to mention his lack of breeding had been faced with one of those duelling pistols the Comte had been polishing this afternoon.

The English Duke had no idea who he was dealing with—but Emilie did. She was already tangled in the Comte's web and she did not wish for anyone else to be ensnared. She remained where she was.

"Tell me how you intend to test our new friend," said the Comte, "but first, shut that cursed door, will you? The chit left it open and there's a draft about my ankles."

Cold dread flooded Emilie's chest. She darted across the hall, padding on the balls of her feet, hoping to make it to the drawing room door before she was seen. She could hide in there under the pretence of fetching the servant to get her cloak and hat.

Just before she made it, a prickling sensation ran down her spine, from her hairline to her lower back.

With icy dread, she halted, and turning silently, she saw Dartois standing in the half-open door. His body blocked her from the Comte's sight, and he was watching her with a half-smile on his full mouth and a gleam in his eyes.

"Has she gone home?" asked Dartois, keeping his eyes on hers.

She could swear her heartbeat was audible. Breath came fast and shallow and she wondered if she might faint.

Dartois' mouth curved and then he pouted his lips in a kissing motion at her.

"I neither know nor care," the Comte hissed. "She tires me with her failure to accept my offer. Forget her—tell me your plan for Tremaine."

The Marquis finally drew the door to a close, all the while watching Emilie, clicking it shut and leaving her frozen in her place.

CHAPTER THIRTEEN

During her sedan chair journey home, fear crowded in on Emilie's mind. Not only was she worrying about her friend Mademoiselle Saint-Val Cadette, but she could not shake the unnerving feeling of Dartois' eyes upon her, nor the disquiet caused by his intimate gesture.

The Marquis had looked almost pleased to discover her eavesdropping. He'd stared at her with such intensity she had been unable to look away and his gaze had unsettled her. The blown kiss had not helped the matter. What was the man about? He knew she entertained an offer from the Comte to be his mistress. Didn't Dartois fear Vergelles like everyone else did? Or was it just some meaningless flirtation?

Emilie could not determine the truth.

By the time she met the Marquis again—at a small dinner party held by a business associate of the Comte—the feeling of disquiet was not forgotten, but it had somewhat abated. This was aided by Dartois himself, who could not have told the Comte about her eavesdropping, for she had received no reprimand on her next seeing her benefactor.

Seated next to each other for supper, Emilie thought it

best not to mention the incident, but the Marquis had other ideas. No sooner had the soup been served, and Emilie's conversation with the man on her other side taken a brief respite, then Dartois leaned over to whisper in her ear.

"I knew you to be more inquisitive than the Comte supposes."

"Inquisitive?" Emilie feigned confusion.

"You are like me—always attentive to the circumstances surrounding you, even if you do not participate. It is survival, non?"

Emilie didn't like the direction of Dartois' conversation, nor the way he spoke so closely to her ear. She could feel his breath upon her cheek, filling her nostrils with the rich scent of claret.

"I have been remiss. I should thank you for not mentioning my hesitation in the hallway at my Lord's residence when last I saw you."

Dartois chuckled, leaning back in his chair and taking a bite of bread, chewing slowly as he observed her.

"Even now, you keep your cards so close to your chest I should barely think you hold any at all. But I have spent time with you, Mademoiselle Cadeaux, and I know your mind to be as sharp as the Comte's. Or mine for that matter. You know the value of wit, as I do, and have risen from the gutters of this pestilent city to sit here, in the drawing rooms of Polite Society."

Dartois had never spoken to her like this. The familiarity implied an intimacy she had not sought—and it closed in around her.

"Why do you talk like this, my Lord?" She hoped that being direct might push whatever this was back past the boundaries she had enjoyed with Dartois before. "Have I upset the Comte with my behaviour? Did you tell him after all?"

"No," he said, partaking of his soup slowly, savouring the

liquid and licking his lips after each spoonful. "The Comte has no knowledge of your eavesdropping."

Emilie sighed inwardly with relief but maintained a collected composure.

"He is too easily rattled," Dartois continued. "Those of us who know who we are, and do not fight to be something else —we are the ones who stand firm."

Emilie subconsciously reached for her right arm to where a bruise had once been. She had received it soon after the Comte had made his offer to her. It was when she had assumed behind his proposition was a basic level of affection for her. Feeling secure in that knowledge, and playing the flirt she knew he liked, Emilie had made a joke about the Comte's purchased title.

Even now she could feel his vice-like fingers closing around her arm. The smell of his cologne. His ignoring her cry of pain. The cool way in which he spoke which meant every word was still imprinted on her mind.

"Do you know why I chose you out of all the beauties at my disposal? Not for your wit, nor your conversation, not even for your beauty. It is because you are nothing. You have no connections, no standing in this world except that which others give you. You are nothing without my offer—even the theatre is done with you—and I can send you back to the gutter in which you were born. If you displease me again, I will do it."

Since then Emilie had never once spoken of his past. Neither had the Comte mentioned the punishment he had meted out, nor the threat. But perhaps most disturbingly of all, he had shown no remorse for his actions. He had shown no feeling at all. Now his warning hung over Emilie, an ever-present danger to the life she had built. She had found out exactly where she stood—on a tenuous piece of ground that might give way at any moment and send her plummeting back into nothing.

After that she had not wanted to be near the Comte. She had been playing for time, but that precious commodity was running dry, and her hope of a way out was becoming desperate.

"Have I ever told you, I grew up poor on the outskirts of Paris?"

Dartois' words drew Emilie from her reverie. "No," she replied, traces of surprise in her voice.

The Marquis was as refined as any other aristocrat she came across. There wasn't a trace of accent, or action, that betrayed anything other than noble blood.

"Oh, yes. Title ground into the dirt and not a penny to the family name. You see, I, like you, have pulled myself up from the muck heap to make a way for myself."

Emilie said nothing, nodding to show she was listening and to avoid censure, but all the while thinking how wrong Dartois was.

He was not like her.

Money he may not have had, but title, connections, and the ease of being born a man were all cards he had to play. What had made the Comte's threat to send her back to the gutter so utterly terrifying was that his words were true.

Emilie Cadeaux was *nothing*.

She had been born in a Parisian tavern to a sad mother and an uncaring father. As she'd grown older she'd blamed her mother less for her lack of affection. The woman had been one to whom life had been unkind and a broken thing found it so much harder to love others. At least, that was what Emilie told herself, to ease the pain. When Emilie's father had died, ten years ago now, her mother had left her, unable to care for a child she saw more as a burden than a blessing. She was probably still out there somewhere, eking out an existence as Emilie had done—until Monsieur Claude had found her singing in the tavern one night.

It kept the men from harassing her—singing to them—so she'd done it once several tankards had been sunk to keep them happy and stop them fighting. Monsieur Claude had been visiting and later Emilie learned it was to listen to her. He'd heard of an adolescent girl with a fine voice and a pretty figure. In Emilie, he had recognised an opportunity, and in Monsieur Claude, Emilie had seen a way out.

It was thanks to him she had found her way onto the stage. Initially it had been small parts, but soon her beguiling voice and her beauty had propelled her onto the centre of the boards.

"You, I think," said Dartois, breaking into her memories like an unwelcome visitor, "are like me. You will not allow yourself to be a victim of life. I have watched you, Mademoiselle Cadeaux, and I have admired you."

The hairs on the back of Emilie's neck prickled. First his unnerving gaze and that kiss of the air outside the Comte's study, and now he spoke of admiring her.

"Tell me," Dartois said, "Will you be happy as Vergelles' prize—always to sit quietly and observe—or do you desire something more for yourself?"

"More?" Emilie repeated, wary of answering his question.

Trying to keep the Comte sweet had only pulled her further into his clutches and now it felt as though Dartois was playing his own game.

"Come now, I have already told you I know you have far more wit and far more intelligence than you display. I know your kind—we are kindred spirits—never satisfied with what life has dealt. I can offer you more."

Emilie already had one offer she was desperately trying to get out of—she did not need another.

"And will you tell me, without your riddles, exactly what

you are offering? I am sure the Comte would be most interested."

She would not give in either to Vergelles or Dartois.

Emilie would not allow life to dictate her circumstances, she would not be a victim of fate as her mother had been. She must keep on the right side of the Comte until she could find a way out of this coil, and she must keep Dartois at arm's length.

The Marquis did not immediately answer, chewing his last piece of bread meditatively, and leaning back in his chair, eyes still fast upon her. Emilie did her best to appear calm, slowly sipping her cold soup, and smiling at various persons around the table as she caught their eyes.

"You are not ready yet—I see that now. Disappointing," he said at length, before leaning in to her again. "You need time to consider your options. I will wait. When you are ready, you may come to me and I shall offer you a new opportunity far more interesting, far more lucrative, than the Comte de Vergelles'."

"And what does loyalty to a friend say to the matter? Your relationship with the Comte bears no weight with you?"

"You mean to ask, am I afraid of him?" Dartois smiled, but there was something menacing about the way his lips pulled thin and tight over his teeth, and his eyes narrowed. "No, Mademoiselle Cadeaux, I am not afraid of the Comte. Nor am I friends with him." The cold words were offered in a strangely jovial voice. "He is useful."

"Useful?"

"I have uses for many people. Like the Duke of Tremaine —you heard me speak of it when you stood outside the Comte's study?"

Emilie knew she was standing on a fine line and must navigate it with poise and care, for the Marquis had just allowed her an opportunity to ask the question which had been begging in her mind since that day. "And if I said I did, would you tell me for what use you are entertaining the English Duke?"

Dartois' eyes gleamed and he smiled at her appreciatively. "There, you see. I knew my measure of you was correct. You smell the opportunity, do you not? You seek far more than a mistress' position. But"—he held up a pale hand—"I cannot give away all my secrets at once, Mademoiselle Cadeaux. If you will not give me an answer to my offer, I shall not tell you what I intend for your friend the Duke."

Her friend. He'd enunciated those words, and his eyes were intent upon her face. Something about Dartois' stare, and the way he was speaking, made the hairs rise on the back of Emilie's neck. She sensed danger, even if she could not define it, and it was not clear to her where she could tread safely with her words.

"Very well." She sighed, toying with a fork on the table and looking about as if for better entertainment. "It was only a passing interest. I shall be quite content not knowing."

Emilie wondered if he would argue, but she refused to look at him. She wished to evade this sudden and intense interest of his.

To her relief, Dartois did not battle her. Instead he dropped the matter entirely and transformed back into his normal self—laughing, joking and flirting. The speed with which he did so and the skill with which he closed the doors on those hidden depths of his was disconcerting. As quickly as he had changed from the Comte's loyal and pleasure-seeking friend to a dark and ominous figure, he reversed the transformation.

Emilie did not question it. Taking his lead, she fell back into her role as the young and beautiful retired actress, potential companion to the Comte, Dartois' friend. Except... he wasn't the Comte's friend. Neither was he acting as

Emilie's chaperone on behalf of Vergelles. Dartois was an unknown.

Emilie had thought she had the measure of him months ago. As such she had let her guard down around him—far friendlier towards her than the Comte had ever been—but now it turned out she had been growing close to a snake. One who was venomous and whom she had a feeling could inflict a nasty bite.

Yet Dartois posed her no immediate threat. He was offering her... she hardly knew what... but she was certain it was illicit. It had to be if it was connected to the Comte's business dealings. But while Emilie was at present safe from the Marquis, the same could not be said for the Duke of Tremaine. Dartois and the Comte clearly had designs on the English noble, and after this conversation with the Marquis, she was sure those plans weren't good.

CHAPTER FOURTEEN

Avers watched Vergelles leave his mistress for the lure of chance in the adjacent room. Dartois also disappeared, either to the tables or cornered by Madame Pertuis and forced to listen to her latest philanthropic endeavours. This left Avers free to approach Mademoiselle Cadeaux.

"We are thrown together once again." He bowed to the lady in question.

This salon was focusing on music, and they were currently enjoying a break between violin pieces played by an Austrian master staying in the Pertuis' household.

"The Comte is at the tables if you wish to find him."

"Thank you for your directions—but do you wish to get rid of me as quickly as I have arrived at your side?"

"I assumed," she said without pause, "that you wished for the Comte's company as you regularly do—and not that of his mistress."

Avers frowned, and made a faux pained expression, sucking in air as though he'd been dealt a blow. "I am impaled upon your wit, Mademoiselle. Yet," he lowered his voice, "I could have sworn the last time we met, you were warning me away from acquaintance with your... benefactor."

This was not why he was here this evening. He knew he should go in search of the Comte and continue his mission for Wakeford, but this woman, with her contrariness, attracted him. He could not figure out the puzzle she presented.

"Nonsense," she said, smoothing her skirts with one hand and gently fanning herself against the heat of the room. It was increasing as conversation broke out across the gathering. "Why should I do such a thing?"

Avers realised from her eyes flicking back and forth that she was taking note of who sat near enough to overhear their conversation. That was the action of someone in fear.

Avers lowered his voice further. "Exactly my thoughts. Why would the mistress of the Comte de Vergelles be sending me secret messages."

"What an imagination Your Grace has," she whispered back at him, wafting her fan in his direction as if he were a pesky fly she wished to shoo off.

Her words were firmly spoken, but belied the unease in her dark eyes.

"True—very true—but in this case, I think not."

She glanced at the other guests in the room, across to the walls on all sides with their gilt and paintings, and finally to the door that led through to the gaming rooms. Was she checking on the whereabouts of the Comte? Or was she viewing the walls of her prison?

"I think," he said gently, "that you are a woman of great heart and that your compassion led you to warn me off."

Now he really was off track. He'd side-stepped his mission in favour of walking through this unchartered territory.

To his surprise, Mademoiselle Cadeaux laughed—but the sound was not pleasant. It was forced, and when she turned towards him, there was a hardness in her eyes along with a challenging gleam. "You think you know me so well, Your Grace?"

Apparently not. He'd assumed reaching out with genuine care might garner trust.

Avers refused to be put off by her sudden change of tone. "No—I barely know you at all. In fact, the more time I spend in your company, Mademoiselle Cadeaux, the less I feel my initial judgements of you were correct."

"Am I to thank you, then—for your gracious re-estimation?"

"Once again your wit is sharp enough to cut. No thanks are needed. I will merely keep any judgements of you reserved until I know you better."

"You can have no judgements of me," Mademoiselle Cadeaux said, her voice calmer.

"How so?"

"Because until you have lived my life, you have no say."

"Touché, Mademoiselle," Avers conceded. "Perhaps that is the realisation I have come to."

He saw a flicker of surprise cross her face. Good. She misread the smugness for insincerity.

"I do not need to be shamed by one who has no concept of struggle."

Avers observed her from beneath his hooded lids and then dropped his gaze to his nails before saying, "Have I done such a thing?"

"Do not play the fool with me, Your Grace. You are well versed in clever talk, but I am better versed in listening to it. I can decipher even the most sugar-coated of insults." She gestured around herself, her voice steadily rising in volume. "I have spent enough time with men like you, born to wealth and name. Your only hardship has been your banishment to your family home in Paris to attend salons and balls and *work* with your cousin."

Avers had found the nerve he had been searching for, and along with it raw, unfiltered emotion. He had done a poor job of hiding his initial judgement, and she was doing an excellent job of scolding him for making it in the first place.

He remembered the young woman on the Île de la Cité—that world that ran parallel to his own yet never intersecting it... until Mademoiselle Cadeaux.

"You decided what I was when you first met me, and you are determined to shame me for it. But I make no such judgements of you in return, despite your dissolute lifestyle, your exile, and your obvious desire to do business with the Comte."

"And there it is again—the implication that doing business with the Comte is no good thing. You warn me away from Vergelles with an analogy about your dog though I so clearly vex you. Why is that?"

"Do I?" she asked, ignoring his question and returning his gaze unwaveringly.

Avers resisted the desire to sigh in frustration. He thought he'd cracked her hard outer shell with that outpouring of honest emotion just now. That with the glimpse of the real Emilie Cadeaux perhaps he had deciphered her, and she would cooperate with him. Or... is that what he wanted from her —cooperation?

"So, you stand by your falsehood?" he asked, the same lazy gaze running over her face as one brow rose. "You have no metaphors you wish to discuss with me concerning the Comte?"

"None that I can think of—about the Comte... or his friends."

"Very well, I shall desist with the analogy. Let us now turn to the matter of the dog biscuit—do not tell me that you dropped such a precious item, acquired at such cost, by *accident.*"

"I am beginning to feel interrogated."

"You do? In that case, I must apologise. My inquisitiveness is borne from your mysteriousness."

Mademoiselle Cadeaux let out a rather unladylike snort.

"Aha!" Avers chuckled, finding the action endearing rather than off-putting. "But it is true."

And now to play his trump card.

"A woman who appears in Society to possess a particular character and yet spends her nights giving to the poor of the Île de la Cité and warning off foolish Englishmen from business with the Comte de Vergelles. What is behaviour like that but mysterious?"

She visibly jumped at his mention of her nocturnal activities and her eyes fixed upon his face, the fan she had been wafting frozen in mid-air.

More than anything, Avers wanted to understand this woman, and why she was mixed up with the Comte.

"Is it not far more common for a woman in love to be her gentleman's champion—not his detractor?"

He let the question hang in the air between them. A question which he knew he was asking far more for his own interests than that of his mission.

"And I thought," Mademoiselle Cadeaux answered, voice even and words deliberate, "that you were a foolish nobleman in Paris looking to find pleasure and abandon. But you are not, are you, Your Grace?"

In that moment, Avers believed that Mademoiselle Cadeaux's dark eyes could see right through him—through the subterfuge and the acting. They knew he was not here in Paris for pleasure-seeking but for some ulterior motive. He had played his hand too freely.

A wave of cold fear ran through him. What was he playing

at? Had he risked the mission—and Wakeford's reputation—in some foolish attempt to understand a woman who intrigued him? Now it was too late. She was suspicious and he had nothing more to lose.

"The more I get to know you, Mademoiselle Cadeaux, the more I believe you and the Comte de Vergelles do not suit."

CHAPTER FIFTEEN

Emilie ignored the Duke of Tremaine's blunt statement about her and the Comte's relationship. One grenade needed to be dealt with at a time, and right now, she wanted to know exactly how the Duke had found out about her philanthropic ventures.

"How did you know about my visit to the Île de la Cité?"

"The night I attended Mademoiselle Saint-Val Cadette's play I was outside the theatre and saw you exit and begin to walk alone. I could not in good conscience leave you to make your way through Paris on foot without protection, and something told me you would not have responded well to my offer of assistance."

Emilie's eyes narrowed as she weighed his explanation. On the one hand she was shocked he had found out about her night-time visits himself rather than through some lackey. And his care for her wellbeing was admirable—if it was genuine. On the other, his secrecy about following her did not ring true.

"I did not need your assistance—nor your surreptitious

following, nor your opinions on whether the Comte and I suit. What makes you an expert on such matters anyway?"

The Duke's mouth pulled down at the edges and his brow puckered as he considered her challenge.

"I am not—though I have seen love matches, and I do not see any love, or affection even, between yourself and the Comte."

"And you believe affection is necessary in such an arrangement? I thought you had already made it clear that I am motivated solely by financial gain. Other considerations are not... considered."

"I was wrong about you."

"Perhaps you are wrong about my relationship with the Comte."

The Duke had judged her and thought the worst of her from the beginning. She had allowed him to think it, and now she did not wish to acknowledge the truth. It felt more mortifying, more vulnerable and dangerous, to tell Tremaine he was right. She must never admit to this man she had no feelings for the Comte beyond that of fear. She couldn't confess it to anyone. That revelation might be used against her.

"I do not think so."

"You are very confident, Your Grace," Emilie said, turning the conversation back towards him. "One would think you were an expert in love."

"Only in that I understand the pain it can entail."

"You have been crossed in love?" Emilie asked before she could stop herself.

His honesty took the wind out of her indignant sails. She had not expected it, nor the earnestness of his tone, nor the agony she could now discern on his handsome face.

No matter how provoking the Duke was, or the judgements he had so ignorantly passed against her, Emilie never desired to cause another pain. She attempted to cover her thoughtless question with humour. "No doubt your désagréable questions put her off."

The Duke was not dissuaded from her original question. "It was not my interrogations."

His gaze was no longer upon Emilie—it had wandered towards where the Austrian violin master had returned to his music stand to review his next pieces. She followed his gaze but was sure that the Duke did not take in the sight before him. There were the shadows of memories passing over his expression, bringing hurt with them, and writing it across his face for her to see.

"It was my lack of prospects."

Emilie frowned. "I find that hard to believe. You have a ducal title and estates. How could any woman view you as anything but an advantageous match?"

The Duke's eyes refocused on her. "I see your point, but I do not have a healthy estate. As you know my uncle has retained control after my father's death thanks to my gambling habits. Doesn't trust me to safeguard the family's fortunes. A duke in possession of title alone is not the catch he might hope to be."

Who was this woman who had captured the Duke of Tremaine's attention and then broken his heart? A woman who had caused him pain that was still evident when he spoke of it.

"Though they may not think it, those without title and fortune are better suited to finding love. They are not prey for fortune hunters—only for hunters of their true love's heart."

"Perhaps you should reform your dissolute ways and no longer pursue opera singers and actresses. Women such as I, as you have implied numerous times, can only be ensnared by money."

There was no malice in his next revelation, as if he forgot it was to Emilie that he spoke. "The woman I spoke of was a lady."

A lady. Those two words segregated Emilie from any woman who might ever aspire to the hand of a gentleman, let alone a Duke. She might sit here conversing with a Duke—she might entertain an offer from a Comte—but she was not a lady. It was as Vergelles had told her. She was nothing. A feeling of worthlessness, hollow and bitter, filled her chest.

She was a common tavern owner's daughter who had trod the boards, and soon she may be a mistress. That was all. There were no other avenues in life down which she might venture. She was a small, insignificant thing, with no chance at love and marriage.

Emilie was so wrapped up in thoughts of her own situation that she almost missed the change in her companion. The Duke shifted in his chair, shoulders rising, arms crossed and the lazy humour on his face thwarted by agitation. Clearly this line of conversation was not one he enjoyed and yet Emilie felt for the first time she was seeing the true Duke beneath all those layers of sarcasm and humour.

She fought the urge to press him. "I have no doubt it was her who failed to see your charm, Your Grace."

Tremaine turned to her and smiled, the gesture so earnest it brought real warmth to her heart. "Finally, you admit I have charm."

The joke took her by surprise as much as the laugh it conjured within her.

"But we were talking of *your* lover, not mine, and I fear our tête-à-tête will soon be drawn to an unwanted close."

Sure enough, the Duke was right. She followed his gaze to where the Austrian master was taking up his instrument and beginning to re-tune it for the next piece.

"I believe your story was more interesting."

"Others' stories are always more interesting. Be that as it

may, I must ask you, Mademoiselle, if you would be so kind as to change the subject. I find questions about it... painful."

The temptation to press her advantage home was tempered once again, this time by the bare and pained expression on his face—one in complete contrast to the Duke's usual facade of bored amusement.

"As you wish," she murmured.

"May we turn back to the matter of your disguised warnings? I shall make myself plain—your benefactor has offered me the opportunity for an investment. I wish to pursue it, but have little knowledge of exactly what he offers, and then you warn me off engaging with him on the Champs-Élysées. What am I to think?"

He was like Lutin with a bone. He would not desist and Emilie began to regret ever warning him.

No.

She calmed her frustrated thoughts—no she did not regret it. Especially after seeing the Duke's humanness just now. But any further conversation along these lines put Emilie at risk. Not only Emilie, but her friend as well.

"Your Grace's thoughts are not for me to discern or persuade. I'm afraid I cannot serve your purpose for you grossly overestimate my importance. I have no knowledge of the Comte's business dealings. I am only his mistress."

She hoped her plain speaking might put him off further questioning. He had shown such aversion to her position before. He might want more information, but he did not realise the danger he put her in. Allowing her gaze to casually survey the room, she tried to spot another seat next to an acquaintance she might move to.

"Yet you warned me—you know enough of his dealings to want to warn me off."

Emilie struggled to cover a huff of frustration. Anxiety

rose within her chest. She needed to get out of this conversation.

"I know nothing," she whispered harshly, holding a tight rein on her feelings that were beginning to buck and plunge away from her, "except that you are a fool determined to involve yourself with dangerous men."

"And what," asked the Duke, leaning closer to her, locking his eyes onto hers, "does that make you?"

Emilie bit her lip, surprised by the sudden emotions boiling within her, and not sure whether she was going to cry or shout for this impertinent man to leave her alone. He had no concept of the trap she was ensnared in.

She tried to slow her breathing, swallowing against the emotions, forcing them into check. "You may think of me what you want—just as you will do whatever business you want with the Comte."

"I have upset you."

Emilie's eyes darted to him and she was horrified to find herself looking through unshed tears. This man was determined to subvert her attempts to keep him at arm's length and scale the defences which kept her real feelings safely away from the prying eyes of others.

"That was not my intention."

During the conversation Emilie had clung to the arm of her chair. Her hand was lying parallel with the Duke's and she felt the briefest brush of his against hers.

"I apologise. You have intrigued me, Mademoiselle Cadeaux. You are unlike any woman I have met before. I find myself unsure what to think of you."

"Then perhaps," Emilie said, the faintest waver in her voice, "you should not think of me at all."

He chuckled, the sound low and rumbling, and she saw a light enter his eyes. The action was so at odds with the emotion of the situation it surprised her.

"Would you believe me if I said you are not the first woman to tell me that in as many months?"

She found the weight of her fears shift. With a blank expression she replied in the affirmative.

The Duke's slow chuckle transformed into a full laugh. The atmosphere lifted and with it her mood.

"At least you are honest," he said.

"I try to be," she replied unguardedly, and then quickly turned the conversation from her. "Are you used to women lying to you?"

The Duke did not immediately answer, his eyes switching between the Austrian master and Madame Pertuis who were discussing something about the next part of the performance.

"Yes."

There it was again—honesty. This man was a bewildering mix of irritating fool and earnest gentleman. It placed another stone in the opinion of him she was building. She had been around enough actors to discern the real from the false. This Duke was disguising who he really was behind the facade of a pleasure-seeking fool.

"I find you—déroutant."

"Confusing? Yes," the Duke murmured, lounging back in his chair, gazing down at their hands lying in parallel but no longer touching. "I have been told that before. I am not easily read."

That she could whole-heartedly agree with.

"But, I might add, neither are you." He exhaled heavily, his expression relaxing. "I shall desist from my interrogation."

Emilie breathed a little easier and the two sat in comfortable silence until they were disturbed by the Comte de Vergelles.

His cool clipped voice came across the room. "There you are Mademoiselle Cadeaux."

An involuntary shiver ran down Emilie's spine. There was

displeasure in his tone and he hardly ever drew attention to himself in public as he had just done by speaking so loudly. She turned towards him and saw him lock eyes with her companion.

The Comte took his time walking across the room, all occupants pausing or slowing their conversation to watch his progress, until he stood before Emilie and the Duke. He leant back on one leg, displaying his clocked stocking to advantage, and was drawn up to his full height, looking down his nose at them both.

"You have been keeping my companion company?" the Comte asked, cold eyes on the Duke and one dark brow raised.

"I have," Tremaine answered, unruffled.

Either he could not read the Comte's obvious displeasure or he was wilfully ignoring it.

"And how were the tables? Did fortune smile her radiant face upon you, my Lord?"

"She did—and now I am well-satisfied, and desiring Mademoiselle Cadeaux's company."

He had come to stand beside her and Emilie felt his cold hand descend upon her bare shoulder. The touch was light at first, but soon his fingers closed around her, the tips pressing into her skin.

"I have been missing your company," he murmured.

The Duke continued to lounge in his chair, smiling up at the Comte. "Mademoiselle Cadeaux and I have been enjoying an excellent conversation."

The English noble's affable tone seemed to irritate the Comte further.

"And what have you found to talk about?"

Emilie's blood ran cold. The Comte's fingertips began to pinch at her pale skin. The weight of his hand grew suffocating. Her stomach dropped. The way Vergelles was behaving—it was as if he had heard everything they had said.

Had he?

No, surely not. How could he have done so? She was imagining it. At least that was what she hoped, because once again she remembered the bruises on her arm and exactly what angering the Comte de Vergelles could lead to...

CHAPTER SIXTEEN

Avers had felt guilty on leaving Madame Pertuis' musical salon. The Comte had clearly been displeased with the Englishman speaking with his mistress. Yet again, he'd become distracted by the intriguing Mademoiselle Cadeaux, and his focus on Wakeford's mission had wavered.

Thankfully, the incident did not affect the invitation Dartois had issued on the Champs-Élysées. Avers received a missive reminding him of the appointment and its location shortly before it was due to take place and thus, ten days after the Austrian master's performance at the salon, he was journeying to the Café Procope.

The establishment was just as he had left it over a week since, filled with pipe smoke, humming with conversation and warm with the candlelight that supplemented the daylight in the areas towards the back. The mirrors which lined the walls reflected the patrons, giving a false sense of the crowds, creating an atmosphere teeming with energy.

Avers walked through the melee towards where he could see the Comte, Dartois and two men he recognised from last time, sitting at the same table they had occupied before. Snippets of conversation found him on his way. One table discussed taxes, another the price of bread, another the King's latest rulings, and yet another the Queen's latest whim of living like a peasant.

It was a political and philosophical melting pot. One argued this way and the other opposed. It was the atmosphere Avers had expected to find at Madame Pertuis' salon on his first attendance. True, there had been discussions, but none like the zealous debate currently taking place at the Procope where untitled voices engaged with the nobility at equal volume and authority.Rolling his shoulders back as he approached the Comte's table, Avers took a deep breath, wrapping the facade of the Duke of Tremaine around himself.

"Bonjour mes amis." Avers made a leg and bowed low to the gentlemen. As he rose, he observed there was no spare chair for him.

No man at the table made a move to rectify the matter.

"Bonjour," said the Comte without deigning to look at the newcomer.

The others in the party followed suit and as they greeted Avers, Dartois signalled the waiter, murmuring something in the server's ear.

The man soon returned with a pewter platter bearing a tankard brimming with liquid.

Dartois grinned. "I thought you would be happier with your country's drink—warm beer for Your Grace."

Something in the Marquis' eyes made Avers suspect the gesture was mocking. He looked at the table, scattered with open bottles of wine and half-drunk glasses, and back at the lack of chair.

"I think, today, I am in the mood for your country's brandy." He turned to the waiter and ordered the said drink along with a pot of coffee. He also requested a chair be brought and implied a fair tip should this be done with all speed.

The server nodded vigorously and hurried off. In less than a minute Avers was presented with a chair which he took in exchange for a silver coin.

"It seems nonsensical," he said, taking his chair, "to sit in a coffee house without the title drink."

"As you say." The Comte's countenance was as implacable as ever and still he would not do Avers the courtesy of looking at him. Instead he was now examining his nails.

"Our English friend is determined to appear the rebel," Dartois said, smiling in that disarming way of his, a gleam in his eye. The Marquis was as warm as the Comte appeared cold. "Very sensible, and that is just the sort of man we should wish to do business with, is it not Vergelles?"

The Comte neither answered nor nodded.

"Speaking of which, would you be so kind as to expand on the opportunity of which you spoke?" Avers spread his arm wide, still attempting to catch the Comte's eye.

How was he to find out the truth about the man's leadership in this spy ring if he continued to evade him? No wonder Wakeford's men had struggled to find the evidence they needed.

"Our English friend is keen, n'est pas?" Dartois chuckled. "Did I not tell you Vergelles?"

"He certainly seemed so when speaking to Mademoiselle Cadeaux at the salon last week," said the Comte, apparently fascinated by the embroidery on his right cuff.

Ah, so that was it. The Comte was peeved at Avers' attention to Mademoiselle Cadeaux. He would have to smooth things over.

The Comte's pale eyes flicked up to lock their gaze with Avers. "She said you asked about me."

Cold fear rose up and began to wrap its fingers around his

chest. All thoughts of Wakeford's mission disappeared as he realised with dread the position he had put Mademoiselle Cadeaux in. There was no way she had offered that information to the Comte willingly.

He shrugged, the action less casual than he had meant it to be, the tension failing to leave his body. He was just constructing a suitable answer to the Comte which might alleviate the pressure of the situation when the server returned with Avers' glass of brandy and pot of coffee.

The wiry man placed them before him and then began to clear some of the empty bottles from the table. As he leant across for the second such bottle, the servant inadvertently caught the Comte's shoulder, nudging the man forward.

"Pardon."

"Cursed dog!" Vergelles snarled, ignoring the apology and slamming the glass of wine he had nearly spilled onto the table. Drops of blood-red liquid sloshed over its rim, trickling down the stem and leaching into the linens.

The Comte ignored the mess, turning quickly and clipping the unfortunate servant around the ears. He swore again, and the poor server visibly shrunk before him, one hand clutching an empty bottle, the other reaching up to his forelock to tug it and bow away from the table in abject apology.

Avers said nothing, masking the distaste that was begging to be shown on his face, and relieved when the servant scurried away before further mistreatment. He had always believed you could tell a lot about a man from the way he treated his servants. What the Comte had just shown him was revealing indeed, and Mademoiselle Cadeaux's warnings came loudly to the front of Avers' mind.

He focused on pouring out his coffee. While he might drink alongside these men so as not to arouse suspicion, he would temper it with coffee to stay as clear-headed as possible.

"You teased me with an investment opportunity," said

Avers, breaking the awkward silence that had descended on the table. The one good thing about that interruption was that it had taken the Comte's attention away from Mademoiselle Cadeaux. Avers intended to keep it that way.

"I would be very much obliged if you would satisfy my curiosity on the subject. Or are we to keep sharing superficial conversation? If you have nothing for me, I have an opportunity to game this afternoon which I may still take up if I leave now. This political hotbed is not exactly my scene."

He motioned at the animated debates surrounding them, and as if on cue, an argument broke out at an adjacent table and a pot of coffee was knocked over when the opponents began gesturing angrily at one another.

The Comte, who had pulled out a lace handkerchief from his pocket to wipe the non-existent spilled wine from his hands, finished dabbing his long white fingers and carefully polished nails. He then looked up at his guest and raised a single brow.

"You do not care for politics—even after your recent appointment?"

Avers felt the coolness of that gaze. "Hardly."

"Bien." The Comte reached for his glass, taking a sip and maintaining the impassive expression on his chiselled face. "The cunning man makes money from politics—he does not get involved in them."

"Spoken like a man who knows his business," said Avers. "I have not been lured here for no account then?"

"Lured?" Dartois shot him a penetrating look, a half-smile on his face. "You make us sound positively... *criminal*."

Avers took refuge in a long sip of hot coffee, unsure of the best response, finally settling on one as he replaced the cup on the table. "That's hardly my business, is it?"

Dartois chuckled. "Touché."

"Are we to bandy words or do business?" Avers pressed his

fingernails into the palm of his right hand in an effort to keep his nerve.

"Patience," the Comte snapped. "We do not go into business with just anyone." Then he fell silent, and it appeared as though he didn't intend to say anything further.

Another awkward silence descended upon the table, the antithesis to the room around them, until finally the Comte spoke again.

"However, Dartois believes our business may suit you."

"Oh yes? And what business is that?"

He was already halfway through his coffee and soon only the brandy would be left to drink. He eyed the bulbous glass.

Dartois gestured to the undrunk beverage. "It's good."

Avers glanced up to see the fair-haired gentleman watching him, and realised just how sharp Dartois was.

"Marcel stocks an excellent cellar. Ever since we bade him to—isn't that right, Lucien?"

The Comte inclined his head, a small sneer curving his lips, allowing just the tips of his teeth to show.

Dartois leaned in towards Avers and smiled as if sharing a joke. "We were most persuasive." The Marquis' eyes caught the light of the candles behind Avers' shoulder and glittered disconcertingly. There was something unreadable in them—calculating—and it made Avers feel as though he were some deer wandering into a snare. Perhaps Mademoiselle Cadeaux was right.

Despite his misgivings, Avers pressed on for Wakeford's sake. "The business?"

The Comte made a signal and the majority of the table rose. Avers cocked his head, raising a single brow in enquiry as the rest of the party reseated themselves at a distance, leaving Vergelles, Dartois and him with an empty table between them and the rest of the bustling café.

"Before we go on," the Comte said, leaning forward just a

little, his face a tightly schooled mask of impassivity, "I must state one thing categorically. Mademoiselle Cadeaux is *mine.*" His voice was hard as flint. "I have seen you singling her out, and I will give you a courtesy that few receive—I will warn you this once not to touch her."

Avers was fairly certain that the Comte was not speaking aloud the rest of his thoughts which were definitely along the lines of 'or I will...' and ending in something violent. His mind once again ran over all the possibilities of what had happened after Madame Pertuis' last salon. How long had it been since he'd seen Mademoiselle Cadeaux last—ten days? The apprehension grew in his stomach.

"Singled her out?" Avers played for time as he constructed the most placating answer he could think of. "That was not my intention. I must offer my sincerest apologies if that is how it appeared. I, of course, recognise her... relationship to you. Truth be told I was in love with a female in Italy recently and it did not end well. I have no intention of foraying into those waters again any time soon."

But neither had he intended any ill-consequences to befall Mademoiselle Cadeaux as a result of his actions.

"I heard you were lately in Greece," said the Comte, a query in his tone.

Dartois grinned, as if this were all some game and there wasn't a seriousness to what was going on. "And yet our English Duke speaks of Italy, a cock pit and now tales of this Italian woman of his. You get around, Your Grace."

Avers winced inwardly at the wound Dartois had pressed. Miss Curshaw was certainly *not* Avers' woman and *not* in Italy. She had not been his woman when he'd left London and she was even less so now. When he thought about it, he no longer felt the acute pain of her betrayal—but rather a general sadness about what had occurred.

No. Miss Curshaw was *not* Avers' woman. And this was

the first time he could say with absolute certainty, he no longer wished her to be.

"That is true." Avers pulled his thoughts back to the Marquis' words. They appeared to know a lot about him. "I had been in the Mediterranean for some years before my recent return."

"And why did you return? I heard you were a fully fledged scholar living out your dreams among the ruins of the ancients."

"You seem well-versed in my history."

"You are interested in the Greeks. I am interested in my potential business partners," replied the Comte without emotion.

"My father died."

"And the prodigal son returned even though Society expected him to live out the rest of his days overseas. The servants in your household hadn't seen you for five years at least."

"I see I have a spy in my servants' hall. If you would be so good as to tell me which one you paid off, I will have them out on their ears without a reference this afternoon."

"A little compassion." Dartois chuckled. "They could hardly turn down five sous."

Even the Comte was smiling now, as though they were both winning the unspoken game they were all playing.

"Well, it's hardly a secret," Avers said with a shrug, making a mental note to be even more discreet while in the Tremaine residence. "I had a penchant for the classic civilisations, but it waned, and upon hearing of my father's death I came home to take up my inheritance. My uncle, however, after hearing of my lifestyle on the Continent and seeing the damage I've done to the family coffers, decided he needed to protect what remains of the estate from me until I can be trusted with the responsibility. He packed me off to Paris under the beady eyes of my dull cousin. Now here I am."

Avers expounded his fake history in pragmatic tones, making no effort to substantiate the facts. If he wanted to be believed he should not try to justify himself.

"I take exception to your rooting around for information on me in such a fashion."

"I only repay you in kind. Mademoiselle Cadeaux told me you did the—how did you say it?—*rooting around*—on me."

Avers' stomach tightened.

The Comte drew his mother-of-pearl snuffbox from his pocket and flicked open the lid with a well-practised finger.

"She assures me she said nothing." He took a pinch up each nostril. "But women—they do run on..." There was an underlying menace in the Comte's voice that triggered a sick feeling in Avers' stomach.

Why had Mademoiselle Cadeaux had to *assure* the Comte? And what had the Comte done to gain those assurances? If Vergelles' temper was short enough that he would hit a servant in public for merely nudging his shoulder, what would he do to a mistress who betrayed his confidence behind closed doors?

"I grow weary of this cat and mouse game," Avers said, emitting a theatrical huff as he decided to change tack. "Either you have business for me or you don't."

The Comte sat very still. His pale eyes were hard upon Avers as he snapped his snuffbox shut.

"Come, Vergelles. I think it is time we let our English friend in on our little enterprise," Dartois drawled, taking a long draught of wine immediately afterwards.

"Very well," said the Comte. "Our business is a lucrative one. There is much money to be made when demand is high and our governments bicker just as much as the men in here."

"'Demand?" Avers asked, sipping slowly at the brandy.

The Comte gestured with the snuffbox still in his hand at Avers' glass. "You drink one of the items."

Avers leant back to stare at his half-drunk glass. Brandy? What had that to do with stolen papers?

"Ever since the French government started financing your colonial rebels in the Americas through Caron de Beaumarchais' business, your English ministers have been raising taxes on French goods in retaliation. I hardly think it makes a difference to either side." The Comte waved one pale hand in the air to indicate how beneath him all this political manoeuvring was. "But to the men in the middle—there is money to be made."

Smuggling. That is what the Comte meant. The smuggling of French goods to England and selling them illegally. It avoided taxes and made a tidy profit.

Even the most respectable English households were not immune to a bargain on tea, lace, or brandy. What did it matter to them if the Crown got their cut or not? And it was far lighter a rebellion than the people of Boston throwing their tea in the harbour in protest against the Crown—there was no sense in that—it was a waste of good tea.

If a man held no scruples about upholding the law, then the Comte's investment in smuggling activities was indeed a good one. But that did not explain the missing papers.

Avers expressed no shock at the revelations. "It sounds like a profitable venture. "What is it you want from me?" He looked down at the nails on his left hand and flicked an imaginary piece of dust from one finger. "Capital for one of these ventures?"

"There are other commodities, in a time of international feuding, that increase in value."

The Comte was being elusive again and Avers was becoming impatient. Either the man trusted him—or he didn't. To move back and forth on the subject of Avers' veracity was not only fatiguing, but a waste of time.

"Cloth? Silk?"

The Comte chuckled, looking to Dartois who joined in with a smile, and then back at Avers as though he were some foolish child.

"It is not just the physical that holds value at times like these."

Now they were getting to it. Avers fought the urge to lean forward in his chair. He furrowed his brows as if trying to work out what the Comte was implying. He tossed off the last of his brandy in an effort to appear reckless. "I'm afraid you've lost me now."

Just then, a gentleman came to the table, moving to Dartois' side and bending to murmur something in his ear.

Avers could only make out a few words. "... Sebastien... our friends..."

While he listened to the message from the newcomer, the Marquis' gaze did not falter from Avers' own. He stared at him, eyes sharp and gleaming, making the hairs on the back of Avers' neck rise.

"Pardon," said Dartois to the table, rising and walking to the back of the café with the gentleman to continue their conversation out of earshot.

Without the Marquis, it appeared as though the Comte was unwilling to continue. He sat in silence, not attempting small talk, only every now and then sipping from his glass between sweeps of the rest of the café with his hard eyes.

"Pardon," said Dartois, finally coming back to the table as the man he was speaking to left the establishment. "Good news, Vergelles. Our friends have arrived in Paris."

"Bien."

Neither gentleman explained of what they spoke and Avers chose to let the incident pass by without comment.

Dartois slipped back into his seat, taking up his glass again and smiling as though this were any social engagement.

"Well, have you asked him, Vergelles?"

"Not yet. I thought it best to wait for you. As I was saying, there are non-physical commodities which have value in times such as these. There are a great number of ways for money to be made. There is opportunity if only we look at the positions we are in and what may be taken advantage of."

Avers bit back his frustration that the conversation was growing vague again and the Comte was resuming his condescending tone. "So, is it an investment you're looking for? If so, I can send you a draft on my bank and be done with it."

"He is eager, non?" Dartois asked the Comte, as though Avers were not present. "Patience, Your Grace. Vergelles is just being careful. We must be wise when it comes to our business and those whom we choose to befriend."

"Naturally," replied Avers.

"You are, of course, welcome to invest in our little enterprise, but we have another business you may be interested in— one that is best discussed outside of Paris. Lucien, I think we may invite our new friend to the hunting lodge."

"As you wish," Vergelles replied, looking as displeased as Dartois was jovial.

The Marquis leant across the table, a generous smile upon his fair face, and no hint of concern at the recent chatter about illegal trade. "You are invited to spend next weekend at my hunting lodge near Versailles. We'll be comfortable there and may discuss our little business opportunity more freely."

Avers' heartbeat quickened. An invitation to the inner sanctum. This was too good an offer to pass up and yet Mademoiselle Cadeaux's warning came to the forefront of his mind. He'd felt uneasy the moment he had sat at this table alone with the Comte and Dartois. Yet, if this was the opportunity to find proof of the group's stealing of Wakeford's papers, he had to take it.

"I'd be delighted."

The party broke up soon after. Dartois bade Avers a friendly farewell, assuring him of how much he looked forward to the following weekend, but the Comte was as cold as ever. The French noble offered the barest of farewells before leaving the café abruptly.

As Avers stepped out of the establishment, he felt one step closer to uncovering the truth... and one step closer to danger.

CHAPTER SEVENTEEN

Emilie folded and refolded the freshly pressed handkerchief in her lap until it was little more than a soft rag. The Comte's carriage turned down a new street, hitting a pothole in the road, and she was jolted sideways against the cushioned wall. It did nothing to calm her frayed nerves.

Since her last interview with Vergelles she had been anxiously awaiting his next summons. She'd considered refusing, but fearing what he might do in retaliation had forced her to accept. So, here she was travelling to meet him at the Café Procope.

Another bump in the road made her look down and see the wilted mess of handkerchief. She sniffed, took a deep breath, and folded the linen square before putting it away. The Comte may have exposed her nerves on their last encounter, but that did not mean she had to leave herself open for him to see them again today.

It wasn't just a matter of protecting herself from the man she now knew was as cruel as she had feared. It was playing the game until she could find a way to deal herself out. After all, the Comte had made her lack of power clear.

The carriage drew to a halt across the road from the café and Emilie dropped her window to signal the servant at the door of the establishment. A few moments later a server crossed the road to her.

"A pot of coffee, s'il vous plait, and a message for the Comte de Vergelles— Mademoiselle Cadeaux awaits his pleasure."

The servant bobbed, turning to dart between passing traffic, and disappeared inside the café.

Emilie flexed the hand she had used to open the window. She'd done so without thinking, and the movement had caused burning sensations to break out across the back of it again.

It was a souvenir from her last interview with the Comte. To illustrate his point that *he* paid for Mademoiselle Cadeaux's apartments, that *he* bought her fine dresses and jewellery, and that *he* had enabled her to enter Polite Society on his arm, he had dashed the contents of his smouldering pipe across her hand. Before allowing her to fetch water to bathe the wound or clean linen to dress it, he had explained at length that his patronage of her, and her insistence on taking time to decide whether she would be his mistress, was becoming untenable.

Then he'd brought up the Duke of Tremaine.

She'd known such an interrogation was coming ever since Madame Pertuis' musical night, but the height of the Comte's anger she had not expected. He'd raged at her for speaking to the Duke and questioned her on what she had found to say to the Englishman for so long at the recital.

Emilie had denied any wrongdoing, carefully skirting the issue of what they had discussed. With much placating and gentle words she had smoothed the Comte's ruffled feathers enough that he had allowed her to attend to her wound.

And he had given her an ultimatum. She had one week to decide on his offer.

He had not reiterated his threats of what would happen if she refused him, but they were clear. She would be ruined. Her friend Mademoiselle Saint-Val Cadette would suffer the same fate, and Emilie would come to physical harm.

The invisible snare around her neck tightened. She had to get out of this mess. But until a plan presented itself in her mind she was trapped, and she must play her part as the Comte's companion.

The door of the Café Procope opened across the road. Emilie slowed her breathing, pressing her hands together to control their trembling, and forcing down the sudden panic rising within her.

She watched several men exit the establishment. First Dartois, then the Comte, and finally the Duke of Tremaine whose eyes immediately caught hers. They did not move on, his gaze locking with hers, his look so penetrating she wondered how many of her thoughts he could read from this distance.

Dartois pointed out the Comte's carriage across the way, and the gentlemen looked to cross the road when the traffic permitted. The whole time Tremaine's eyes did not leave Emilie's. She pressed her legs together beneath her skirts, willing herself to calm down as her breath came faster.

She must act indifferent. She could show no emotion if she wished to protect herself against the Comte's wrath. Yet the Duke's gaze would not leave her. They came to the other side of the carriage, out of the road, and she dropped the window to greet them.

"Good day, Mademoiselle Cadeaux," Dartois called in a jovial voice.

When Emilie met the Marquis' eyes, she remembered his

conversation with her two weeks since. It was not just the Comte she had to tread carefully with.

"Bonjour," she murmured.

The Comte merely inclined his head. His failing to greet her, despite summoning her here, did not bode well.

"You remember His Grace, the Duke of Tremaine—our English friend." Dartois' manner was so pleasant Emilie could almost believe she'd imagined his ominous offer.

"Bonjour, Your Grace." Emilie inclined her head.

"Mademoiselle Cadeaux, your obedient servant." The Duke bowed a little lower and longer than he needed to. "I trust I find you in good health?"

In spite of her best efforts, he managed to catch her eyes again as he rose, and she saw in them a real earnestness.

"Quite well," she murmured, breaking her gaze and finding something in the middle distance to focus on. She could still feel him looking at her, and as she'd turned away she'd seen a slight furrow in his brow.

"We all get along so well," Dartois said, ever-immune to the tension rolling off the Comte. "We shall make a très joyeuse party at my hunting lodge, n'est pas?"

"We shall?" Emilie asked, eyes flicking between the Comte, the Duke and Dartois.

"Oui—next weekend," the Comte replied. "We will attend."

Her fear took a brief hiatus in the face of a sudden flash of irritation. She had borne the Comte's wrath for nothing. The Duke was ignoring her warnings.

Only those who were trusted were invited to Dartois' hunting lodge. It was where matters of business were discussed to which Emilie was not privy. She had only been there twice during her relationship with the Comte and both times she had spent the majority of her days there alone, occupying herself in the gardens when she was turned out of the gatherings of Vergelles and his men.

Emilie had intended to visit her friends in the Île de la Cité on Friday. Mademoiselle Saint-Val Cadette had sent her a note to tell her another collection of the actresses' tips was ready to be dispensed to the poor. Those plans would have to wait.

"You shall be the belle of the party," Dartois said, leaning in at the carriage window, his hand inches from where hers rested.

The action was harmless enough to those who had not experienced the Marquis' conversation with Emilie. She could not help removing her hand to her lap to avoid an involuntary touch. Just as she did this, Lutin—who had been very content curled up under her skirts, acting in lieu of a warming brick between her feet—woke up.

The canine's ears had not failed him. He took one look at Dartois—his sworn enemy—and erupted into a series of angry barks.

"Urgh!" Dartois lept back as the dog jumped up at the window. "Maudit ce chien infernal!" He began checking his hand and arm for bite marks.

"You brought that infernal dog of yours?" snapped the Comte.

"Ah, the petit diable," the Duke of Tremaine murmured, smiling over at Lutin's fierce little face.

The Comte shot the Englishman a venomous look.

"I have tried to be his friend," said Dartois testily, "but he will have none of me. I cannot like him."

"Animals have a sixth sense when it comes to humans. His penchant for snapping at you is no doubt driven by it."

Was the Duke saying Lutin sensed something he didn't like in the Marquis? Emilie's eyes darted to the English noble as she simultaneously grabbed Lutin's collar to stay his jumping. Tremaine's comment was as if he could read Emilie's recent fears about the Marquis right out of her own mind. But when she saw the Duke smiling in that languid way of his, a gleam in his eye, she realised he was simply funning at Dartois' expense.

The tension which was still very much present in her body intensified. If the Comte saw the Duke exchanging meaningful glances with her, even if only in humour and nothing else, she was sure he would exact a payment.

"Pardon."

A servant from the Café Procope had crossed the street and was now attempting to gain access to the carriage window. He carried a pewter tray bearing a pot of coffee and a single cup.

"Merci," Emilie said as the server threaded his way skilfully between the nobles and held out the tray for her to serve herself.

Lutin made no demur as she released his collar and began pouring the hot drink, tendrils of steam rising and twisting in the air.

"Are we to wait for you to finish?" Vergelles asked.

Emilie halted halfway through pouring, glancing at the Comte and then back at the pot in her hands.

"I'm sure the lady may finish her drink before we set off," Dartois said smoothly.

Emilie found herself grateful for the Marquis' intervention, once again confused over his seeming split personalities.

"Very well, but I will not travel with that beast." Vergelles pointed his ebony cane at Lutin's head, just visible over the carriage door, as he still stood on his hind legs. "Must you go everywhere with that thing?"

"On this point I must concur, Mademoiselle Cadeaux," Dartois said. "Your canine companion is less than affable."

A sudden wave of irrational fear crashed over Emilie as she thought of being parted from Lutin. The little dog made her feel marginally safer. She could hardly reply to the Comte and Marquis with that as her reasoning.

Before she could think of a suitably placating response, Vergelles commanded her to get out of the carriage so they might walk to Sebastien's.

"My driver will take that dog of yours back to your lodgings where he belongs."

Without waiting for her consent, the Comte signalled for the driver to let down the steps, and then turned to the Marquis de Dartois to discuss the particulars of their meeting with Sebastien.

Emilie, having not taken a single sip of coffee, replaced it on the server's tray and paid him for his vain service. She picked up her gloves from the seat beside her, having previously removed them to warm her hands with her coffee. The movement caused the wound on the back of her right hand to sting afresh.

It was a raw reminder of the Comte's anger and her current inability to escape it. Emilie tried to school her breathing into a steady pace. It had grown fast and shallow with the Comte's foul mood and the memories the pain in her hand conjured.

As the door of the carriage opened she took a steadying breath, stroking Lutin's head rhythmically, telling herself that the ringing in her ears would abate. The idea of leaving the safety of the carriage and her little white shadow behind... Breathe, Emilie... Breathe.

As she placed an unsteady foot on the first step a strong, steady hand took her elbow. It took her weight, guiding her down from the steps as she focused on a single cobble below. As she reached solid ground, she looked up to find it was neither the Comte nor Dartois who aided her.

It was the Duke of Tremaine.

"Mademoiselle." He bowed towards her, his gloved hand

slipped down her arm to hold her hand lightly.

His continued support caused her breathing to slow and the ringing in her ears to abate.

Emilie glanced towards the Comte, but Vergelles' back was still turned as he was now in deep discussion with Dartois, speaking forcefully in rapid French. She couldn't risk them suddenly turning and seeing Tremaine holding her hand. She tried to pull back from the Duke's grasp, but his grip tightened on her fingers in response.

Emilie gazed up into his eyes and was startled to see concern there.

"You have injured yourself?" he murmured, too low for their companions to hear, and looking meaningfully down at the bandage on her hand.

She tried to pull her hand away again, mild panic rising within, and this time Tremaine released it. A thread in the bandage caught on his sleeve, tugging it loose as she dropped her hand.

"I do not wish to alarm you."

The Duke had misread her gasp of pain as one of shock.

"You seem... anxious."

Her eyes darted again to the Comte and she scolded herself inwardly for allowing her feelings to be interpreted so easily. Then she looked down to the bandage that had unravelled from her hand. She turned her back to Vergelles and Dartois, reaching for the loose strip of fabric and raising her hand to unfurl it and rebandage the injury.

For a brief moment the red, ugly, blistering skin was revealed.

"That's a nasty wound."

She tried to hide it from the Duke, the pain fraying her temper. "It's nothing."

"It doesn't look like nothing. You would do well to cover it with a poultice to prevent infection and encourage healing. I can send my old housekeeper's best recipe to your address. Tell me how you came by the burn?"

Emilie sighed, the pain overcoming her resolve. "I told you, there are consequences when one gets involved with dangerous men. But please," she pleaded, loathing the fearful tone in her own voice, "we must not be overheard."

"Of course." The Duke's eyes—as they looked upon her—were the softest she had ever seen them. When he glanced over at the Comte, the change was swift and remarkable. Fury transformed his features and brought a blazing light to his eyes.

"You warned me. I have been careless. I ignorantly believed your warning only applied to me. Why did he hurt you?"

Emilie shrugged impatiently. "The Comte is jealous of his privacy. He wished to know exactly what I had said to you. What secrets I had divulged. I told him none. He wished to be sure."

He bowed his head in apology. "Please forgive me."

She struggled to concentrate fully on the Duke's apology for fear that the Comte might overhear their conversation. She glanced over at her benefactor whose back was still turned to them. Vergelles' foot tapped on the floor, and Emilie could see the conversation between him and Dartois was petering off. No doubt he was waiting for Emilie to come to his side. His anger at her bringing Lutin meant he would not deign to turn and take her onto his arm.

"It is not *you* who burned me. Will you now desist whatever obsession you have with doing business with the Comte?"

She looked imploringly up at the Duke and saw his troubled brow furrow, his eyes more apologetic than ever.

"I cannot explain to you why I am unable to do as you advise. Please trust me that it is important I engage the Comte in friendship."

Emilie's lips parted a little as she stared at him in bewilderment. He had inadvertently seen the damage the Comte had done just because she spoke to Tremaine and yet the Duke would still pursue this relationship?

"Then I will beg of you to stay away from me. I do not wish to be burned twice by whatever foolishness you pursue. And there are others whose wellbeing relies on me." She stepped forward and the Duke immediately bowed and moved away to allow her passage. She did not look at him again or loiter any longer. Coming alongside the Comte, she curtseyed to him and apologised for upsetting his morning by bringing Lutin.

"I await your pleasure, my Lord."

The French noble looked down at her from the corner of his eyes and gave the smallest jerk of his head in acceptance of her submission. He then raised the silver head of his ebony cane, signalling the coachman to leave, and there emitted a new stream of indignant barks from the Comte's carriage as Lutin was taken—unwillingly—away.

Emilie felt her heart squeeze at her poor pet's confusion.

"I can walk you as far as the Hôtel des Invalides," said the Duke of Tremaine from behind her. Emilie refused to turn and catch his eye again. "And then I must return to my cousin's offices."

The party struck out, Dartois explaining the location of his hunting lodge to Tremaine, and the Comte maintaining his characteristic silence. Emilie did the same, not wanting to rouse any more ire from her benefactor.

When they reached the spot where their paths were destined to diverge, the group stopped to say farewell.

"And if you should have news of the investment before next weekend," asked Tremaine, "how can I expect to hear from you?"

Feeling safe to look at him once more, Emilie noticed that the bored facade was back in place upon the Duke's face, and his characteristic drawl had overcome the earnestness in his voice from when he spoke to her earlier.

"I cannot vouch for my cousin not intercepting my post. He's my uncle's spy at present, I have no doubt."

The Comte's arm stiffened beneath Emilie's hand.

"We will contact you, should we need to," the Comte replied coolly.

"We have our ways." Dartois expanded on his friend's answer. "Have no fear."

The Duke looked as if he might say something but thought better of it. Instead he tapped his cane to the brim of his hat and bowed low to Emilie.

"I shall bit you all adieu. Take care, Mademoiselle Cadeaux."

He rose without catching her eyes again and turned on his heel to saunter away.

"And what do you think of the English Duke attending our little house party?" the Comte asked Emilie as soon as they were on their way again.

This was a trap.

"I am surprised," Emilie said with a shrug. "I find him très ennuyeux, and I thought you did too, my Lord."

Dartois laughed. "Très bien, Mademoiselle. He is a bore with his constant crass chatter about money. Do not worry your pretty head about it. We shall keep him from boring you, shall we not, Vergelles?"

"Oui—though I could have been fooled into thinking you thought him engaging by the way you spoke to him previously."

"Politeness," Emilie said quickly. "Not interested in his conversation."

Dartois erupted into laughter again. "Your Mademoiselle Cadeaux is so very sharp-witted, Lucien, I would not be surprised if she were cleverer than us all."

"Not clever enough to understand the Duke of Tremaine's usefulness," the Comte snarled. "And I thought you were quite taken with the Duke of Tremaine, Mademoiselle."

Emilie would not be baited. "No, my Lord. But if it pleases you to have him at the hunting lodge, I shall bear the tedium."

"Tedious people have their uses," Lucien said.

"Indeed they do," Dartois said. "And this tedious Duke might prove very useful indeed."

CHAPTER EIGHTEEN

Avers landed another blow on the defenceless dummy. The silent figure jolted backwards. Shaking off the dull ache in his striking hand, he bounced back and forth on the balls of his feet, sizing up his mute opponent. He delivered another blow, then another and another.

With each strike, the overwhelming fury he felt towards the Comte de Vergelles poured out and abated... for a moment... until the next strike, and the next.

Beads of perspiration ran from Avers' hairline, down his temples, and onto his neck. He wiped a bandaged hand across his brow. The boxing club on the rue de Grenelle, opposite the Fontaine des Quatre-Saisons—the monumental fountain in Faubourg Saint-Germaine—was neutral ground on which to meet Wakeford.

Avers had decided to make the most of his time while waiting for his friend and it also happened to be easing his temper. Stripped of his jacket and waistcoat, his linen shirt hung open at his neck, and his stockinged feet were bare of shoes. He padded silently back and forth on the wooden floor.

The vision of Mademoiselle Cadeaux's blistered hand

came back into Avers' mind and he struck out at the dummy in the next moment with more force than he intended. Pain ricocheted up his arm. He inhaled sharply, snatching his hand away from the padded figure, and turned to walk it off.

Stupid! That was what he had been in hitting the dummy so hard. And stupid is what he'd been, in putting Mademoiselle Cadeaux in harm's way. The anger Avers felt at the Comte was only matched by the anger he felt towards himself. He had initially believed Mademoiselle Cadeaux was complicit in the Comte's business dealings. Then he'd seen her real character come to the fore. But he'd never appreciated the position she was in. Hadn't she said that to him—that he could have no concept of her position in Society?

Now, thanks to Avers, her position with her malevolent master was precarious. The sooner they could stop the Comte and his associates, the better.

"Avers?"

He turned and saw Wakeford entering the deserted sparring hall. His friend's face was unusually pale.

"*Cousin*," Avers said, reminding his friend of their pretend relationship.

It was clear from Wakeford's verbal slip that something was wrong. Along with a lack of colour in his face, his wig was mussed, his clothes crumpled and the lace cravat at his throat badly tied.

"Dash it!" Wakeford exclaimed, slapping a palm to his forehead. "*Cousin*." With the correction from Avers, he appeared to come to himself and took in his friend's appearance. "Who've you been fighting?"

He removed his hat and made to place it on a nearby table, missing the surface, and dropping it on the floor. He bent to pick it up and put it next to the half-drunk pot of coffee already on the table.

Avers rang for a fresh pot. When the server arrived he ordered a large one. Wakeford clearly needed it.

Once the young lad had disappeared again, Avers began unbinding his hands, the knuckles hot and swollen. He'd gone at it too hard.

Wakeford looked fit to fall down. Avers gestured to the chair, not offering, but commanding his friend to sit.

Dropping the fabric that had been bound around his hands on the seat which also held his discarded clothes, he came over to the table and sat in the chair opposite the one Wakeford had just collapsed into. They were next to a tall window on the first floor of the club which afforded a view of the public fountain opposite.

"Trouble?" Avers asked.

The door opened and Wakeford glanced anxiously over as the server reappeared with a tray, two new cups and a steaming pot of coffee. Both men remained silent while the young man cleared the old items and placed the new ones on the table. Avers murmured his appreciation and the lad bobbed a quick bow before retreating, tray in hand, and clicking the door shut behind him.

"This morning I got word from Stormont that his spies at the French court have found Versailles is teeming with information about our troop numbers in the colonies."

Avers poured the coffee silently, as his friend's words sunk in. "The information from the stolen papers?"

"That's right. It's been sold or given to the French."

"But as we said before, surely it's no great secret. The men on the ground must have more up-to-date information than us anyway. It takes a full month for word to reach the Americas."

"That's not the problem—the French have also received information on our munition stockpiles. They know the powder supplies are low and which forts are most at risk. It could help them determine where to strike next."

The import of Wakeford's words dawned on Avers, and for the first time that morning, Mademoiselle Cadeaux's face faded from the forefront of his mind.

"This was in the papers that were stolen?"

"Yes." Wakeford rubbed a hand over his miserable face, a sigh of defeat escaping him. "It's exactly what we feared. Now the French will channel their finances through Caron de Beaumarchais' company to outfit rebels who can attack our weak points. Even if we send word now—which we have—as you said, it'll take a month at best to get there and likely arrive at the same time as the French intelligence."

"I don't understand."

Wakeford looked at Avers between his fingers and said in exasperation, "It's not that difficult. We've failed."

"No," Avers replied calmly, leaning back in his chair and taking a sip of coffee. His gaze drifted out of the window as he mulled over something in his mind.

Outside water bearers from the local area were lining up in front of the fountain to fill up their buckets.

"What I mean is—if this was the key information they had to sell from the stolen papers—then what deal are they intending to involve me in? What are they planning to discuss with me at the hunting lodge this weekend?"

"You said yourself in your last missive that they are profiting from smuggling. Perhaps they're just looking for capital."

Something nagged at the back of Avers' mind—something he couldn't quite put his finger on.

He rubbed his chin, then moved his hand to the back of his neck, working the muscles there. "What will we do now?"

"There is no more *we*, my friend. I will be recalled in dishonour. You—you may do as you please—stay on at the

Hôtel du Tremaine if you want. My family have no use for it at the moment."

"You're giving up?" Avers' eyes flicked from the window to his friend, their gaze straight and piercing.

"Did you not hear me?" Wakeford said, an edge to his voice. "We've failed. It's a miracle I wasn't recalled when those papers went missing. I had hoped that if we... if we could have retrieved them... "

Why did Avers feel as though this tale was not yet over? "There was more in them, wasn't there? You said something about personnel and provisions as well?"

"They've sold the valuable information—the rest is collateral," Wakeford replied, hanging his head.

"If there is one thing I have learned from my aunt—the most voracious gossip in London—it's that *all* information is valuable. There is more afoot here. Why else would they invite me to Dartois' hunting lodge?"

Wakeford didn't answer. Avers had lost him in a sea of melancholy and his friend was now obscured by the waves. The poor man stared disconsolately at the coffee pot.

"How long do we have until London recalls you?" asked Avers.

"Hmm?" Wakeford still didn't break eye contact with the coffee pot. "I've already reported to London. It will take three days to reach them, then another three for their reply. No more than a week."

"Then a week it is." Avers put down his empty coffee cup decisively. "That's time enough to go to the hunting lodge and find out what the Comte and his cronies are really up to."

"It's no longer necessary. Don't waste your time on this vain mission anymore."

"I refuse to believe it's vain yet," Avers replied firmly.

"It *is* man!" Wakeford raised his voice in a flash of frustration, but it quickly died back down. "But do as you wish.

There's likely nothing more you will find out, but if it will amuse you to spend a weekend at the Marquis' hunting lodge, I shan't stop you."

Avers recognised it was not the time to argue with his friend. In Wakeford's current mood no amount of rationalising would help. But he wouldn't give up. He couldn't leave Wakeford to face dishonour— or worse, imprisonment—for something his friend had not done.

Three questions circled round and around in Avers' mind. Firstly, what business opportunity were the Comte and Dartois offering Avers if the papers' contents had already been sold? Secondly, what was so secret that it made it necessary for them to meet outside of Paris at Dartois' hunting lodge? And thirdly, if there really was nothing more to discover, as Wakeford surmised, then why had the Comte burned his mistress' hand for fear of her revealing information about their enterprise?

No, this business was not done. There was more afoot here and Avers needed to get to the bottom of it. He needed to do so for the sake of Wakeford's innocence—and Mademoiselle Cadeaux's safety.

CHAPTER NINETEEN

Over the following week Avers had to resist the temptation to send a message to Mademoiselle Cadeaux to ask after her welfare. Not trusting the servants of Mademoiselle Cadeaux's household, as they were likely in the Comte's pay, he had no way of getting a note to her without fear of interception.

In lieu of direct contact, he visited both the Champs-Élysées and the Jardin des Tuileries every day in the hopes he would find her there walking Lutin. He did not.

On Friday afternoon, Avers bade his valet pack a small trunk, and set off for Dartois' hunting lodge. He was fortunate that the Tremaines kept a stable in Paris in spite of the irregularity of their visits, so Avers was conveyed beyond the bounds of the city in a crested chaise and four, two pairs of smart, matching greys carrying him forward.

The first leg of the journey was easy enough. The roads were fair and the weather on their side. That was until they reached Chaville. At that point, a storm that had been threatening finally broke, and the less well-travelled roads became a quagmire. The pace was reduced to a crawl in order to prevent laming the horses, and Avers could not see more than ten yards away from the carriage window, thanks to the torrential rain.

After a time, they passed Versailles and beyond this point the traffic lessened considerably and the roads worsened at an equal pace. Three miles further along the road, they entered a settlement of less than ten houses.

Avers felt the coach come to a halt and the vehicle creak sideways as the driver climbed down off his box. Were they here? He could see no grand house, just a few cottages and a run-down inn.

When the driver knocked on the window, Avers dropped it down, the rain lashing inside before the coachman filled the gap.

"I'm sorry, Your Grace, but the horses may lame if we keep going in this weather. Begging your pardon, but I would as lief wait out the rain for half an hour in the hopes the ground will soak it up, rather than risk getting stuck on the open road. There's a coaching inn just here we can stop at." The coachman gestured to the questionable looking establishment.

Avers had no idea where they were. Neither did he like the idea of frequenting that inn. But there was sense in what his driver was saying and the sight of the sodden man helped make his decision.

"Very well, Hendricks—until the rain eases. But if it doesn't let up in half an hour, we'll have to try the rest of the journey at a crawl." As soon as he saw the coachman nod, he threw the window back up to keep out the rain.

Hendricks was quick about climbing back onboard and in the next five minutes the carriage was pulling off the road into the swampy courtyard of the coaching inn.

It took Avers less than a minute after descending from the carriage to realise his decision to shelter in this place had been a mistake. The building before him was dreadfully run down, its roof patched, and cracked plaster across its facade no doubt letting in the rain. It was doubtful this was a hostelry well-frequented by Avers' class. The lack of other carriages and horses in the courtyard gave it an unnerving feeling and he wondered whether this establishment made its money from catering to travellers or less legal means.

"Hendricks, come here if you please," Avers commanded.

A youth, no doubt the landlord's son, appeared from the stables and came to the horses' heads. Despite this, Hendricks hesitated. He looked at the horses, the boy, and then back at his master.

There might at least be a stable boy to tend the horses, but Avers could not ignore his gut. There were plenty of inns in England who made their living from thieving off unwitting travellers.

The coachman came reluctantly over to where Avers stood. "Yes, Your Grace?"

"I've changed my mind. I think we should carry on, even if it's slowly."

"But Your Grace—" Hendricks looked back at the boy who was staring at them. Then at the inn, then back at his master.

Avers was just about to give the man a tremendous scolding for failing to obey his orders when the heavens re-opened. Rain came down in heavy sheets, lashing across the courtyard, forcing Avers to run to shelter by the wall of the inn beneath the overhanging roof.

"Very well!" Avers shouted across the downpour. "Stable the horses and then come dry yourself off by the fire."

If this place *had* a fire.

"Yes, Your Grace," Hendricks said immediately, running off to tend the horses.

Following the wall to keep out of the worst of the rain Avers headed for the inn's door. On trying it, he found it locked. Not a good sign. He rapped on the wood.

A middle-aged man, presumably the landlord, finally opened it to a rather vexed Avers.

"Good day to you," said Avers in passable French. "A room, if you please, in which I might partake of a modest repast?"

Droplets dripped from the brim of his hat and despite wearing his roquelaure with its high collar up around his face, he felt moisture over his cheeks.

The landlord did not immediately greet him. Instead, the beady eyed individual peered around Avers at the coach in the courtyard. There was the flicker of a smile across his face and then he focused back on Avers and bobbed his head.

"Yes, Your Grace."

That was an exceptionally good guess at Avers' title from a brief glance at the crest on the Tremaine carriage.

"But there is no cook on the premises."

Of course there wasn't. Avers' stomach rumbled.

Behind him, the sound of the carriage wheels turning on the wet cobbles indicated that the stable boy was helping the coachman to unhitch the horses.

"I have a room with a fire lit that you may have," said the man, head nodding vigorously. "You must come in and dry yourself."

That was more welcoming than Avers had so far experienced.

"And some drink you might rummage up?"

"Oh yes, yes, come in, come in."

From no greeting to practically pushing him into the hostelry. This was an odd little man indeed. But by now the rain had seeped its way through the gaps in Avers' clothing and that fire sounded very appealing.

They crossed a dimly lit and dirty floored passage into a taproom of sorts. A few men were dotted here and there. They glanced over at the newcomer and several whispered behind tankards to each other. What had he walked into? Avers thought of the blunderbuss beneath Hendricks' seat on the carriage and wished he had it about his person right now.

At least the landlord had understood his request for a private room. He took Avers through this public space into another passageway and finally through a creaking door into a tiny, rudely furnished boxroom with a small dusty window set high in the wall.

"A candle perhaps?" Avers requested. "And what drink you have."

"Oui." The landlord bowed away, leaving Avers to take a seat on an uneven chair as the latch of the door fell into place with a resounding clunk.

It did not fill Avers with confidence. He was hard pressed not to imagine he'd just been locked in and was immensely relieved when the landlord returned with his requested candle and drink.

He was once again shut into the room, but this time felt less like the prisoner he had before. Passing an uncomfortable half-hour in what Avers was fairly sure was a storeroom and *not* a private parlour, he tried his best to drink the acidic ale he'd been served. He stomached it for the sake of his parched throat and was thankful that at the very least he'd determined their location from the landlord—a small hamlet called Buc.

When the coachman finally knocked on the door to tell him the rain had lifted, Avers was the most thankful man in all of France.

Hendricks went on ahead while Avers settled his bill. Leaving a third of his drink untouched, he paid what he was sure was an inflated sum to the innkeeper, and donned his cloak with gusto. Leaving the questionable establishment in his wake, Avers entered the courtyard once again, expecting to see Hendricks and the coach waiting.

He saw neither.

Looking right towards the yard entrance did not reveal the Tremaine vehicle or the smart greys waiting on the road. Just as he was about to turn back into the inn, the door slammed in his face. He tried the handle. Locked.

An involuntary shiver ran down his spine.

Releasing the door, all his misgivings coming to the fore of his mind, he slowly turned to face the deserted stableyard again. An unnatural silence greeted him.

Rain dripped from a broken gutter into a pile of sodden hay, the sound oddly muffled, but aside from that nothing stirred. The lack of human presence in a place which should have been bustling with activity fed the uneasy feeling in Avers' gut.

He considered calling out for Hendricks, but thought better of it, checked by the feeling in his stomach. Instead, he headed to the stables to discover what had become of the missing greys, carriage and driver.

The cobbles and muck beneath his boots clicked and squelched alternately. The pattering from the gutter into the hay slowed. The abnormal quiet continued.

Arriving at the entrance to what passed as a stable he peered down the long passage formed by the lean-to tacked onto the side of the ramshackle inn. No natural light penetrated the interior passage which Avers assumed was home to several looseboxes for the horses that were regularly stabled at the inn. Thanks to the heavy rain clouds, the lack of any artificial light, and that dusk was now falling, Avers could make little out in the darkness.

He was debating whether to venture into the gloom in search of Hendricks or a sign of the horses when someone grabbed him roughly from behind.

Avers was thrust forward into the darkness, forcing him to stumble and flail to catch his balance. Just as he saved himself, a second set of hands reached out from the darkness to Avers'

DUKE OF DISGUISE

left and pushed him into an empty loosebox. He was sent careening downwards, mercifully onto a freshly made bed of straw. Scrambling, Avers turned to face whoever was attacking him, his mind struggling to catch up with the sudden turn of events.

"Tell us what you know of the Comte de Vergelles," a voice hissed through the darkness at the same moment a flint was struck and an oil lamp blazed into light.

The glow revealed three men, heavily garbed in greatcoats, faces half-obscured by mufflers. Each looked at Avers with the eagerness of a pack of hounds staring at a cornered fox.

Avers played for time, gaining his bearings and surveying his captors as he brushed several strands of straw from his cloak, which had become horribly tangled up around him. "I shall do no such thing, after being manhandled by strangers."

His apparent nonchalance seemed to wrong-foot the men. There was a moment of hesitation. Avers thanked God that while he might be seriously shaken, he had an uncanny ability to present a calm front.

"You will do as we say," repeated the man who had spoken before, this time in English. His accent was rough and common.

"What are you about—manhandling me in such a way? It's not the done thing, not at all." Avers was trying to make out their features, but the one who held the lamp must have seen him squinting for he raised it higher, dazzling him.

"You will tell us what you know about the Comte de Vergelles and his dealings."

"The Comte de what?" Avers now sat cross-legged like a naughty schoolboy looking up at them.

"Don't play games." The third man came forward and levelled a pistol at Avers' forehead. "Tell us what you know."

For a moment, Avers' words failed him. His breath came

155

quick and shallow. The barrel of the gun looked as dark and ominous as the passageway of the stable had done.

"About this Comte fellow?"

Who were these men? And how on earth was Avers going to get out of this mess? Whatever the Comte was involved in was not over as Wakeford's superiors might hope. It was very much still happening and very much still dangerous.

"You're trying my patience," said the man with the gun, his accent definitely provincial. "I suggest you stop doing that. We know you have dealings with the Comte. You will answer our questions in the name of the King."

That brought Avers up short. The King?

"You're working for Louis?"

"Oui—we work for His Majesty against all enemies, including those from within. Tell us what you know."

What on earth? Avers' mind sped back and forth over the last few weeks trying to work out how the French government might be involved in the Comte's spy ring. More importantly, why had they targeted the faux Duke of Tremaine? And how had they known he'd be here?

"A dead English Duke means nothing to us," hissed the man with the gun, pressing its cold barrel against Avers' forehead.

"Are you sure? I imagine it'd be the devil of a thing to explain away if my body should show up in a backwards inn at Buc."

"Perhaps the silly English lord stopped at the inn and got set upon by ruffians."

The coldness of that barrel against his head brought a great deal of perspective. Suddenly the melancholy he'd felt since Miss Curshaw had thrown him over seemed like a colossal waste of time. Not only that, but what of those he'd leave behind—his dear Cousin Sophy and Aunt Goring?

DUKE OF DISGUISE

What about Wakeford and his papers? What about... Mademoiselle Cadeaux?

Mademoiselle Cadeaux... It had only been her, the Comte's circle and Wakeford who knew of his departure from Paris. And would French agents *really* be willing to kill an English Duke?

Avers had an idea. A wild one. What if this wasn't the French government at all, but rather the Comte's men? No. Surely not. And yet...

What had Avers got to lose by testing his theory? He already had a gun to his head.

"I'm afraid you'll have to do your worst—for I have no idea what it is you think I should know—but I do know that I don't know it."

The confusing sentence hung in the air. Two of the men exchanged glances, but the third, who held the gun, kept staring at Avers.

Then something unexpected happened. The man with the pistol began to... *laugh*. Avers blinked, thinking he misheard the sound from beneath the man's muffler, but sure enough, the man was actually laughing. It started as a bark of laughter, rolling into a chuckle, and quickly deteriorating into something akin to a crazed cackle.

Avers watched the gun bobbing up and down in the man's hand. He clutched at the straw beneath him, holding his breath, unblinking—as though each of those actions might have some control over staying the lead bullet from travelling down the barrel of the gun.

At any moment his unhinged captor might pull the trigger by accident.

"Well, well, well, Your Grace. Très bien. We never thought you would pass my test—the Comte was convinced you would fail—but here we are." The provincial accent fell completely away and in its place the smooth and precise accent of the upper ranks.

Avers recognised that voice.

Realisation that he had been right brought with it not relief, but horror. The man with the gun pulled down his muffler to reveal a charming smile.

"Dartois!" Avers finally let out the breath he had been subconsciously holding.

The Marquis threw back his cloak, a suit of aquamarine shown in the lantern light, and swept a low bow before Avers. The pistol still dangled from one hand.

"Oui! It is I. And a fine joke I have made of this." The Marquis waved the loaded gun around to take in the other two men and the dank domain of the stable. "Did you really think I might shoot you?"

"I hardly thought you'd hold me at gun point," said Avers, the shock quickly giving away to abject fury, "so who's to say?"

Dartois burst into laughter again. The sound still held that edginess which suggested someone not quite in control of their faculties.

"The courage in this one—" Dartois gestured towards Avers with his pistol as he looked around at his men. "Impressionnant, non?"

The fear for his life now in full retreat, Avers pressed his lips firmly together to prevent himself from saying something he'd later regret. He chose instead to focus on standing and brushing the straw from his person. That and smothering the desire to throttle Dartois.

He tugged his cuffs down one at a time before saying, "Pray tell me, what have you done with my poor coachman?"

"Ha!" Dartois exclaimed, his gleaming eyes quickly seeking out Avers' own once again. "As cool as a winter lake." The Marquis smiled, the lamplight catching his teeth and giving the impression he was bearing them at Avers. "You need not worry. Your little coachman has been paid handsomely for stopping here and has been enjoying the landlord's ale while we've been having our little chat."

"As long as he is rested—"

Dartois broke into a laugh, and it was just as well he did before Avers spoke his mind about the duplicitous Tremaine coachman. Hendricks had used the rain as a ruse to bring him here and known exactly what Avers was about to face. The Tremaine servants were proving overly susceptible to the Comte's bribes.

"And this little play act—" Avers continued, now focusing on brushing the stable dust off his sleeves. "I presume it was to test my ability to keep a secret."

"Oui. But don't be angry, my English Duke," Dartois said jovially. "We thought it the ideal place to have a private tête-à-tête."

"Paid off the owner, did you?"

"A waste of money—no, Sebastien knocked him out cold and locked him up in the inn."

Dartois had not put the pistol away. From the feverish excitement in the Marquis' eyes, Avers had the uneasy feeling that—had he not passed the so-called test—he would have witnessed the weapon going off.

For the first time since this whole adventure began, Avers could no longer feel the ground. He was out of his depth. And that was not a pleasant feeling at all.

"Are we to stay here all night?" he asked, raising a single brow and doing his best to hide his anger.

"Non," Dartois replied, looking even more amused. "That would never do. Let no one call me a poor host. Come, we can still make my hunting lodge by nightfall and my chef will have a feast ready for us when we arrive."

Avers followed Dartois out of the stable, the other men

coming behind like jailors, and the Marquis chattering all the way about what his chef would have prepared for dinner. A mere five minutes ago Dartois had held a loaded pistol at Avers' head—now he discussed favourite jellies. It was enough to leave Avers questioning the Marquis' sanity.

The entourage made its way out of the courtyard and around to the other side of the inn where the Tremaine coach was located. Hendricks would not look Avers in the eye when his master approached and the latter chose not to address his disloyalty in the present moment.

Installed back in the carriage, Hendricks atop, and the Marquis and his men in their own chaise, the party set forward together. Avers was thankful for the mercy of an empty carriage for the remainder of his journey. He needed the time to regain his composure and process the ordeal he had just been through.

He should perhaps have felt relieved at knowing he had passed the Comte's test. Instead, as his mind ran over what had happened, a sense of foreboding grew within him. With every mile they gained, Avers felt closer and closer to being thrown into the lion's den.

A den in which Mademoiselle Cadeaux already dwelt. Avers wondered what tests the Comte's mistress might have been subjected to. More than that, he wondered exactly what Vergelles' business dealings were that they required levelling a pistol to test loyalty. And at an English Duke no less. It took a brazen man to risk such a thing and Dartois had done it with a smile.

This dramatic episode in Buc did not bode well. No, it did not bode well at all.

CHAPTER TWENTY

The Comte had been looking furtively at the clock on the mantelpiece throughout dinner. Emilie and Vergelles sat alone in the dining room of Dartois' hunting lodge and no explanation had been given as to the whereabouts of the rest of the party.

Emilie had not queried it. The burn on the back of her hand still stung and she knew better than to tempt the Comte's anger.

Dartois' chef was excellent. They were served several small plates of game and soup before the main course of duck à l'orange with vegetables and crisped potatoes. Emilie did not have much appetite. It had yet to return since her altercation with the Comte and whenever she was in his presence, she found all desire for food abated.

"An excellent bird," said the Comte, attempting to engage her in conversation.

"Oui," she replied. "Very tasty indeed." To substantiate the statement she cut a slice from the leg on her plate and popped the succulent meat in her mouth.

"You are settled in your room? It is close to mine—should you need anything. Only one door across."

Emilie nodded, saying nothing. It was the second time Vergelles had mentioned the proximity of their rooms. She had the distinct impression he had arranged the locations with Dartois and expected something to come from it. The thought conjured a nauseous sensation in the pit of Emilie's stomach.

She had played her hand well, but soon she would be out of cards.

"With such an arrangement in our rooms, perhaps now is the time to—" The Comte's speech was interrupted by the sound of voices in the hall. "Ah! I believe our guest has finally arrived."

He rose and went to open the dining room door. The moment his back was turned Emilie breathed out in relief, trying not to guess what his next words would have been. Thankfully she was saved from her imagination by the thought of the new arrival—the Duke of Tremaine. The man of contradictions.

Emilie rose, placing her napkin on the table and smoothing her hand over her stomach, willing it to be calm. She slipped into the hallway without being noticed by the gathering of men. There were Dartois, Sebastien and two others of the Comte's circle, all dressed as though it were the middle of winter with their cloaks and mufflers. Behind them came the Duke of Tremaine.

"Bonsoir, Vergelles," said Dartois jovially, taking the Comte's hand and shaking it in the way Emilie knew he disliked. "Has my chef been looking after you?"

"I'm fit to expire!" said Sebastien. "Tell me you will not make us change for dinner, Dartois?"

"I have no aversion to the suggestion. Though I expect the Comte will want us to discard our cloaks at the very least."

"I would," Lucien said, glancing at the others with a hint

of disdain. "But this is your house, Dartois. Whatever you desire."

"Whatever I desire?"

For a fraction of a second, Dartois' eyes flicked over the Comte's shoulder and looked directly into Emilie's own. She froze, the memory of Dartois' offer all too vivid in her mind.

The Marquis turned away to throw his cloak on a waiting servant. "Off with our outer garments and let us eat before Monsieur Gardoin's dinner is spoiled. I am sure our friend the Duke will appreciate some restoring victuals after his *ordeal*."

A rumble of laughter ran around the men.

"I expect so. Your Grace." The Comte offered him the merest incline of his head rather than the full bow his status deserved. "A pleasant journey, was it?"

For a moment, the usually talkative Duke appeared as though he would say nothing. He stared at the Comte, his hooded eyes hard as flint, with a look upon his face Emilie had not seen before. But after a few seconds, his expression shifted, the hardness cracking away, replaced with his usual ennui.

"It could have been a little more so—had I not met your welcome party at Buc." Tremaine's lips curled into a half-smile, but it was without sincerity and no matching joy appeared in his eyes.

Welcome party? What had the Comte and the Marquis done to the Duke?

"Come now," Dartois said affably, turning and slapping a hand across Tremaine's shoulders. "A bit of fun to determine your loyalties."

"Necessary," the Comte agreed, looking down and flicking an imaginary piece of dust from his sleeve.

"Let us not bore Mademoiselle Cadeaux with our talk," said Dartois. "I can offer you brandy for your nerves, if you need it, Tremaine. I guarantee I stock an excellent cellar."

"I have no doubt," the Duke murmured, apparently seeing Emilie for the first time and bowing towards her.

Dartois laughed, slapping Tremaine on the back again, and the party moved towards the dining room.

"I shall take you up on your offer, though I do not need it for my nerves."

"Bien," Dartois said, making his way to the sideboard and pouring drinks for the party.

The Comte resumed his seat at the far head of the table, and Emilie made her way back to hers, only to find the Duke coming to hold her chair for her. She glanced up into his face as she sat and murmured her thanks.

What was that in his eyes?

Agitation? The warring of strong emotions? An almost imperceptible furrow appeared on his brow. His gaze did not linger upon her for long, however, turning back to the gentlemen and their impenetrable conversation.

Something had happened on the road out of Paris. It was clear Dartois and his men had met the Duke of Tremaine on his way and the Marquis was acting as if it were all a grand joke. But if Emilie had learned anything in the last month, it was that Dartois was unpredictable and whatever that test of loyalty had been, it did not appear the Duke had enjoyed the experience.

The men were soon served with the food the chef had kept warm. They all devoured it ravenously and soon Emilie left them to their pipes and port.

She waited in the drawing room for half an hour, but the men did not appear and the questions in her mind grew. What had happened to the Duke on the road? What were Dartois and the Comte up to? After another quarter of an hour, Emilie assumed she was dismissed, and that the gentlemen would continue their conversation in the dining room. She sent a message via one of the servants to let them know she had retired, and went up to her room.

One of the housemaids was sent up to attend her, and before long she was dressed in her nightgown, her hair brushed out and plaited down her back. She dismissed the girl and followed her to the door, closing it behind and turning the key in the lock. Emilie might be in for a disturbed night's sleep thanks to the questions whirring round in her head, but she was determined not to be disturbed by the Comte.

CHAPTER TWENTY-ONE

Avers did not spend a restful night. His usually steady mood was feeling altogether frayed the next morning. The shock from being held at gunpoint had not abated until the small hours and any sleep he had gained had been fitful at best.

He needed to clear his head. Once he was up, he decided to venture out into the grounds of the lodge. Fresh air was what he needed to overcome the feeling of being trapped at the Comte's mercy. Descending the stairs and not knowing his way, he opted to go out the front door.

The day outside was uncertain, the sky covered in white-grey clouds and the air, which had started true to early autumn, had turned cool and damp. Rain threatened. Skirting the front of the building, the gravel of the drive crunching under his boots, he followed the shrub line around to the rear where the formal gardens were laid out. To his right was the entrance to the stableyard, an archway leading through to where the Tremaine greys must be resting. Directly behind the lodge the gardens were simple lawns divided into quarters by gravel paths for promenading.

It was likely he could be seen from the house, so to gain time away from prying eyes, Avers turned left towards the rest of the gardens. He passed a line of manicured trees, his pace now a brisk stride and his mind fully occupied—despite his best efforts—with replaying the events of yesterday. He turned off the main path, heading towards one of the garden's stone walls, and was just going around a set of rose bushes to come parallel with it when his booted foot connected with something soft.

"Ouch!"

Avers tried to pull back, off-balance from his forward momentum. He failed, lurched sideways and plunged several steps further before coming to a stop and jerking round.

Mademoiselle Cadeaux knelt on the path, rubbing her ankle beneath the hem of her skirts.

"I beg your pardon." The tension running through Avers' body, which had already been at an all-time high, was pushed over the edge by surprise and his apology came out more like an angry question.

Mademoiselle Cadeaux glared at him, then bent down to examine her ankle again, muttering something in French. He took in the soil on her hands and the nearby basket of cut roses.

"It is nothing."

"I've hurt you," he said, failing to curb the anger in his voice. First yesterday's incident and now he'd inadvertently hurt Mademoiselle Cadeaux. "What were you doing crouching on the path in such a fashion?"

"I was weeding—before I was interrupted."

She rose, batting down her skirts and smearing yet more mud on them, before placing her hands on her hips and throwing him a challenging stare.

He felt her dark-eyed gaze keenly. There was a gentle flush to her cheeks from the morning air and her hair escaped in floating tendrils framing her face. His eyes dropped down, taking in the gown she wore that had clearly seen better days, the floral material a little faded, the cuffs frayed. It wasn't the glittering, pleated and bowed gowns he had seen her in before. Her appearance was so altered, he supposed some might see her as dowdy in such a garb, but they would be wrong. He had never seen her look more beautiful.

Avers had been staring for too long.

"Do you mean to chastise me with your stare, Your Grace? I realise weeding is not the work which women of your rank undertake, but I am not a lady, remember?"

She had misunderstood his look. It was anything but critical. Her sudden appearance set off a whole different range of emotions to the ones he had been feeling. Unfortunately, it left him even more discomposed and before he had the sense to stop himself he snapped back at her.

"I apologise. Being held at gunpoint has a way of disconcerting a man."

Shock fractured her expression. "Gunpoint?"

She took a step forward and then jerked to a stop.

"You weren't privy to your Comte's little game? His test of loyalty?"

His tone made it sound like an accusation and he saw the flash of anger in her eyes. He didn't care. What was wrong with this woman? She stayed with a madman, putting herself in harm's way, getting burnt for speaking to him. If Vergelles had been willing to order a Duke to be held at gunpoint to test his loyalty, there was no telling what he would do to a mistress of no name or rank.

"I'm amazed at your foolishness in choosing to continue in such harmful company," he said.

"You kick me and now call me a fool?"

Her knuckles turned white as she dug her fingertips into

her hips. "And what are you, if you paid no heed to my warning? Now you have put us both in danger."

Guilt lanced his chest.

"But you are determined to think the worst of me," she said, bending to pick up the basket of flowers, "so I should not be surprised. I shall do you the favour of sparing you my company."

The stab of guilt transformed to an ache in his chest. She made to walk past him back to the lodge, and before he could stop himself he reached out a hand to grasp her arm, arresting her step beside him.

Mademoiselle Cadeaux looked up at him, her dark eyes full of surprise. He could smell the earth on her, mingling with the scent of roses and... what was it? Lavender? This close he could see the delicate flush of her cheeks from the cold morning air. It deepened under his gaze. His eyes dropped to her mouth, taking in the rise and fall of her slightly parted lips.

He instinctually dropped his head an inch. Stopped. Recognising the overwhelming desire he had to kiss her. The realisation shocked him into releasing her, yet he didn't move away.

Had she just shivered before he let her go?

He remained close enough to her that his legs felt the press of her skirts. Something indefinable was passing between them in this moment and he knew it was transitory. Soon enough it would be broken. Before it was, he needed to apologise.

"Forgive me," he said huskily. "My fear has made me bullish, and you have borne the brunt of it."

He reached for her hand, and traced a thumb lightly over her bandage that still covered the burn. "Not just fear for me."

Her brow puckered, and her eyes widened in comprehension. What was that expression on her fair face? One of surprise mingled with disbelief?

His fingers found her wrist and continued tracing their

random pattern. There, she did it again—she shivered. He had not been this close to anyone in a long time. The desire to be known, to be understood and cared for, he thought he had grown past, but it seemed those feelings had just been lying dormant.

"You need not fear for me," she said, a hint of a waver in her voice. "I only repeat my last plea to you, that you stay away from me."

"I am finding that hard to do," Avers replied honestly.

"You despise me and then you wish to protect me. I find you contrary, Your Grace." She said the last part quietly, attempting to escape his gaze by looking to the path behind him.

She was considering walking away from him again.

He sighed, releasing her hand, and stepped back to put an appropriate distance between them.

"I cannot... I carry a wound that runs deeply, given to me by the woman you quizzed me about at Madame Pertuis' last salon. I have not found a way to heal just yet. When I am pressed on it, I am afraid I do not show my best. I am not a... a whole man. I have been broken and I cannot find the way to become whole again." His honesty, his rawness, shocked even himself.

This woman had a way of drawing from him the infection that had festered in his heart since it had been broken. While she lanced it, the hurt came out, but he was starting to feel relief too, as the pressure released. As though acknowledging it somehow gave it less power to define him.

"I am not your healing."

Her blunt words caught him off-guard. She no longer avoided his gaze. Her eyes found his and conveyed a frankness matching her words.

"I didn't—" he began, but she cut him off.

"What you speak about is unforgiveness and it is the

enemy of contentment. No other person is the elixir for that ailment but God."

"You are an expert in the matter?" he said, dropping into his usual provoking tone as a defence against the painful rawness of what they spoke.

She raised a single brow at him and he felt the challenge. She would not be giving anything away.

"You're suggesting I must forgive the one who broke my heart?"

"I am not suggesting you *must* do anything."

Avers chuckled softly. This woman continually surprised him. "But you advise it?"

"I know that unforgiveness is disfiguring to the soul, and before you throw my position back at me, I also know the irony of speaking about my soul when you believe me a common mistress."

Believe me. That was an odd turn of phrase.

"You have no wish to walk a different path?"

It was her turn to laugh, but the sound was maudlin. "Consider yourself blessed to have been born a noble *and* a man. You have options where others do not." She looked past his shoulder again. "We should go back to the house before you are missed, or we are seen alone together."

He didn't want this interview to end.

"May I escort you? It is the least I can do after kicking you."

"Yes, it is."

The atmosphere between them lightened. Avers offered her his arm but she shook her head.

"I believe it would be prudent to return to the house separately."

Avers was disappointed, but she was right.

"A wise choice. You are *not* a fool, Mademoiselle Cadeaux."

He saw the corner of her mouth crook upwards. Her eyes twinkled as she inclined her head in acknowledgment of the compliment.

"Thank you, Your Grace. I wish I could say the same about you."

Avers laughed, watching her turn on her heel and make her way back towards the lodge's south side. He waited a short while, taking a turn around the garden and going over all the words they had shared, his amusement dying down into thoughtfulness.

He had wanted to kiss Mademoiselle Cadeaux... That was not a desire he had felt in some time. And the more she spoke to him—the more wisdom that poured from her lips and candour that she operated with—that feeling had strengthened. But she had pushed him away. She had made it clear she was not the solution to his discontent and that action made him admire her all the more.

Unforgiveness is disfiguring to the soul.

The words hung clearly at the forefront of his mind. They deserved careful thought. But as he turned into the lodge's entrance, he resumed his alter-ego and made ready to play his part. Deciphering the mixture of emotions Mademoiselle Cadeaux had stirred within him would have to wait.

CHAPTER TWENTY-TWO

The Duke's question echoed back and forth across Emilie's mind. *You have no wish to walk a different path?*

She scoffed aloud as she skirted the shrubbery edging the walls of the lodge and turned into its south entrance. It was a boot room, designed for the return of the men from hunting, with large flagstones making up the floor, various pegs in the walls for the hanging of hunting gear, and a broad oak trestle table running down its centre. She placed the basket of cut roses on the table while she changed out of her dirty boots and into silk mules appropriate for inside.

It was easy for the Duke of Tremaine to ask such a question of her. His ignorance was understandable when he enjoyed the security of his position. His place in life had been on firm foundations from the beginning. Emilie had been born clinging to an uneven surface, forced to carve out her security, making footholds above the treacherous waves of life below.

Yet... the Duke's words ran around her mind again. She

was choosing to remain in her current position with the Comte's suit hanging over her.

Was it a choice?

Emilie's standing felt more precarious than ever and it was not only herself she must think of. There was also Mademoiselle Saint-Val Cadette and those who depended on her in the Île de la Cité. She was staying where she was for the moment to protect others and herself until she could find a way out. Piece by piece, the Comte had taken away her freedom. The final piece was still hers, but it was clear Emilie was nearly out of time.

Even before this English Duke had bowled into her life and begun challenging her decisions, she had already been questioning her choices. But that inner questioning had been easy to ignore. The Duke of Tremaine was not. Especially when he had looked at her as he had just now.

It had been desire in his eyes.

But Emilie would not be trapped a second time. She had learned from Vergelles. And what she had said was true. She had seen the pain in the Duke's face when he had spoken of the woman he loved. Whatever emotions he felt towards Emilie, they were superficial, while the wound below was real. The fact that for an instant she had wanted him to kiss her was... by the by.

She brushed down her dress with her hands, removing any loose pieces of mud, and headed into the house with the basket on her arm. Just as she came into the hall, Dartois appeared.

"Good morning, Mademoiselle." He bowed to her. "I see you have been making use of my gardens?"

"Yes," Emilie replied, realising how forward she must look. "I asked your housekeeper if any cut flowers were needed for the house, and she furnished me with a basket, scissors and a trowel as I like to weed. I wished for fresh air. I hope that was all right?"

"But of course." Dartois opened his arms wide. "What's mine is yours, Mademoiselle Cadeaux." That disconcerting gleam that had been in his eyes when they were last alone reappeared.

Emilie felt the atmosphere shift from a polite morning greeting to something else. The Marquis came towards her, feigning interest in the basket of flowers on her arm.

"Beautiful, aren't they? And that scent—the very scent of heaven." He was close, smiling down at her, and one finger found the bandage on her hand and traced over it. "The gardens here were all in ruins when I bought the place. It used to belong to my grandfather before he had to sell it off. I persuaded the new owner, an elderly widow, that she was better getting the property off her hands, and I have been bringing it back to life ever since. Roses were my choice—have you ever noticed how hardy they are? They may be cut back harshly by the gardener, but they come back more vigorous than ever."

His touch on her hand made her shiver, but not with the pleasure Avers had evoked before.

"They are beautiful flowers. I should get them to the housekeeper to put in water before they wilt."

Dartois completely ignored what she said. "Have you thought about whether you want more than your position as the Comte's mistress, Mademoiselle Cadeaux?"

With his words Emilie's entire frame tensed. The unease his touch had induced was magnified by his question. She had hoped to get away from him before he had the opportunity to bring up this subject.

Dartois pointed at the bandage. "I should not mark such a pretty thing if I was its owner."

Owner. The word made her feel sick.

"I guess it is not sensible to damage what you are investing in," she replied, nausea giving way to anger.

Dartois smiled. "Exactly."

The heat of her fury gave her sudden courage. "No, my Lord." How dare he treat her like an object to be bought or sold. She may be a nobody, without name or wealth, but she would never be owned. "I have not considered it."

"You will," Dartois said confidently. His arrogance repulsed Emilie even further. "But I will not press you. Unlike the Comte I am not interested in coercing an answer."

"I think you mistake my value, my Lord," Emilie replied. "I am only a woman." If he was going to talk about her as an object—and paradoxically, he had before called her a creature of wit and curiosity—then she would use his words against him.

"Correct," he replied. "But as I said before, you have potential that could allow you to do so much more within your position as a mistress. I have plans you would fit into so well, Mademoiselle Cadeaux. Lucrative plans that would see us gain wealth we couldn't have dreamed of."

A servant appeared in the hall. The Marquis broke off his conversation and both of them watched the maid carrying a basket of wood into the morning room to make up the fire. He seemed about to resume his petitioning when sounds above indicated the other inhabitants of the house were now awake and moving around. She heard Tremaine's voice from the dining room as another servant appeared from the kitchen and entered the room with a tray of food.

"You had better get those flowers to the housekeeper, Mademoiselle Cadeaux, and then come in to breakfast," said Dartois.

"Yes, my Lord," she replied, inwardly sighing with relief.

She left Dartois' presence as quickly as she could and made her way to the kitchen with her basket. The Duke of

Tremaine's questioning and the Marquis' talk of 'ownership' had sparked a fire within her.

Up until now she had been biding her time, waiting to see what happened and how she might play her hand to protect herself. She had been operating from a defensive position fuelled by a growing fear. But now she could feel the corner into which the Comte's impatience and Dartois' menacing offer had backed her, her fear transformed into anger.

Life may be outside of her control, but she would not sit idly by any longer and allow it to happen to her. Her tenacity grew. She wasn't sure how. She wasn't sure when. But she had to get out.

CHAPTER TWENTY-THREE

"We have some sensitive information," said the Comte, his cool eyes observing Avers over the top of his steepled fingers.

They sat in the study of the lodge. Avers noted the floral wall paintings that peeped between the many books lining the walls. It was entirely at odds with the otherwise masculine domain, and yet somehow it suited Dartois, the noble who was at once pleasantly affable and terrifyingly unhinged.

"Information? So, it isn't just brandy and lace you are selling after all," Avers replied, feigning disinterest by observing the cuffs of his jacket and straightening one, then the other. "I assume, whatever it is, the information must be high profile for you to have asked me outside of Paris and to—ah—test my loyalty?"

"Still sore over it?" asked Dartois who sat behind the ornate desk, his booted feet carelessly resting on its polished top.

"Not at all," Avers replied, keeping his tone even. "I am only pleased the experience had purpose—I hope, a lucrative one."

DUKE OF DISGUISE

Dartois smiled. "*We* hope you may help us with that." He nodded to the Comte.

"It is your cousin's offices that have provided the information," Vergelles explained.

Avers gasped, as if surprised. "No wonder my cousin has been in such a foul mood. How did you come by it?"

"The important part is that we did," Dartois said, brushing off the question, "and this intelligence is worth a small fortune to interested parties." He tapped a finger on a set of innocuous looking papers on the desk.

Avers eyed them. "Are those the documents?"

"Yes," Dartois replied casually. "We have identified a buyer for the information, and we believe with your connections, you will be able to meet with them for the exchange without attracting attention."

Avers shifted in his chair to face Dartois. While the Comte had started this conversation, and the Marquis had handed over to him once, it was feeling more and more as though Dartois was leading. The relaxed and amusement-driven Marquis had an air of authority about him since they had left Paris.

Avers glanced towards the papers again. They were there—the stolen papers that Wakeford's career rested upon. Not wanting to attract attention, he allowed his gaze to drift lazily up to Dartois again and raised a single brow. "And the buyer is?"

Their explanation of the business they were offering him did not add up with Wakeford's recent conversation. According to his friend all the valuable information had already been sold to the French. There had to be another party.

"Have you heard of the Commissioners of the Continental Congress who have lately arrived in Paris?" asked Dartois.

The colonists from the Americas? Wakeford had mentioned them in his initial briefing.

"Franklin isn't it? And two others. Over from the colonies."

"When there is rebellion," Dartois said smiling, "information is as valuable as weapons, and we have enough here to interest them."

But if they had already sold the information to their French compatriots, wouldn't they pass it on to the colonists? After all, the French were subversively financing the colonists against the British already. Or was the Comte doing a double deal before the information could pass between them? Make them pay twice for the same information.

"And you think I can draw out the Commissioners with my connections in the British government?"

"They are here to petition the King for French aid, but that does not mean they would be averse to speaking with a British nobleman, especially one who may have information to help their cause. You have far more reason and influence to meet with them, thanks to your position at your cousin's offices."

He remained quiet while he allowed the information to percolate in his mind. The Comte continued to watch him and Avers couldn't help but wonder why he was suddenly the submissive one in the partnership with Dartois. Was it because he did not trust Avers and so he was sitting back and observing?

Avers' eyes were drawn back to the papers beneath Dartois' hand. If he could get hold of them, he might save Wakeford's neck and do a service to his government in one fell swoop.

"And the prize?"

Dartois laughed. "Are your uncle's strictures pinching so much?"

"Yes."

"I told you, Vergelles, that this was the man. He is so very *willing*."

The Comte's face remained impassive, but he inclined his head in acknowledgement.

"When would you like me to arrange the meeting?"

"Tuesday," Dartois answered without missing a beat. He picked up the papers and dropped them in the top drawer of his desk, shutting it and turning the key. "In the Place Dauphine on the Île de la Cité."

"Very well," Avers said with a nod. "And the price I am to negotiate?"

"Twenty thousand livres should suffice. You would enjoy twenty percent—naturally."

"This is promising indeed," Avers said, rising from his chair and forcing a smile, all the time wondering how hard it would be to force the lock on the desk drawer.

"And you're quite happy, not knowing the information you're selling?" asked Dartois, leaning back in his chair still holding the key in his hand. "You have no curiosity over its contents?"

"Need I? I'm sure our colonial friends will see any potential leverage over my fellow countrymen as worth the risk of a meeting."

Dartois chuckled. "Bien." Finally dropping his legs from the desk, he walked over to the sideboard upon which sat several crystal decanters holding liquids of varying hues. "Will you not stay and toast to our enterprise?"

"That excellent brandy of yours couldn't hurt," Avers replied.

Once the drinks were poured and handed out, Dartois and the Comte fell into a discussion about the hunting trip, and Avers was left to sip his drink in quiet reflection. He'd learned a great deal in the last half an hour, and with all the information at his disposal, his mind was fast at work hatching a plan to steal the papers.

CHAPTER TWENTY-FOUR

The hunting around Dartois' lodge offered excellent shooting and, had Avers not been completely preoccupied with a theft, he might have enjoyed himself. It was not until half the afternoon had gone and they had bagged a good number of game birds, that he conjured up an adequate reason to slip away.

Inspiration struck when he caught his boot on a firm tuft of grass in the uneven clearing where they had set up their base camp. He'd picked himself up just in time so as not to plunge headlong onto the ground, but the realisation of this opportunity struck him.

"I say, this ground is treacherous terrain—" He broke off as he faked another trip, making out he couldn't catch his balance and landing in an unimpressive pile on the floor. "Dash it all—my ankle!"

The false claim of injury drew polite sympathy from his comrades, the Comte clearly more concerned that his sport was interrupted. After Avers pretended that putting weight upon that leg was impossibly painful, Dartois sent him back to the lodge to be attended to by the butler. The cart upon which the caught game had been strung up by one of the gamekeepers was requisitioned as a makeshift stretcher to carry the Duke.

Avers arrived back at the lodge near three o'clock in the afternoon, and with the majority of the party out, the menace of the place dissipated and he had to concede it was a handsome and well-appointed residence. On his exaggerated hobble into the hall, he learned that Mademoiselle Cadeaux was in the gardens. He ordered a cold compress and a tankard of ale to the drawing room, and upon the servant delivering it and retreating, he was left alone.

Avers cocked his head to the side, listening until the servant's steps echoed into nothingness. After a short time, he dropped his 'injured' foot from the footstool that had been placed out for him and stood up. Leaving his discarded boot and stocking where it was on the floor, he put the cold compress back on the silver tray resting on the side table, and took one of the linen strips from the medicinal wrap to wind around his ankle.

He then made his way over to the door. Should he need to, he could return to the room in a hurry and replace the compress as if he had been sitting there all along. In the meantime, the linen around his ankle would hide the lack of swelling from any servants he should meet.

Avers placed his ear to the door and listened. Movement appeared to be limited to below stairs and nothing stirred in the polite chambers of the lodge. The servants were no doubt using their master's absence to rest from their toils and even the return of the injured Duke was not disrupting their plans.

Now was the time.

Resting a hand upon the door handle, he waited a moment more before pressing it slowly down and inching the door open. The hallway beyond was deserted. Avers slipped silently from the room, closed the door behind him and made quick work of the space between the drawing room and the Marquis' study. Heartbeat quickening, he tried the door and mercifully found it open.

Entering the room and realising how close he was to seeing his ambition through, his mind moved onto the following step. Escape. He would have to leave the lodge immediately after getting the papers. What of Mademoiselle Cadeaux? Could he warn her to leave as well? Would she listen?

He didn't pause long over such thoughts. If he was caught in here, all pretence would dissolve, and the threat he'd been given at the inn at Buc would likely be renewed and carried out. Driving thoughts of Dartois' pistol from his mind, Avers strode over to the desk, circling round to the side with the chair, and tried the drawer into which he'd seen the Marquis place the papers.

It didn't budge.

Avers hadn't expected it to. He scanned the desk for the letter opener he'd seen the Marquis use and found it lying with the pens in the carved-out tray of the ink stand. Snatching it up quickly, he slid the tip between the desktop and the drawer and eased it along until he hit the lock.

First he just tried to push it against the lock hoping the mechanism wasn't fully home.

No good.

Then he began working the blade, twisting it and manipulating it to try and gain some sort of purchase on the lock and force it to withdraw.

Still no good.

His final option was to force it open. It would damage the desk, but his hope was to be long gone by the time his handiwork was discovered, and the papers were found stolen... again.

He risked a rattle of the desk, putting more pressure on the knife, hoping it wouldn't snap.

"What are you doing?"

The plainly spoken question made Avers jump so much he hit his left knee against the desk, sending a cracking pain through his joint.

"Blast it!" he swore, swinging around to look at his questioner.

Mademoiselle Cadeaux stood by the door which she had already shut behind her.

He froze. One hand was on the knife jammed in the locked drawer, the other clutching his throbbing knee. His mind raced to find a suitable excuse for being found in such a compromising position.

"You are stealing from Dartois—and I had it from the servants you had twisted your ankle on the hunting trip. A ruse to get into the Marquis' study secretly, I see."

There was no getting out of this. He stared back into those frank brown eyes and knew his only choice was running or taking Mademoiselle Cadeaux into his confidence. He could not lose this opportunity to acquire the papers. He was still hesitating when she spoke again.

"What is it an English Duke needs so badly he must steal it from a French noble?"

Curse it! He still hadn't said anything. He always had something to say.

Mademoiselle Cadeaux muttered in rapid French. Avers didn't catch it all. Something about knowing this nosy English Duke wasn't what he appeared.

"Tell me the truth—what are you doing here?"

He finally relinquished the knife, leaving it jammed in the desk, and straightened. "I am—"

He broke off, coming around the desk towards her. She

backed away, a wary look in her eyes, and he responded by raising his hands in a show of peace.

"Your benefactor has stolen papers from the British government. I am tasked with retrieving them."

Her gaze was hard upon his, interrogating, measuring. Her expression was focused, emphasising the largeness of her eyes, the fine point of her nose and the arch of her shapely brows. She was achingly beautiful and Avers found himself willing her to believe his words. To believe he was not a bad man.

"A spy?"

Avers nodded, disliking the moniker but acknowledging its aptness.

With a suddenness that made him step back, she came to life, striding forward. For a moment he thought she meant to strike him, but instead she passed him quickly and came to the desk.

Removing the lid from the left-hand ink pot, she poked her slender fingers inside and began to root around.

The action was so odd, and the explanation so totally lacking, that Avers could do nothing but stare.

After a few moments of wiggling her fingers she withdrew them and to Avers' surprise they were bare of ink. There appeared to be no reason for her action until he saw the fine chain she had pinched between her first and second finger. She drew it out and upon its end dangled a key.

"Dartois' hiding place. The gentlemen—they do not notice when I am still in a room," she said by way of explanation.

She did not pause, making her way around to the side of the desk housing the drawers, and positioned herself in front of the one Avers had been trying to open. Taking hold of the knife, muttering something in French that Avers believed was not entirely ladylike, she gave it a yank.

By the second yank, Avers realised what was transpiring.

She was helping him. He came to her aid, standing beside her and leaning over to lend her his strength, when it suddenly came loose. Mademoiselle Cadeaux was sent careening backwards into him.

His hand connected with her waist, her body fell against his arm, and he instinctively pulled her against him so she didn't hit her head on the wall sconce beside her. By the time she had lost momentum, she was fully in his arms, and turning surprised eyes up at him.

She felt *good* against him.

He stared down into those dark eyes of hers and got a waft of lavender water. Then he glanced inadvertently at her lips.

Now was not the time.

He shook his head and then looked back into her eyes and realised she was looking at *his* lips. Was that a tentative desire in her expression? A rush of the same feeling ran over Avers and he instinctively dropped his head lower so that his lips brushed hers. She was soft, warm. He gently pressed his lips against hers and she responded. Pleasure flooded his senses and awareness of their circumstances very nearly deserted him.

Very nearly.

Avers raised his head from the pool of sensation he had been submerged within, and saw a similar look of realisation on her face. Releasing her, he stepped back. With a shake of her head she drew her shoulders back, and focused on the task at hand.

As if they hadn't just shared a kiss, Mademoiselle Cadeaux stepped forward, placed the key in the lock, and turned it. The well-oiled mechanism slid back easily, and she pulled the drawer open.

After a few seconds staring at its contents, she stepped back, looking over to Avers. He identified the stolen papers quickly enough, taking them from the drawer and searching through the remaining contents to make sure there was nothing else from Wakeford's office that had found its way there.

The drawer thoroughly searched, he turned back to the woman who had aided him, who now stood by watching.

"Why are you helping me? I have already caused you trouble before." He gestured to her burnt hand.

"Perhaps—perhaps I wish to make the right choice, not the easy one." Before Avers could respond, or even take in the profound statement, she spoke again. "What do you intend to do now? Fly?"

"Yes, if I can—I must go before they return." On a sudden impulse, he blurted out, "Come with me. If they even suspect you've helped me it will be more than a burnt hand you'll need to contend with."

"I—"

But whatever reply had been coming died on her lips at the sound of voices in the hall outside. Both their heads snapped round to the door, eyes wide, breath held.

Avers made out Dartois' voice, then the lower timbre of the Comte's. This was not good.

Mademoiselle Cadeaux came to life first. Snatching the papers from his hands, she thrust them back in the drawer, and shut and locked it before he could react.

"I will get the papers to you, but you cannot take them now. There's no way you could escape. We must not get caught." She dropped the key back in the empty inkpot and replaced the lid.

How cool and collected Mademoiselle Cadeaux appeared. Avers felt overwhelmed with admiration for her.

The Comte's voice sounded again in the hall.

He glanced to the door, half-expecting the nobleman to walk through it at any moment, but it remained closed—for now. On looking back to Mademoiselle Cadeaux he saw that, in spite of her quick wit, there was fear etched across her pale face.

"The window," he whispered urgently. "We cannot be found alone in here."

He strode over to it, thankful the latch and hinges had been recently oiled, and swung it open easily enough. Turning back to Mademoiselle Cadeaux he held out his hand.

She looked uncertainly at it, then back to the door, the voices in the hall growing louder. Looking once again at his outstretched hand, she gave the slightest nod, and, as if deciding the situation in her mind, she started forward.

"You will have to—"

But she was already scooping up her skirts with her free hand, exposing her stockinged legs, and lifting one over the window ledge before he could finish his instructions. The wooden heel of her silk mule clicked against the stone on the other side.

"Lift me," she commanded, bearing her weight on Avers' arm so she could gain enough purchase to sit astride the ledge. She let go of his hand and swung her other leg over, dropping down silently to the ground below the window outside, her skirts snaking after her.

Giving one last cursory glance around the room to make sure nothing appeared out of place, Avers followed the resourceful woman out the window. Upon reaching the ground he drew the glass window closed—knowing he couldn't fasten it, hoping it wouldn't be noticeable.

Their tracks covered, he turned to find Mademoiselle Cadeaux looking perfectly composed, waiting for him. His mouth curved in appreciation. What a remarkable woman.

"It is an odd time to be smiling, n'est pas?" she asked, her fine brows rising.

"I'm sorry," he said with a half-chuckle. "I've just never met a woman who would do what you have just done and appear moments later as if nothing untoward had happened."

To his surprise, a flush appeared in her milky cheeks. "I would not normally, but the circumstances demanded it. I realise it was very improper—"

"No, no!" Avers immediately raised his hands in supplication. "That is not at all what I meant. It is just that most women I have met would have had an attack of the vapours. Here you are, all calm collectedness. I admire it."

To his surprise, the flush deepened, and he saw the ghost of a smile on her lips.

"Perhaps," she said, a challenge appearing in her tone, "you have not met any women of substance before."

It was a bold statement and now she would not hold his gaze, instead focusing on smoothing her already smoothed skirts and looking down the path that ran outside the study window. But though she avoided his gaze, he continued to look at her and saw tiny dimples appearing either side of her irresistible mouth. Was she... flirting with him?

"Perhaps not," he concurred, coming quickly beside her and offering her his arm. "We had best not be found here."

She did look at him then, and there was the lightest and most beautiful smile on her face. It transformed her expression, eradicating all the hiddenness it usually contained. She appeared open and free and... yes... very, very beautiful.

Taking his arm, they both focused on the path ahead, winding around the rear of the hunting lodge towards the formal gardens.

"Ah!" he exclaimed, suddenly remembering. "I left my boot and the compress from the housekeeper in the drawing room."

It would not do to be found wandering around the gardens with Mademoiselle Cadeaux after bemoaning a twisted ankle, the treatment discarded in the house.

"I had them sent up to your room," she replied.

Avers' jaw dropped.

191

"I wasn't sure where you were and Dartois is particular about mess. After your encounter with him on your way here, I thought it best you didn't anger him."

"I thank you, my resourceful lady, for your care over my person."

"Once I found you in the study I realised the cold compress was likely a ruse to leave the hunting party."

"Resourceful and intelligent." He smiled and then added, his tone far softer, "And kind."

She remained silent.

They came to a bench and Avers invited her to sit. "Please."

He sat down beside her, but before she could settle, he pressed a hand to hers.

"I owe you an apology. I sorely misjudged your character. First you show yourself to be charitable to those less fortunate, and then you try and warn me of danger at your own expense. Yesterday you cared for my feelings, and now you aid me. I don't deserve such treatment from someone I so wrongly judged. Thank you."

Her pink lips parted in surprise.

"I should tell you—"

"Ah! There you are." Dartois' voice broke across Avers' words as it sailed across the shrubbery.

Avers removed his hand from Mademoiselle Cadeaux's and they both looked over to where their host approached down one of the formal paths. The Frenchman greeted them both, eyeing Avers' bandaged foot which he had propped up on the bench in a show of his fake injury. The Marquis invited them both in for refreshments. The couple rose, Dartois giving aid to Avers' faux hobble, and the party headed inside.

As they met with the Comte for tea and sweetmeats, Mademoiselle Cadeaux's actions replayed through Avers' mind. Even when she left his presence to change for dinner, those deep eyes of hers followed him through his thoughts. He had spoken the truth. He had never met any woman like her before, and he was beginning to think, he never would again.

CHAPTER TWENTY-FIVE

Over the next two days, Avers ran over the details of how he and Mademoiselle Cadeaux had covered their tracks. They had been careful. The Comte did not appear suspicious. But Avers was realising how unpredictable Dartois was. He made a point of remarking on Avers' swift recovery from his ankle injury several times. The affability that emanated from the Marquis and the feeling of ease in his speech cloaked a sharpness that caused Avers discomfort.

As a result, he was relieved to find out that the hunting party would be breaking up on Monday and returning to Paris. Clearly, there had been no need to prolong it, now that the Comte and Dartois has finally revealed their business proposition. The party's only other purpose had been to test his loyalty at the ambush in Buc.

Avers was told the Commissioners would soon receive an invitation, via the Comte and Dartois' communications network, and the meeting would be set. He should have been satisfied at the success of his mission, but the idea of leaving Mademoiselle Cadeaux the following morning filled him with disquiet.

DUKE OF DISGUISE

No opportunity presented itself to speak alone with her and attempting to manufacture one could put her in further danger. As a result, sleep that night evaded him, only descending in fitful bursts, and when he took his leave the following morning, he felt as though he left her, a lamb, among wolves.

He was back in Paris less than a day when he met with Wakeford. The information he had learned weighed as heavily on his mind as Mademoiselle Cadeaux. He could not escape the memory of that kiss as he travelled through early morning Paris.

When he arrived at the boxing club, the lad who had served him last time opened the door, bleary eyed. It was barely seven o'clock. Avers had paid the owner of the club to open early, and the lad showed him to the same private sparring room where he had met Wakeford less than a week before.

His friend was already there, back to the window, where he had likely been watching for Avers' arrival. He had a beaver hat pulled low on his brow and collar turned up to obscure his face.

The door clicked shut behind the serving boy.

Avers greeted him, grasping his friend's hand warmly. "Thank you for meeting me so swiftly."

"Of course—your note said urgent?"

Neither gentleman made to sit. Avers couldn't have even if he'd wanted to. He felt incapable of sitting still. Instead he threw his hat and gloves upon the table, resting his cane against a chair, and then he ran his hands through his loose hair.

"My excursion to the hunting lodge has proved fruitful. You know already that the papers the Comte de Vergelles' circle stole from your offices contained information helpful to the colonists' cause in the Americas and that they have sold the intelligence to Louis' government. Well, it appears they plan to sell it twice over before the French have a chance to pass on the information. They're intending to sell the papers to the Continental Commissioners who are currently here in Paris."

Wakeford inhaled sharply. "Devils!" He reached a hand up to rub the back of his neck, not taking into account his hat, and knocked the beaver-skin creation off his head. Its stiff brim made an odd thud on the floorboards of the largely bare room.

"It's serious, yes—" Avers began after a few moments, but Wakeford cut him off.

"Gracious!" he exclaimed, half-stumbling towards the table and falling heavily into one of the chairs. He stared disconsolately ahead of himself. "I'm ruined."

Avers followed him over to the table calmly, tapping the top lightly with his fingers to capture his friend's attention before speaking.

"The situation appears dire." He ignored a groan of unhappiness from Wakeford. "However, bringing me into it has finally paid off, my friend. They've offered me a handsome payment in return for being their go-between with the Commissioners."

Wakeford's ears pricked up at this, his eyes refocused intently upon him. "Yes? Go on."

"It appears my connection to your offices will legitimise the information in the colonists' eyes. I have the details of the meeting, where and when it is to happen, and that means we will have the chance not only to catch the Comte red-handed, but to recover the papers as well."

"You've arranged all this in the last few days?" asked Wakeford, astonished.

"I'd have the papers for you as well," Avers said ruefully, "if it wasn't for an untimely interruption by the Comte and Dartois. "It's only thanks to Mademoiselle Cadeaux that I was not caught in the act of stealing them."

"What?" Wakeford demanded in astounded accents. "The mistress?"

The title hit Avers' chest uncomfortably.

"The woman is not party to their dealings. I had to tell her what I was doing when she caught me in Dartois' study trying to retrieve the papers. She helped me evade capture. When we arrest the others she must go free."

If Wakeford had been less dazed he might have noted the warmth, almost fierceness, in his friend's voice.

"I suppose if you vouch for her, and she's not at this meeting that's been arranged, then there's no point bringing her into it."

"She isn't a part of it," Avers reiterated.

But Wakeford was already onto his next thought. "Where is the meeting?"

Avers spent the next several minutes explaining exactly what had transpired at Dartois' hunting lodge, including the test of his loyalty and the plans for the meeting with the Commissioners.

"Dash it, but they're brazen fellows to hold up an English peer in such a fashion! I can only be sorry I let you go alone without support. I had no notion they would be so dangerous. And such an enclosed space for sale of the papers. They must have no fear of being caught."

"Brazen appears to be their modus operandi," Avers said, thinking of the ambush in Buc, "but we can be thankful for it in the case of the meeting with the Commissioners. It should mean they're unlikely to get away if you send people with me to arrest them."

"*With* you?" Wakeford dropped his hand from where he'd been rubbing his chin. "Gracious no, man! You won't be going anywhere near that meeting. No sense in it! If they're not afraid to hold an English Duke at gunpoint on the road, there's no telling what they might do when they're backed into a corner. Far better to keep you out of it entirely.

"I'll send a note to Lord Stormont and Viscount Weymouth directly to apprise them of the situation and request a retinue of men to be positioned in the gardens ready for the meeting—discreetly of course—and as soon as the Comte and his men show their hand we'll bring them in."

"You're sure I won't be needed? I have no problem seeing this through if it should result in their apprehension." Avers wasn't sure he wished to leave the work so wholly out of his control, not when it would indirectly affect Mademoiselle Cadeaux. The Comte needed to be taken into custody without issue if she was to be kept safe.

"I'm positive. You've put yourself in harm's way enough for me already." He reached over and put a hand on Avers' shoulder, patting him soundly. "For that I'm immeasurably grateful. Mind you, if I had known there was still something afoot, I wouldn't have let you go to the hunting lodge at all."

"I knew the situation wasn't done yet."

"I should have listened to your gut," Wakeford replied ruefully. "You have more of a knack for this sort of work than I would have thought—espionage that is."

"I'm not sure what that says of my character," Avers replied, with a mock-frown. "Not a gentlemanly pursuit with its falsehoods and trickery. But seriously—you are absolutely sure I am not needed for the exchange? I'm happy to continue playing my part if it will aid their arrest. It could be our only chance to get them."

"I'm well aware of that, and yes, I'm certain. You've done your part and I'm confident that now we have a solid meeting arranged, we'll be able to bring them to justice. My reputation and my neck will be forever grateful to you." He rubbed at the skin between his chin and his cravat.

Avers refrained from saying what was in his mind. It was not only Wakeford's safety he was concerned about.

"It's the Comte you want," said Avers unnecessarily. "He's the ringleader, so you must make sure you pick him up at the earliest opportunity."

Once Vergelles was under arrest there would be no further danger to Mademoiselle Cadeaux.

"I know. Thank you."

Wakeford rose and Avers reluctantly followed suit, realising his friend's mind was made up—he wouldn't let him take part in the meeting on the Île de la Cité.

"You've saved my skin." Wakeford threw his arms around Avers to embrace him. "I shan't ever be able to repay you."

"Just get the Comte." Avers broke his friend's hold, nodding, the business settled.

But his feelings were no easier than they had been all night when they parted. The prospect of remaining at the Tremaine's Hôtel while the Comte and his accomplices were apprehended was intolerable.

It was not just *their* fates which hung in the balance. Nor was it only Wakeford's. It was the fate of Mademoiselle Cadeaux—the woman who had aided Avers at the expense of her safety. The woman who had proved herself a lady of character despite his judgements. The woman who was increasingly consuming his thoughts no matter how hard he tried to fight it.

The idea of that woman being in danger, and Avers being unable to aid her, was almost too much to bear.

CHAPTER TWENTY-SIX

The fine weather Paris had been enjoying since Avers' return to the city broke on Tuesday afternoon. Grey clouds crowded in above, obscuring the sun, but they failed to release the rain they threatened. A mist came up the Seine, creeping out into the streets, clinging to the buildings like some ominous being. It provoked an odd closeness in the air, one of cold and damp. Everything about the atmosphere of the city became heavy and depressive.

It was the perfect backdrop for an exchange of stolen British documents. Avers couldn't have written it better himself—though, perhaps, he might have chosen a different hero. For despite Wakeford's best efforts to keep his friend out of any further dealings with the Comte and his circle, Avers was entering the Place Dauphine on the Île de la Cité in person for the exchange.

Both Wakeford and Avers had naively assumed that the Comte and his men would meet the faux Duke of Tremaine with the papers at the rendezvous point. It had been the lynchpin of Wakeford's plan to keep Avers out of the situation. However, shortly before the meeting, a note appeared on the Tremaine hall table, reading as follows:

Our friend,

We hope your ankle has sufficiently healed from your unfortunate fall to undertake our agreed business on Tuesday at 2 o'clock.

You're invited to attend us at our known address before the meeting. We will journey together to rendezvous with our mutual friends and offer them our gift.

We hope it will be less eventful than our meeting in Buc—

The sardonic tone and the mention of the meeting at Buc had all the strokes of Dartois' hand. When the Tremaine servants had been questioned as to who had delivered the note, none could confirm having received it. According to the retainers it had simply appeared in the hall. The idea that the Comte's circle was not only able to communicate amongst themselves without being caught, but could enter the very home of another, without any sign, was disturbing.

As there was no signature on the note it could not be used as evidence, and Avers had no way to respond to Dartois and the Comte to counter with an alternative plan that might keep him out of harm's way. Truth be told, the alteration to Wakeford's plans was a welcome one to Avers.

So it was that he was journeying with the Comte and Dartois to the Île de la Cité a little before two o'clock through the dim mist of the Parisian streets. The Comte remained largely silent while Dartois' casual attitude and speech set Avers' teeth on edge. There was no mention of Mademoiselle Cadeaux, and Avers chose not to bring her up, despite wanting to know of her well-being with every irritating word that came out of Dartois' mouth. Soon enough she would be free of the Comte and Avers could check on her himself. For now, he must focus on the business at hand.

Shortly before the carriage reached its destination, Dartois handed him a leather portfolio containing the papers. Avers resisted the urge to check the contents. His persona of uncaring Duke would hardly bother with the particulars, and even if he'd wanted to, the next moment they arrived.

Disembarking from the carriage, the portfolio beneath his arm, he entered the Place Dauphine. The grounds before him were set out in formal sections with gravel paths intersecting them. While the blooms that were out might have looked vibrant in the sun, they appeared now like a mockery of the season among the green leaves and branches.

Behind Avers, the Seine flowed around the base of the Pont Neuf, the architectural feat of the previous century that severed the island from its tip and made up the road next to the square. Here and there creeping tendrils of mist had snaked their way over the bridge's balustrade to dissipate slowly across the thoroughfare.

Up ahead the boundaries of the Place Dauphine opened up to a square end and Avers made a circuit before taking up position in one of the far corners. From this vantage point, with no one behind him, he would be able to observe everyone who arrived in the gardens. That would be the best place to wait.

Through the avenue of buildings leading back onto the

Pont, he saw the mist swirling, expecting some ghoul to rise up from the murky Seine and break through the fog.

None did. The mist ebbed and flowed and the dark, fast flowing waters could be heard in the distance undisturbed by malevolent apparitions. Avers turned back to begin his vigil.

The wait was interminable.

He had wrongly assumed the weather would turn walkers away. A steady stream flowed into and around the gardens, indistinguishable at first in the gloom, each one causing Avers' heartbeat to quicken and his body to tense in anticipation. At least ten individuals came and went, none appearing to be promenading for leisure. Most had purposeful strides and were deep in conversation with companions. It was obvious from the staid clothes and old-fashioned wigs that several of them were taking air between sittings of the judicial courts which were housed on the island.

These men of the law and the middling sort were nothing like those with whom Avers had been mixing since coming to the French capital. These weren't men of leisure who idled away their hours at play and amusement, appearing at Versailles when summoned to court by the King, and enjoying a tax-free existence. No, these were the Frenchmen who made up the machinery of government, whose existence was driven by more than the desire for pleasure. The individual Avers was due to meet was not likely to be among their number.

Sat on a bench about fifty yards from him, Avers saw a gentleman who did not appear to be of the judicial bent. Neither did the man seem totally at ease, his eyes working their way around the square and back again. Avers recognised him as one of Wakeford's men he'd met before. He'd been told there would be men planted throughout the Place Dauphine. He hoped they would not appear obvious to the Comte and his men.

The clouds above shifted a little and Avers glanced up to

see watery sunlight, pale and harsh to his eyes. The bright daytime star was up there, trying to break through, but failing to burn off its adversaries in the atmosphere.

Avers ran a finger around the inside of his collar. It was sticky, yet he felt cold. Was it the humidity or the tension causing him such discomfort? The cravat his valet had so studiously starched wouldn't stand a chance against these elements. No doubt it was wilting already.

Another gentleman appeared on the left path. He was dressed differently. He wore his hair unpowdered, and a wool suit far more at home in a pastoral setting than the city—its cut not in the current style, and too full in the skirts and heavy in the cuffs to be considered *à la mode*. The man paused every now and then, scanning the park, looking for someone. Then his eyes settled on Avers and he struck out directly for the English Lord.

Avers' breath quickened. He clasped the leather portfolio a little tighter. That was the agreed sign—the portfolio—and even from this distance, he had seen the approaching gentleman's gaze drop to what was beneath his arm.

The man was closer now.

Twenty yards.

Fifteen.

Ten.

Avers' mouth went dry. He suddenly had an absurd desire to walk in the opposite direction as quickly as he could. Then straight after, an overwhelming feeling of idiocy. What was he to say to this man? The thought hadn't occurred to him before now. He'd been so intent on considering the impending arrest of the Comte that he hadn't considered he might actually have to speak to one of the Commissioners.

The gentleman was upon him, halting and executing a neat bow.

"Your Grace, Tremaine?"

"Good afternoon." Avers' voice cracked a little after being silent for so long. "At your service," he added smoothly, bowing and making a leg as he did so.

As he rose he took the opportunity to observe the man before him. The Commissioner was middle-aged, not handsome, with shoulder length untied hair and a weathered face out of which looked steady grey eyes. There was a humorous lilt to his wide mouth and Avers understood it with the man's next words.

"And what service is that?"

The blunt question did Avers some good. It jolted him out of his overwhelmed state, and he became the Duke of Tremaine once again. Perhaps for the last time.

"Information that may aid your cause." He raised the hand that clasped the portfolio and widened his eyes in a meaningful manner.

"And what business does a subject of the Crown have in disclosing such information? Or false information, as the case may be."

The Commissioner might have been unassuming in appearance, but he had a way of speaking that assumed authority. The situation was one of danger and treason and yet this man appeared unruffled by either consideration.

"Our cause goes beyond petty rivalries and individual interests," the Commissioner said, all the while those steady grey eyes on the faux Duke. "We will not be knocked off course."

Avers shifted uncomfortably. It felt like the man was settling in to give a speech in this very public garden. He glanced over the Commissioner's shoulder. Where the devil were Wakeford and his men? The meet had happened. They needed no more proof to arrest the spies.

"I wouldn't dream of knocking your cause off course," Avers said, playing for time. "I owe little allegiance to—"

A shot cracked through the air. Avers jolted, instinctively ducking. Where had it come from? Before he could look around, the Commissioner—who had also jumped at the shot—fell forward. Avers was overcome by the gentleman, dropping the leather portfolio to the floor and catching the Commissioner up in his arms to stop him hitting the ground.

"Good gracious man—are you hurt?" cried Avers, trying to pull him up enough that he might examine him.

The Commissioner scrambled to regain his footing.

"I'm unhurt," the man panted in shock. "But you aren't—your arm!"

Looking down, Avers saw it, bright crimson blood, all up the sleeve of his jacket. He flexed his muscles automatically, feeling for injury, and immediately the shock wore off and a burning sensation laced around his arm.

"Blast it!" Pulling a handkerchief from his pocket Avers pressed it to his left arm, groaning against the pain, which now lashed at him.

"Is it bad?"

"I don't think so." Avers breathed out through his mouth and in through his nose, telling himself to be calm, determined not to pass out as he felt the warmth of blood on his hands. "But I will sit." He lowered himself onto the path, almost crumpling at the end.

Leaning back against a low stone wall, the ringing in his ears abated a little and he looked across the gardens.

There was a man on the floor, struggling in vain against a heavy-set fellow who Avers recognised from the bench, kneeling on his back. Thrown a little distance away lay a pistol, still smoking. Across the way, two other men were manhandling a third into submission.

"You there!" shouted the Commissioner. He, too, had been taking in the scenes across the garden. "Release my man at once! He had nothing to do with the shooting."

The Commissioner started away from him toward where the three men struggled. Unable to focus on anything but breathing through the pain, Avers closed his eyes, a faint whiff of sulphurous gunpowder entering his nostrils.

"John!"

His eyes sprang open and there was Wakeford bounding towards him. His friend came to his side, kneeling before him, worry etched into his pale face.

"You've been shot."

"So it appears," said Avers on a groan.

"I must see if the bullet has exited." Wakeford began teasing Avers' fingers and bloody handkerchief away from his arm. "A knife!" he barked at one of his men who had followed closely behind and was now standing over them.

The man ran off immediately to procure the object.

"Well," murmured Wakeford, turning back to his friend and replacing the handkerchief over the wound causing Avers to grunt in pain. "That did not go according to plan."

"A plan to kill me?" asked the Commissioner who had come up behind Wakeford, his now freed man standing a little in front of him in a protective manner. "Your man is a poor shot. Perhaps now you'll do me the service—after trying to assassinate me—of ordering your men to allow me to leave the Île."

"Not our man," Avers said, eyes rolling back as Wakeford tied the handkerchief around his arm to staunch the flow of blood. "Or our assassination attempt." He managed a crooked half-smile.

"And for your protection," said Wakeford testily, "we will not allow you to leave the gardens until my men have ensured the shooter and all his accomplices are in our custody."

At that point, the man who Wakeford had sent in search of a knife returned and handed over the requested instrument.

"You mean to tell me that I have not been lured here under

false pretences for you to kill me?" snapped the Commissioner. "I recognise you, Lord Wakeford. You are a King's man."

Wakeford did not answer immediately. He had removed the handkerchief from Avers' arm again and was taking hold of the sleeve, pulling the fabric taut.

"I'm sorry to ruin such a beautiful suit," he said, and then ran the knife as high up the sleeve as he was able, parting the fabric and revealing the bloodied limb below. After wiping as much of the blood away as he was able, he examined the wound, pulling and prodding, causing Avers to flinch. "Thank the Lord, it's a graze. Just caught the edge of your arm. Probably hurts like the devil and bleeding no end, but not a direct hit."

"I shall have a scar, I hope?" Avers asked, that crooked smile still upon his lips.

"Yes, you'll have a scar," Wakeford replied ruefully. "Here." He undid his cravat and used the length of linen to bind up Avers' arm. He doubled it over with the cravat of the man who had fetched the knife and nodded, satisfied, when he had finished.

"We should get the doctor to see you."

Finally feeling as though the pain was no longer increasing, and being told the wound was not serious, Avers began to think more clearly. The only people who had known about this meeting were the Comte's men, Avers and Wakeford. It followed that it was one of them who orchestrated the attempted assassination.

"I demand you allow me safe passage off this island," said the Commissioner, making both Wakeford and Avers realise he was still standing there.

Wakeford rose. "As I said, not until we know there is no further danger to your person."

"You English—ordering us about as though we are still

your subjects when we have declared independence from you. And now you expect me to believe you did not attempt to assassinate me? It would benefit your King and his government very well if me and my colleagues did not succeed in securing King Louis' backing."

"Benefit?" Avers murmured.

Who benefited from the Commissioner's death? Perhaps Britain in the short-term, but ultimately it would only promote more anger in the Colonies and a determination to fight their cause. It would also undermine Britain's relationship with France if they were seen to be interfering with the colonialists on French soil. And that is exactly how it would appear, because it was an English noble who had arranged a meeting with one of the Commissioners to share supposed secrets. An English noble who had lured him somewhere to be assassinated... The animosity between the age-old enemies Britain and France would be stoked and the repercussions would start with trade embargoes and...

Trade.

War with France would mean the boom of free trade and the Comte and his cronies were perfectly positioned, with their operations already in place, to make a fortune. All the parts of this nefarious plan began to fall into place in Avers' mind. He had been their pawn all along. They had never really trusted him. That test of loyalty in Buc was nothing but show. They had wanted him as a scapegoat for their assassination. How could he not have seen it? He had thought he had played the game well, but instead he had been played a fool.

"At least we have the Comte in custody now," Avers murmured, head leant back against the wall and eyes closed.

"Avers, where are the papers?"

He cracked open his eyes and saw a flash of anxiety pass across Wakeford's face.

"There." Avers gestured with his good arm to where the portfolio lay on the path a little way away.

Wakeford stood and walked quickly to pick them up, untying the leather strap and allowing the soft covers to fall open in his hands.

"Curse it!"

Avers' eyes were fully open now. Something was wrong. He struggled to his feet, light-headedness making him lurch sideways.

"What is it? You do have the Comte?"

Wakeford held the open portfolio out to him in silence and Avers saw what his friend had seen. It contained pamphlets, half a dozen of them, all displaying grotesque cartoons mocking King Louis and his Austrian wife.

"You lured me here with filthy pamphlets?" the Commissioner asked, peering over Wakeford's shoulder.

Both Avers and Wakeford ignored the Commissioner.

"You're searching the Comte's house?" asked Avers.

"Yes—but so far we've found no sign of the papers. We've found no proof at all. The shooter is all we have, and he's refusing to speak. The Comte and Dartois left as soon as you were dropped off. We have Vergelles at his house, but we've found nothing incriminating, and the Marquis has managed to give us the slip."

Avers looked again at the pamphlets in his hand. It was like some grand joke had been played on him. He had thought himself carrying precious secret papers, meeting for a financial exchange, and instead he had been the bait and the one to be framed. The dark humour of it, the joke of the pamphlets—it all felt too similar to the incident in Buc. Avers had thought he was playing the game, but what had really been played?

As he looked back at the portfolio in his friend's hand, the pamphlets slipped, and a flash of script caught his eye among the printed words.

"Wakeford—pass that here." He reached out with his good arm, retrieving the hand-written note from amongst the propaganda.

To our English friend,

We hope you enjoy the little pictures of the King and Queen. We realised we could not trust you with our precious items when we found them in Mademoiselle Cadeaux's keeping and she informed us, after some persuasion, that she intended to give them to you.

It appears your loyalty has been somewhat divided and so has hers...

We are sorry that you have not proved a faithful friend and we regret to inform you that as such, we will not be able to continue our business relationship with you. Please do not be too disheartened, you have been a most useful asset to us.

—

"Where is Mademoiselle Cadeaux?" Avers asked in a strangled voice.

"The Comte's mistress?" Wakeford asked. "She wasn't at the house. We assume she's at her lodgings."

Cold, suffocating fear rose in Avers' chest, forcing the air out of him and making it difficult to breathe it back in.

"Has anyone confirmed it?"

"No, but why—what does the note say?"

Avers handed it over, his expression now one of horror, his mind racing.

What had he done? What had he done?

CHAPTER TWENTY-SEVEN

Avers did not know the whereabouts of Mademoiselle Cadeaux's apartments, making the Comte de Vergelles' Hôtel the only starting point for finding her. Despite Wakeford telling him to go home and rest—and assuring him he'd send word if the Comte shed any light on his mistress' whereabouts—Avers could not obey. As soon as his gunshot graze was properly dressed, he took his leave of Wakeford and headed, not for the Hôtel du Tremaine, but for the Comte's residence in Faubourg Saint-Germain.

He could not allow anything to happen to Mademoiselle Cadeaux. The possibility of the dangers she could be facing at that moment was unbearable. The very idea doubled his suffering—the physical pain in his arm matched with a sharp ache in his chest.

He should never have left her in Vergelles' company. Or allowed her to consider helping him by stealing the papers herself. He'd been a fool to do so, believing he had control of the situation and his ruse as the Duke of Tremaine had been effective.

But how could Mademoiselle Cadeaux risk her safety in

such a fashion? What had she been thinking, taking the papers? Knowing what kind of man the Comte was, and doing it anyway to aid Avers? He was torn between admiration and exasperation. Once again, she had shown her character to be one of worth and proved Avers' initial judgements to be superficial and flawed.

Whatever frustration he felt towards Mademoiselle Cadeaux, with every jolt of the carriage and fresh stab of pain in his arm, it was dissolving before a very real anger towards the Comte. The emotion was hot and volatile, and by the time he reached the Comte's Hôtel, he was ready to unleash it.

Bounding up the steps two at a time, he rapped upon the door with a fury that might have loosed the knocker from its nails.

It was finally opened with interminable slowness and Avers recognised the man behind it as one of Wakeford's.

"Percy." Avers jerked his head and strode past the man into the antechamber before he was invited. Spinning on his heel to face the fair-haired man, he asked bluntly, "Where is the Comte?"

"My Lord?" Percy closed the door and turned a measuring look upon Avers.

"Out with it."

"We're holding him for Lord Wakeford," Percy said, clearly displeased at being interrogated by someone who wasn't his superior.

"I'm aware," Avers said with equal ice in his tone. "But I asked you his whereabouts." He levelled the man with an exacting stare, his eyes unrelenting beneath his heavy lids.

"Does Wakeford know you're here?" Percy's gaze took in the torn sleeve of Avers' jacket and the bandage tied around his arm.

"No."

"Do you need to sit down?" Percy gestured at the wound.

"I need to speak to the Comte." The pain in his arm was reaching new heights and it took Avers' best efforts to maintain a hold on his temper. He had to remind himself, it wasn't Percy he was angry at. "The Comte's mistress, Mademoiselle Cadeaux, is in danger after helping our cause. I've come to discover her whereabouts."

Percy said nothing, his measuring stare steady on Avers' face.

"Please."

For a brief moment Avers thought he might need to continue his persuasions, but all of a sudden, Percy relented.

"He's in the drawing room with Terry and Brown."

Giving a curt nod of thanks, Avers strode off in the direction Percy indicated.

Taking a hold of the drawing room door handle, he turned it, throwing it open with more force than he realised. The wood flew back on its hinges and smacked against a table behind. The room's occupants turned as one towards the newcomer.

"It's His Grace, the Duke of Tremaine," the Comte said from a wing-backed chair on one side of the unlit fireplace. "Do not be alarmed," he said, addressing his guards, who stood either side of him. "He's had a petite shock this afternoon."

"Vergelles." Avers practically spat the name, striding into the room, shoulders back, chest out and hands clenched ready to strike whoever got in the way of his purpose.

The Comte did not flinch at the rapid movement. He sat irritatingly calm in his chair, observing Avers over steepled fingers, his expression cool and collected.

"I believe all of this"—the Comte broke his fingers apart and swept his hands out towards the strangers in his house—"is your doing?" An almost imperceptible curve spread across

Vergelles' thin lips. "I can't think what they are hoping to find here—can you?"

The calmer the Comte presented himself, the more heightened Avers' emotions became. How dare he taunt and provoke him when Mademoiselle Cadeaux's safety was in question.

"A pity to have such a misunderstanding. Dartois was right about you—a useful man, but one who would turn out not to be a... *loyal friend*."

"*Friend?*" Avers spat back, the hold he had on his anger growing taut.

This was all a game to these men. Unbeknownst to Avers, they had been playing with him, and without knowing the rules, his ignorance might have cost a good woman her safety.

"Apparently not," the Comte replied in mock-surprise. He drew his fingertips back together and observed Avers' growing agitation with a dark glee. "According to these men you think us... spies?" The Comte arched one elegant brow, laughing faintly.

"I know exactly what you are."

"What a tale you spin. Your imagination is to be applauded. And you—Tremaine—what are *you*? From my vantage point it seems you have been playing a part all along."

Avers ignored the Comte's question. "Mademoiselle Cadeaux—where is she?"

"How should I know?" Vergelles separated his fingers and flicked both hands away from him as though disassociating himself from the woman they were talking about.

"She was under your protection," Avers said from between clenched teeth.

"She *was*—but I tired of waiting for her to make up her mind. Such elevated ideas of her own virtue."

Avers was about to launch a repeat of his interrogation when what Vergelles had just said hit him. Virtue—did that mean? The flames of Avers' anger were doused for a moment. He strode away from the fireplace to do a circuit of the drawing room and give himself time to think.

All this time he had judged Mademoiselle Cadeaux for being mistress to the Comte and yet she had never given in to the man. Avers was left in more admiration of the woman, for despite his disagreement with the practice, he had come to understand her position in life was one of little choice or security. And yet, after all his assumptions, she had not given in to the Comte's advances.

"She was nought but a tavern brat," Vergelles called out across the room, a taunting tone to every word. "I should have known. You cannot wash the common off from one such as her."

Avers came back to face the Comte. "You have no concept of her worthiness."

"Mon dieu! You have it bad, do you not? To be so defensive of nothing but a low born harlot."

Avers snatched up a book from a nearby table and slammed it down just as quickly. The crack it made caused Terry and Brown to jump and even the Comte jerked in his chair.

The force of the impact sped through his body, jolting his injured arm and causing a wave of pain, but Avers was too angry to pay it any heed. "I'm warning you, Vergelles. Watch your words."

The Comte laughed viciously. "My words? My, she has you firmly in her talons. But I warn you, *Tremaine*, she is a slippery one, Mademoiselle Cadeaux. She will not give up her charms as easily as you might think."

"You realise your attempts at denigrating her are actually elevating her in my eyes?" Avers retorted, his inner thoughts coming out before he could stop himself. He immediately threw up a hand to stop the Comte from replying. "Where is she?"

"Not here—you're welcome to look. Your men have already been scouring the place." The Comte leant forward so he might stare at Terry and Brown. "And just what is it you've found, eh?"

A flash of uncertainty passed over the faces of the two men. Leaving the Comte for a moment, Avers walked over to them and asked in a low voice what Vergelles meant by his words.

Terry spoke first. "We haven't found anything, my Lord. Percy's already sent word to Wakeford."

"The papers?"

"No, my Lord, not a thing that incriminates him."

"We have the shooter," said Avers, more to reassure himself than the others. "And the note that Dartois sent to me —" He broke off, remembering with a sick feeling that the taunting note had not been signed.

The case against Vergelles and Dartois, which Avers had thought so solidly built, block by block, now showed itself to be made of ice. Each fact was slowly melting away before his eyes and soon there would be nothing at all to hold them.

Swinging round suddenly, he demanded, "Vergelles, tell me where she is, and do not test my temper any further."

The Comte smiled, an infuriating, sly, smug smile. It crept across his face slowly as he took in Avers' agitation until he was grinning wickedly up at the man. "I've thrown her out. A woman like that is only good for one thing and as she was not willing to—"

Rage overcame Avers. Leaping over the low table that separated them, he took the Comte by his cravat, twisting the lace and linen around in his hand, tightening it like a noose. Fiery pain shot down Avers' injured arm. The Comte's breath hissed out, his neck growing dark, and his veins bulging out from the skin.

"I know how you treated Mademoiselle Cadeaux," Avers whispered, inches from the Comte's face, the rage within punctuating every word. As he tightened the cravat and his eyes imparted all the fury within, he was satisfied to see a hint of fear in the Frenchman's eyes. "I saw the burns you gave her."

The man in his hands was nothing. A pathetic being, who preyed on the weak. One whose false sense of his own power enabled him to take advantage of others. He needed to be taught a lesson.

"A low-born woman she may be, but *you*," Avers hissed between his teeth, "are no better than a filthy cur. She transcended her place in life. You have sullied yours. You've no idea the treasure you had in her. You're an ignorant fool and if it weren't against God's holy law, I'd kill you."

In spite of his final words, Avers turned his hand again, tightening the noose. The Comte's breath came in rasps. Just a little more and Vergelles would be...

Avers half released him. "Mademoiselle Cadeaux—tell me where she is."

"I've given her to Dartois," he wheezed, smiling perversely, the flush of his skin making him appear half-crazed. "He seemed happy to find her with our precious items. Says she has potential if she will only submit to him. He commanded me to hand her over and I was only too happy after being tired of waiting. He's less patient a man than me though." He attempted a gasping laugh and Avers finally released him, throwing the Comte back in his chair and striding away.

He took up pacing, rubbing the back of his neck, staring at the carpet he traversed. Silence descended for a few minutes until Wakeford's voice came from the doorway.

"Av–Tremaine!"

Avers glanced up, taking in the surprise on his friend's face.

"What are you doing here?"

"Come to find that harlot he's taken with," the Comte called out, still wheezing, his neck coming up in angry red welts.

Ignoring Vergelles' provoking words, Wakeford came and took Avers to one side.

"What the devil are you doing here? I sent you home."

"I told you," Avers said impatiently, "we must find Mademoiselle Cadeaux."

Wakeford searched his face and then appeared to relent. "Anything?"

"No—except he says Dartois commanded him to give the woman over." *Commanded.* Something about that didn't sit right with Avers.

"Well, it's the deuce of a mess out there," Wakeford replied in an undertone. "The shooter's refusing to admit any relationship with the Comte or his men. I've had it from Terry and Brown that they've been unable to find the papers here, so I've come as soon as I could to confirm it."

"Curse it!" Avers hissed, the feeling of doom growing with every passing moment. "What does it all mean?"

"We have to find the papers here, otherwise we have no evidence, and there's nothing to connect all of this together."

A sick feeling entered Avers' stomach. No papers. No connection with the Comte or Dartois. No Mademoiselle Cadeaux. What had started out with such promise had turned into an utter disaster.

"I'll check in with my men." Wakeford made to signal Terry and Brown.

"It's no use," Avers replied harshly. "They've found nothing."

"But how can that be? I've had this place under watch night and day. The papers have to be here."

"Well, they aren't." Avers raked a hand savagely through his hair, pulling it painfully, but enjoying feeling anything but the fear over Mademoiselle Cadeaux's welfare. They'd played their hand and lost and there appeared no way to turn the game.

Game!

It wasn't a *game*. It was her life. *Hers*. The woman Avers... he couldn't stop his mind running to all the worst scenarios. What if they hurt her? What if they took her... life?

CHAPTER TWENTY-EIGHT

"I don't know you," Mademoiselle Saint-Val Cadette repeated, staring at her own reflection in the dressing table mirror, not even deigning to glance at her male visitor.

Avers had realised on leaving Vergelles' residence that the best place to start trying to find Mademoiselle Cadeaux was at the Théâtre des Tuileries. If he could persuade her friend Mademoiselle Saint-Val Cadette to trust him, he might just discover where she lived. He had confronted her in her dressing room, but the lady was not inclined to be helpful.

"As I told you," he said from between clenched teeth, trying his hardest to keep his voice level as his impatience spiked. "My name is Tremaine."

The actress tilted her head at various angles, observing all aspects of her visage, in the mirror before her. "What was her name—Cadiz? No doubt some minor player. I can't be expected to remember all those who tread the boards behind me." She put a finger to the corner of her mouth to wipe away a smudge of rouge.

"*Cadeaux*—I'm concerned for her welfare."

The actress sighed, assuming the pose of one of her characters, a lavish open silk robe hanging carelessly from her pale shoulders. It draped over her body like a Greek goddess, falling across her limbs, her stockinged legs peeping daringly out at him.

"And how do I know that to be true—that you are seeking to ensure the welfare of this... *Cadeaux* you speak of?"

"I give you my word as a gentleman. She was here barely a month ago attending one of your performances. I have it on good authority that she's known here."

Cadette sighed again, her pale decolletage heaving and a diamond necklace she wore rising to be seen above the line of her chemise's ruffle. The stones caught the candlelight winking and hinting that the actress had a rich admirer.

Despite it being afternoon, there was no natural light in here, the only window high up in the wall and covered in thick brocade curtains. Wax candles flickered and glowed over almost every surface in the room and their heat and smoke mingled with the scent of the actress' perfume and the fumes from her clay pipe to create a heady atmosphere. It was one in which Avers was fairly certain many an admirer had come to seduce the famed tragedienne.

But Avers wasn't here for that. He was here to save a life.

"I only wish," he said, a hint of the desperation he felt in his tone, "to know where I might find her—her lodgings—to ensure she is safe and well."

"I thought the whole of Paris knew—" Cadette took up a feather powder puff by its little wooden handle and blotted it in a pot of cosmetics before applying it to her face. "She is companion to the Comte de Vergelles. Why don't you ask him?"

Avers' ears pricked up and the slump of his shoulders gave way to sudden alertness. "You say you don't know her and now you do?"

The actress stilled her ministrations.

"The Comte has thrown her off—or so he says—handed her over to one of his friends. But I have reason to believe she has not gone willingly."

"Ha!" Cadette shot him a condescending look. "I am sure no woman likes to be handed over like a prize horse." She turned back, the sheepishness at being caught out gone, and resumed powdering her face. "And you wish to become her new protector, is that it? Perhaps she does not want one."

"I hold no such pretensions, and have no doubt she would not want one, as you say. I only desire to ensure her safety and I believe her in danger." Avers' mouth went dry at the thought. "Please—please help me."

The actress put down her powder puff and turned to face him. Her eyes locked onto his and she gave him a hard, measuring stare.

"What you forget, you little Englishman, with your advantages, is the world she comes from. You are not of it, and you cannot possibly understand it, nor what she needs to keep her safe. You nobility are all the same—you cause more harm with your so-called honourable intentions, not thinking of the consequences to those who have neither birth nor fortune to fall back on. One man decides he wants her, then another, now you. You would do better to leave her in our world and go back to your own—at least, if I knew her, that is what I would think."

She turned back to her dressing table and Avers recognised he had been dismissed.

"Please take my card." He put it on a side table. "And if you should change your mind and choose to remember Mademoiselle Cadeaux and where I might find her, you may send me a missive."

Mademoiselle Saint-Val Cadette waved her little rouge brush at him to send him on his way and he reluctantly bowed and left the room. Short of taking the woman by the shoulders and shaking the information from her, he was at a dead end.

He was in one of the main passageways now, leading past what he assumed was the side door from which he'd seen Mademoiselle Cadeaux leave the theatre all those weeks ago. Avers was just about to ascend some steps into the front part of the theatre when a hand reached out from the dark and tugged at his coat tails.

If the hand had exerted any real strength, Avers might have struck out at the interloper, and forced them off. As it was, the tug felt tentative, and when he turned to the cause, he found himself facing a girl.

The lass was likely no more than thirteen, standing back in the shadows of a doorway, hands fidgeting with each other as she looked nervously up at him.

"May I be of service, Mademoiselle?" Avers asked, taking a step back so as not to loom over her.

"I—" She shrank back, doubting her impulsive decision to stop the nobleman.

"It's all right," he said quickly, softening his tone. "You have nothing to fear from me—what is it you want?"

The girl's large blue eyes watched him like luminescent pools and then, discerning whatever she needed to see in his face, she spoke in quick common French. "Mademoiselle Cadeaux, she is a good woman, she is kind to me. Mademoiselle got me this job sweeping backstage. She gives me her old clothes and money for food when I need it, and she keeps the gentlemen away. She says I don't need them with her to look after me." The girl was not pausing for breath. "I heard you speaking to Mademoiselle Saint-Val Cadette and she would not help you, but I—I know that Mademoiselle Cadeaux spoke of an Englishman. She said—" The girl broke off.

"Yes?"

"She said you were good and I—I do not want Mademoiselle Cadeaux to be in danger. You must help her. When I went to her apartments earlier today, she would not answer the door, but I could hear her dog Lutin barking within. She does not go anywhere without her dog. I am so worried."

Avers pushed the reappearing feeling of cold dread down, trying to ignore whatever assumptions the girl's revelations were setting off in his head. "Her apartments." Avers stepped forward without thinking, making the girl flinch. "Where are they?"

She gave him the address in a less than wealthy neighbourhood in Paris.

"Thank you." Avers pressed several gold coins into the girl's hands. "I am in debt to you, dear girl."

She nodded dumbly, eyes wider than ever, and watched as he turned and ran to the exit.

Finally, Avers had a heading.

CHAPTER TWENTY-NINE

Mademoiselle Cadeaux's apartments were situated in a modest street in an unfashionable part of Paris. Avers found them easily enough and paid the unscrupulous landlord to let him in.

The moment he opened the door a barrage of barking sounded. Within seconds a white rocket of fur darted from what Avers took to be a bedchamber.

"There, there, you devilish sprite!" Avers cried out in a booming voice to slow the animal.

It only worked a little, the dog catapulting itself a moment later into Avers' arms which he opened in anticipation. The dog, whose teeth had been bared just seconds ago, recognised the intruder and transformed into a licking, sniffing, quivering mess.

"Come now." Avers deposited the dog back onto the floor and patted his little rump.

Lutin immediately trotted over to a couple of empty bowls and nosed one of them hopefully. Avers looked around, and seeing a ewer nearby he filled one bowl with water, and then discovered a biscuit barrel full of dog treats. He scooped a generous handful into a bowl and the poor little dog had his fill of both.

Avers straightened, finally taking in the room before him. "Right, let's find your mistress, shall we?"

The apartments before him were small and modestly furnished with items that had been carefully selected to fit the petite space. All of it was fairly plain, with a more expensive piece here and there. There were a number of well-thumbed books on a side table next to a tattered green chaise longue, at the end of which a thick blanket lay in swathes. It looked as though the reader had just got up for a glass of wine between chapters.

Scanning the room he saw elements of life littering the surfaces. A vase of dried flowers, a framed miniature of some unknown woman, letters sealed waiting to be sent, a half-burnt candle in its holder. They were all elements of *her* life. A life he thought he knew, but standing here, he felt he was only aware of it in part.

Did she like to read? Did she stay up late devouring chapters? Where did she pick those dried flowers from? Who was the woman in the frame—a lady dear enough to Emilie that she wished to see her likeness every day?

A deep ache appeared in the depths of his chest. He desired to know all of her and yet at this very moment, she might be in mortal danger. Springing into action, he ignored the feeling that he was invading her private domain, and scoured the room for any clue as to her whereabouts.

That was when he noticed the hat and discarded ribbon on the floor behind the chaise longue. He followed the trail of clothing into the bedroom and on entering was confronted by a mess of clothes and cases and brushes.

On the freshly made bed were garments of all types, thrown and crumpled as though someone had been packing in a rush. Scattered on the floor was a brush, a handheld mirror, two more hats.

Lutin followed Avers, jumping onto the bed into what appeared to be a nest he'd made among the clothes, and gave a bark as if to agree with Avers' unspoken thoughts. Yes, Mademoiselle Cadeaux had been packing in a hurry.

Avers exhaled heavily, not even realising he had been holding his breath, finally acknowledging the fear he had carried into this room. He had thought he might find Emilie dead in here. The thought, now clearly articulated in his mind, sent a shiver down his back.

He clenched his fists. This was not a scene of violence but of great haste. Turning on his heel, his small white shadow jumping from the bed and trotting behind him, Avers came back into the main room and scanned it again. His eyes stopped on the pile of letters.

Striding over to the table on which they lay, he scooped up the pile and began flipping through the directions written on them. One was to the actress Saint-Val Cadette, care of the Théâtre des Tuileries. Avers clenched his jaw. As he had suspected, the actress *had* known Mademoiselle Cadeaux. The next was to an unknown lady. He flipped through them faster, hope running dry, distracting him so he almost passed by his own alias. The Duke of Tremaine was scrawled across one letter.

He dropped the rest and turned it over. It wasn't sealed and the address was missing. His breath quickened. She'd been writing it in a hurry and if it wasn't sealed, but in the middle of the pile with the others ready to be posted... had she hidden it there for him?

He wasted no more time, unfolding the letter and quickly scanning its contents.

. . .

'Your Grace,

I have been instructed by my benefactor to make ready to leave. I was discovered with the stolen papers—for I tried to retrieve them for you, but like a fool I was caught—'

She was not a fool. Avers had been the fool to allow her to put herself in danger.

'I thought my life forfeit, but Dartois ordered the Comte to give me over to him.

He will not tell me where we are going, but I paid one of the men who came to collect my trunks, and he says we head for the coast.

I don't know if you will find this, and you owe me nothing, but I ask that you take care of Lutin, for I'm unable to do so, and that you—'

The letter was cut off. Avers could see splotches on the paper where the ink had not dried before she'd folded it closed. She'd been interrupted.

Dropping the hand that held the letter, Avers stared at the wispy-haired dog waiting at his feet.

The coast.

That could only mean one thing. Dartois was fleeing across the Channel. With their smuggling operations it would be easy enough.

But what was the reason? No evidence had been found at the Comte's residence of their spying. They couldn't be linked to the assassination attempt. Whatever Dartois' plan was, it wasn't clear, but Avers couldn't stand here trying to figure it out any longer.

The Marquis already had half a day's head start on him, and while Mademoiselle Cadeaux was alive for now, there was no telling what his plans were for her. Avers scooped up Lutin in his arms and left the apartments.

He would chase them down. The faux Duke of Tremaine was leaving Paris.

CHAPTER THIRTY

Emilie sat in the private parlour of an inn on the road to Cherbourg staring at the uneaten food she had been served. The nausea which she'd felt ever since leaving the French capital had not abated.

Dartois had already finished his pigeon pie and downed a glass of claret and was now staring at her. He had been doing that since leaving Paris, his eyes gleaming in that disconcerting way of his, making Emilie feel like a bird and Dartois the cat.

"I've thought for some time that Lucien hasn't appreciated you."

She said nothing. The statement was no doubt meant as a compliment, but the implications added to Emilie's discomfort. She could see it in the Marquis' face—he coveted her, and not as a person, but as an object to be owned and possessed. Hadn't those been his words to Vergelles when she had been found with the papers in her possession. *Give her to me.*

"Lucien was surprised by your betrayal, but I was not. You are neither stupid nor weak. You are a survivor—like me."

Emilie had no wish to provoke him, so she swallowed the retort on the tip of her tongue.

"The bastard child of a lesser noble with no place in Society, like you—an unwanted tavern brat—and yet we have carved out a place for ourselves on this muck heap of life and we will be cursed if we'll give it up to any lesser mortals. Lucien could not see your potential. I can."

Emilie looked up from her plate and, holding his penetrating stare with some effort, she finally spoke. "And what do you intend to do with me and my potential?"

That gleam in his eyes which she had always taken for funning, appeared differently in these circumstances. Suddenly there was an uncontrollability to it, a darkness, a sensation of Dartois being somewhat maniacal. She had the strongest feeling she needed to choose her words carefully or this man might turn on her without a second thought.

She took a steadying breath and continued to return his stare, waiting for his reply.

"What do you think I intend?" Dartois leant back, one hand dangling from the chair arm, the other clasping a freshly poured glass of wine.

"I wouldn't presume to guess."

Dartois broke out into amused laughter. "Aha! Very good —the survivor in you will not allow you to risk a wrong guess." He raised his wine glass to her in salute and took a sip.

"I know we are making for the coast," she said, playing some of her hand in an attempt to both appeal to his view of her and to show her intelligence. "We left the city by the north road." She would not mention the servant she had bribed. Why throw another poor soul into this man's clutches?

"Very good, my little bird."

The hairs prickled on the back of Emilie's neck. He desired her.

"Will Lucien be following us to where we're going."

"You heard me ask him for you. He has delivered you into my care now. I will take responsibility for your... *needs*. So, to answer your question, no, he will not be joining us in England." Dartois' gaze grew more intense as he revealed their destination. "At least not yet. He has work to do for me here."

"England," Emilie repeated, keeping her expression neutral and nodding her head in acknowledgement.

"I may require him, after a time, but I have business in London, and Lucien is caught up with your English Duke at the moment." He spoke of the Comte as if he was merely a lackey. Had appearances really been that deceptive? Was Dartois the one pulling the strings?

"I am sure"—Dartois took a draught of wine, the deep red liquid glistening on his lips as he replaced his glass on the table—"I can do something to remove that man from your mind. Whatever he promised you—money, security—I will not be outdone."

Emilie let out an involuntary laugh.

"I have amused you?" Dartois fingered the stem of the wine glass, tapping it with his fingernail, a challenging look in his eyes.

But despite the hint of displeasure from the Marquis, Emilie refused to become any more intimidated. She was already furious with herself for not making more fuss when Dartois marched her from her lodgings with a pistol at her back. Then there was the carriage ride through Paris—that would have been the perfect opportunity to jump out and escape, but she had failed to take the chance.

Her only solace was her friend Mademoiselle Saint-Val Cadette would now be safe. But in hedging her bets, hoping for the perfect opportunity to run away, Emilie was now in the middle of nowhere, with an unpredictable man and no means of escape. Soon, there would be a choice. She could feel it in her gut—surrender or fight.

"Lucien offered me both," she replied, choosing to

wilfully misunderstand the Marquis. If she had answered according to the real object of his sentence—the Duke of Tremaine—she would have said the man had offered her nothing.

The Marquis would not be put off. His gaze grew more intense. "I do not speak of Lucien."

"Not Lucien—oh! You mean His Grace, the Duke of Tremaine? What makes you think he offered me anything?" she said, a little too lightly.

"Not his name—that I am sure of. But perhaps an agreement. It is plain to all he holds a tendre for you."

Dartois' words both surprised and stung her. As a fallen woman it was beyond anyone's comprehension that a gentleman might offer his name to her. Yet the acknowledgement so bluntly delivered still hurt and because he spoke of Tremaine, it seemed to deliver a sharper pain.

Her mind flashed back to that moment in the study of the hunting lodge, when they had been alone trying to get the papers from the locked drawer, and she had fallen back into his arms. When he had stared down at her, his gaze warm, falling onto her lips. When they had... kissed.

"You are unwilling to share what he offered?" An edge appeared in Dartois' voice. "It is no matter—what I offer you is financial freedom, if you will be my companion and aid in my operations."

"Aid?"

"All in good time." He leant forward and traced a finger over the back of her gloved hand.

She shivered. The involuntary action was not one of pleasure.

"I shall allow you to consider my offer after we discuss it on the crossing. Whatever you may think of me, I am not a monster, and I will not take an unwilling woman."

"And if I refuse?"

Dartois shrugged, his eyes wandering over to the window, the fingers of his right hand playing with the knife on this plate. "Eat. It is time we were on our way."

CHAPTER THIRTY-ONE

Avers hastily scrawled a note to Wakeford on the Tremaine crested paper of their Parisian Hôtel. With the ink barely dried he attached a wafer and rang the bell for a servant. Exiting the study, so he might hand over the missive all the faster, he met the butler in the hall, and thrust the letter into his hand with rapid-fire instructions for its immediate delivery to Lord Wakeford. Before the servant disappeared to carry out His Grace's commands, Avers also requested his horse be made ready, a valise packed and gave suitable instructions for Lutin's care while he was gone.

It was the closest Avers had ever come to treating the Tremaine staff as his own. Once the butler had been sent on his way, and hurried footsteps and calls sounded out below stairs, Avers ran up the main staircase two at a time, making it to his bedroom before his valet.

Before half an hour was up, with the valise strapped to the back of his saddle, he cantered through the streets of Paris causing outraged street sellers to cry out at the reckless rider.

Avers knew where Mademoiselle Cadeaux was. Returning to the Comte's residence, he demanded the location of his shipping concerns through which he conducted smuggling operations. While Vergelles was less than helpful, a scan of his business papers had revealed their whereabouts easily enough.

Now Avers was heading for Cherbourg. There was no time to waste. Nothing would delay him. Not even the devil himself.

He had to get to her before she disappeared.

The journey out of the French capital was painful. Every street seemed three times as busy as it had during Avers' entire stay. Twice he was stuck behind an overturned cart and the third time saw him urge his horse to jump a series of crates that had been unloaded outside a shop. The shopkeeper's wife, upon coming out of the building to the sight of a fine hunter clearing her orders with a foot to spare, stumbled backwards and swooned into her husband's arms.

Once Avers had left the capital, the journey was significantly quicker. Without the distractions of physical barriers to negotiate, he found his mind wandering. What was Dartois' purpose in taking Mademoiselle Cadeaux? Why was he making his way to England? How would the papers serve him there?

Avers had little idea about the latter. With the spy ring's connection to England, he wondered if they had fostered connections in London and information flowed both ways. Perhaps their plan was to sell the papers there while Paris proved too dangerous.

Yet, Mademoiselle Cadeaux's kidnapping formed no logical part of this plan. The only reason he could think of was her being taken for revenge. Dartois' disconcerting laugh when he'd pointed a pistol at Avers' head in Buc came back to mind. The sick feeling, which had been birthed on reading Mademoiselle Cadeaux's urgently written note, grew in Avers' stomach. How far would this man go to enact his revenge for Mademoiselle Cadeaux's betrayal?

After two days travelling through the night with only a few hours rest at the roadside, his arm aching from his injury, Avers entered Cherbourg as dawn broke. The dock town was cast in a demoralising grey, mirroring his thoughts as he contemplated what may have happened to Mademoiselle Cadeaux while he travelled.

Avers approached two men smoking pipes, on a break from loading their ship. The first refused to admit he spoke English despite appearing to understand Avers' question. After asking again in French, the man still feigned incomprehension, but his companion responded well to money.

He led Avers through the waking docks and pointed out a ship at the quayside with a couple of sailors tramping kegs and boxes aboard looking as happy to be up as the miserable morning was to greet them.

Avers took cover at the start of the quay behind a pile of boxes almost head height, dismissing his guide with another payment, and turning back to analyse the situation. A few minutes revealed that there appeared to be only two men loading the boat. Either Dartois and Emilie were already below deck waiting for the tide, or Avers had arrived before them. The latter was likely if they travelled by chaise. Avers hadn't stopped for more than a few hours overnight, thanks to a full moon, and he'd managed to change horses twice, leaving the Tremaine's fine hunter in an inn west of Breteuil.

As if corroborating his theory, he heard a carriage approaching. Skirting to the far side of the boxes to keep them between himself and the newcomers, he peeked out to see a finely painted chaise approaching the grubby dockside. The horses appeared fresh, without a sheen of sweat on them, indicating that Avers had been right—they must have stopped overnight.

The coachman pulled up on the other side of the quay and a groom jumped down from the back of the carriage to let the steps down. The door flung open, almost hitting the servant in the face, and Dartois appeared, springing down from the carriage and turning back to hand down the other inhabitant.

Avers felt both relief at catching up with Dartois and an overwhelming fury at the sight of him. He drew his shoulders back instinctively, clenching his fists and becoming taut with the expectation of a fight.

But if he'd been on the verge of making a rash decision, he was stilled by the sight of Emilie being handed down from the carriage. She looked so small and fragile, standing over there next to a man who was both deranged and unpredictable.

Avers couldn't see her expression properly from where he stood, but he could see enough to know she wasn't smiling. The Marquis gave instructions to the coachman and soon the trunks strapped onto the back of the carriage were unlashed and placed in a neat pile on the dockside.

The two sailors who had been on the deck of the ship came down the quay to fetch the luggage on board and Avers ducked down quickly behind the boxes in case they saw him.

At that moment, a man came out of a nearby tavern to his right. Avers quickly looked down, pretending to be occupied with something in his left pocket in case the man from the inn should glance across.

If the salty fellow did see Avers it held no weight with him. He passed by, a worn leather tricorn on his head, and an oiled greatcoat flaring out behind him. Shaking hands with Dartois, he began speaking to him in low French and Avers realised this was likely the captain of the ship.

Emilie waited silently while the men spoke and after a few minutes, Dartois and the captain nodded to each other, and the latter set out down the quay to the ship where his men were busy making ready for sail on the top deck.

The Marquis made to follow, taking Emilie by the elbow, and bringing her towards the waiting boat. In an instant she burst out of her placid state. After taking one step forward she pulled back, trying to free her arm from Dartois' grip. The French noble was not so easy to shake off, yanking her backwards so she crashed into him, and hissing something in her ear.

Avers started forward. Stopped. The distance was too great. If he rushed out now Dartois would have time to react and there was no telling what he might do. He needed to wait until they were about to walk down the quay and would pass by him. Avers felt for the loaded pistol nestled in his pocket. Not for the first time in the last two days, he thanked God that the graze he'd sustained in Paris was on his left arm. He pulled back the trigger.

The couple had made it ten steps when Emilie pulled back again, turning and trying to run. Dartois pulled the same move and this time whatever he said to Emilie worked. Shock transposed itself onto her face. She stopped pulling away from him and schooled her countenance back to impassivity. Her shoulders drawn back and her chin raised, she walked obediently beside her captor towards the boat.

This was Avers' chance. He glanced towards the ship and saw no sign of the captain or sailors who must be below deck. Three more steps and Dartois and Emilie would be beside the boxes. Avers' grip on the pistol tightened, his index finger curling around the trigger, drawing the weapon silently from his pocket.

Three.

Two.

One.

Avers stepped out from behind the boxes and shouted, "Unhand Mademoiselle Cadeaux!"

For now, he kept the pistol hidden in the folds of his coat, but his shoulders were thrown back and he was drawn up to his not inconsiderable height.

Dartois halted mid-stride, yanking Emilie to a stop beside him, causing her to stumble, and a flash of pain crossed her face.

"Tremaine," Dartois hissed.

Down the quay, Avers saw the sailors come back on deck followed by their captain. They stopped to watch and he saw one of them pick up a nasty looking cudgel.

"How unwelcome," Dartois continued. "Your wish, I'm afraid, is not one I'm willing to fulfil. Mademoiselle Cadeaux is coming with me."

Avers attempted reason. "The game is up, Dartois. Your leader, the Comte, is under arrest. It's only a matter of time before my colleagues uncover his free trade from this port and then it will be over—you have no hand left to play."

"*His* business?" One of Dartois' fine brows rose and a smug smile curled across his lips. "You're more ignorant than I imagined. This enterprise—" The Marquis gestured at the ship and Avers noted the sailors were now walking along the quayside, edging closer to where they were standing.

He took a step back, creating an arc in which his gun might be fired, that encompassed the men and the Marquis.

"—it was never the Comte de Vergelles'. Do you really think such a man could control all this—not only free trade that might bring in considerable wealth, but the economic and diplomatic conditions to feed it? Why do you think you have found nothing at the Comte's residence?" Dartois' smile grew gleeful, and he was laughing now, the sound high and uneven. "Genius, is it not? Set up the Comte as the figurehead while I pull all the strings undetected. He was always fond of being feared—small men like him are all the same.

"But then you came sniffing around. Your game was obvious from the start and while the Comte disliked it, I saw the opportunity. It was so very easy to get you to do what I needed. With a Commissioner dead, the war between your King and the colonialists will ignite further and then—"

Avers played for time. "You haven't heard?"

The sailors were still moving closer and he felt his exposure acutely. He should have waited for Wakeford's men, but by the time they arrived, Dartois and Emilie would have left with the tide.

"The Commissioner lives."

"Indeed?" The Marquis hid any disappointment at the news. "No matter. The attempt will be enough to stoke fear and mistrust. The colonists will fear British interference whatever you say, and my government will play on their anxieties to weaken the British hold over the colonies. It will work just as well to our advantage, for trade ties between England and France are bound to be cut as a result of the hostilities. And what is it you hoped to achieve by coming here alone?"

The hairs on the back of Avers' neck rose. The Marquis knew him to be at a disadvantage. He gripped the pistol so tightly that his arm began to ache.

"Could you not bear the thought of this in my hands?" Dartois thrust Emilie forward like some prize of war. Then he yanked her back harshly against his side and breathed in her scent in a perverse manner. "I thought the Comte made it clear—she's not available to you. This woman's been bought and paid for many times over with my spoils."

Avers seethed. "Mademoiselle Cadeaux can no more be bought than I." He raised the pistol from the folds of his coat and levelled it at Dartois. They were less than ten yards apart. There would be no missing at this distance. "Release her —now."

"Ah, the path of true love never did run smooth," the Marquis scoffed, pulling Emilie in front of him like a human shield and placing his cheek next to hers. "Tell me—how much do you value her pretty face?" The French noble pulled a knife from his boot and held it to her neck, starting to retreat slowly down the quayside towards the boat and pulling her with him.

"What have you still to gain from keeping her?" Avers called out, desperation setting in. "Hand her over and I will let you leave with the papers. We have no more need of them, thanks to your dealings."

"Please." Emilie finally spoke, her voice strangled, trying to crane her neck further from where the knife pressed against her skin. "Please, just leave." She looked Avers directly in the eyes and he saw an earnestness there that almost broke him.

She was giving up.

"Thank you, Arnaud," said Dartois taking the proffered pistol from his captain as they came alongside one another. The Marquis continued to hold the knife at Emilie's throat with one hand and levelled the pistol at Avers with the other.

"How small your mind is, that you should think there is no more for me to gain from these papers. That's the problem with you English—so stupid and blind—you cannot see the possibilities this world offers. You have no idea of the connections I have, of how far my operation extends. I see value in the papers and in the woman—I will not be giving up either."

He thrust Emilie into the arms of the two waiting sailors who dragged her along the gangway into the boat. She struggled against them, skirts flying, arms beating at them.

"Unhand her!" Avers cried, leaping forward, trying to force his way past Dartois.

A shot sounded.

Searing hot pain lanced through his arm. Emilie screamed. Avers stumbled backwards, hit his head on a crate, and fell.

Everything went black.

CHAPTER THIRTY-TWO

Avers awoke to the smell of fish.

The aroma came from a fisherwoman who was leaning over him, staunching the blood oozing from his wound, while she babbled away in rapid French about the poor Englishman who had been shot by the wicked monsieur.

She helped him back to her cottage and laid him on a rough cot bed where he promptly lost consciousness. Regaining it some time later, Avers sent word to Wakeford of his whereabouts, and recruited his strength while he waited for his friend to arrive with Tremaine's physician in tow.

Upon arrival, the medical man ascertained the shot had passed straight through Avers' upper arm. Miraculously it had missed the bone. If Avers hadn't been lunging past Dartois to get to Emilie, he might have got the bullet straight in his chest.

Immediately after the wound was dressed, Avers announced his intention of leaving to follow Mademoiselle Cadeaux. He was argued back into bed by both the physician and his valet Simmonds who had arrived with Wakeford to help. The fact that Lutin then took up residence across Avers' legs on his sick bed, went some way to keeping him stationary.

Simmonds apologised about bringing the dog, explaining the Tremaine servants had refused to look after the lively animal without the valet's supervision.

Proving one of the worst patients the physician had ever treated, Avers' bed rest lasted only a day. The following morning insisted on setting off in pursuit of Mademoiselle Cadeaux. The physician cast his hands up in despair and then reluctantly gave Avers' valet fresh dressings and laudanum to aid with his master's recovery. Avers paid the fisherwoman handsomely for saving his life, and then quit Cherbourg for London with his servant and furry companion in tow.

The journey proved tedious and uncomfortable, and he arrived back at his London lodgings late the following afternoon to find them cold and the only greeting one of despair. His arm was painful and the lack of sleep getting to him.

Laying down for half an hour, he listened to the activity of the servants, who were all energy setting the apartments to rights after his Lordship's unexpected return. After a fitful sleep, he left his room in search of some brandy only to find two of his footman whispering together at the end of the hall. They broke off on seeing their master and the latter asked if he might fetch his Lordship something to eat or drink.

Avers felt an unreasonable irritation at their tittle tattling, wondering what intrigue they spoke of, if it was about their injured master, his unexpected return to London and... he had a sudden epiphany.

Gossip.

Servants knew everything that happened in the noble houses of London. And his aunt had at least one from each residence on her payroll. Lady Goring—an insufferable busybody who prided herself on curating a plethora of the most infamous gossip—might just be his salvation.

Normally limiting his exposure to his relative, Avers decided—for the first time in his life—that there was no one he'd rather see. Her vices were the very thing which might bring Mademoiselle Cadeaux's whereabouts in reach.

"No," Avers said. "I am going out to pay a call on my aunt."

He took a hackney from his apartments to Lady Goring's residence and strode into her dining room without ceremony.

"Aunt," he said, observing his stout relative sat down to a rather generous and varied repast for a single individual.

"John!" she exclaimed, pulling her silk open robe closed and touching a hand to the matching turban on her head.

Clearly she had no engagements this evening and had been expecting to spend a rich dinner alone in a state of casual dress. She was even naked of the customary powder and rouge which she so often overdid. For once, she looked human and Avers was shocked to find he felt a little comforted by the sight of his relative.

"I have just sat down to eat," she said in irritated tones. "If you were not my nephew recently returned from France, I would send you away to come back tomorrow at the correct hour for visiting."

"Then I am indebted to you." Avers bowed low.

"Oh, do stop being horrid! Your sardonic words do you no favours. It's exactly why you are not yet married, mark my words, dear boy."

"Thank you for your sharp insight, madam. I shall endeavour to take note." He straightened, grimacing a little as the tightness of his jacket sleeves pressed on his wound. "I am only just back from the Continent and wished to pay my respects to you first and foremost, my Lady Aunt."

Lady Goring huffed at his insincerity. "First you interrupt my repast and now you mock me. I am more and more inclined to cast you out."

Avers did not respond to this last comment. He knew for a fact—attested to by her bright, beady eyes—that she would no more turn him away than she would a stranger if she thought them in possession of a Societal secret she had yet to hear. And a nephew lately arrived from the Continent, one who had not apprised her of what he had intended to do in Paris and from which she had received no letters while he was gone, was a veritable vein of potential information for her to bleed.

"Though," she said at length, placing a miniscule piece of pheasant in her mouth and chewing it thoughtfully before swallowing and carrying on as though she'd come to a large-scale epiphany, "I confess, it has been quiet without my dear Sophia to keep me company." His aunt was referring to Avers' cousin who had lately married a Mr Malvon. "And I am a little touched you came to call so soon after your return—which was when exactly?" She motioned for another place to be set for her nephew.

The questioning had already begun.

"This morning, aunt. I have barely stopped at home to change before running to your side."

She huffed again and frowned. "Do stop being sycophantic, John. I know very well you say those sweet words in jest at my expense."

"Never."

He meant it in humour, but she took it as earnestness and her expression transformed to one of gratification. "Well, now that your mood is settled," she said smugly, "how was Paris?"

"Interesting," was all he offered. He knew it would vex Lady Goring, but he needed to find news of Mademoiselle Cadeaux as soon as possible. He refused to be drawn into long explanations of a trip he could not in all honesty discuss with her and gave no space in which she might complain. "But I hear some of my new acquaintances have lately arrived in London."

"Bah!" Lady Goring exclaimed, throwing her cutlery down with a horrid clatter and casting her gaze away from him. "So, that is why you have returned. Not for your poor lonely aunt, but to chase your friends. I should have known you were gallivanting on the Continent with no thought to familial responsibility." She paused, looking back at him with narrowing eyes. "*Friends?* Or perhaps... a female friend? Am I to think you have finally banished the Curshaw girl from your head?"

Avers masked a grimace, the only sign of it the tell-tale muscle jerking at the corner of his jaw. His aunt could be so dreadfully blunt at times.

"It's just as well," Lady Goring continued, not bothering to wait for his response. "For she's taken London by storm since returning from her honeymoon as the Duchess of Gravesend. She's hosted no less than three balls and two routs already. The routs were nothing special, I would say, but the balls—even I have to admit the girl has flare—no expense spared. Do you know she even had an array of exotic birds in the gardens of Gravesend House?

"She would have made an excellent wife for you, John, but I doubt you would have had pockets deep enough to keep her satisfied. The girl has ambition."

And Avers did not. His lack of desire for social mobility, the antithesis of both the new Duchess and his aunt, continued to frustrate and bewilder the Dowager Countess.

He might have cracked a sardonic smile at his aunt's unknowing astuteness had he not been surprised by the sudden onset of painful emotions. It had been some time since he'd considered his heartbreak at the hands of the beautiful Duchess of Gravesend, and while the pain had dulled, he still felt it twinge at his aunt's sharp words. The same repulsion at the weakness such pain engendered reared its head. How he loathed to be subject to it.

"I couldn't agree more, aunt," he said, regaining some of the power he'd lost. "We were not well-suited. I am pleased to hear she is doing so well as Her Grace, the Duchess of Gravesend."

That was odd.

Avers really meant those words.

Since Emilie had thrown out that challenge of forgiveness to him at Dartois' hunting lodge, Avers had chosen to take it up. He had realised it was a choice. He could choose to continue to be a slave to the hurt of the past or to forgive and look to the future.

It did not mean Miss Curshaw had not hurt him, nor did it mean his feelings would change immediately and he would no longer carry the wound of that previous heartbreak. But the seed of bitterness which had taken root in his heart had been pulled out and now the hurt he carried was healing. Instead of an open injury, it was a scar that when poked—as his aunt had just done—might provoke discomfort.

"I am sure you are," Lady Goring replied in less than convinced tones. "As for your new French friends, I've had it from one of my footmen who went out on an errand for me yesterday, that the French consul's residence has some new arrivals. A man named the Marquis de Dartois—I have not heard of him before, so I doubt he is of much consequence—and a woman. An *unmarried* woman. *That* has caused quite a stir." She raised her brows, or at least what she had of eyebrows without her usual use of khol pencil to fill them in. "Is that your friend—the gentleman named Dartois?"

"Your connections and sources never cease to amaze me," Avers replied, ignoring her question and playing for time as his mind raced. He could not believe his fortune in finding out so easily where Dartois and Emilie resided in London and yet how was he to get to her when she was in the French consul's residence? Dartois truly did have connections in high places.

His aunt fanned herself absently, no doubt overheated as the fire was lit and the window shut in spite of the mildness of the day. She had always been scared of catching cold. "There you go, mocking me again, but I have expended a lot of effort curating a network of informants and there really is no substitute for a well-placed servant."

Something fell in the back of Avers' mind. He tried to grasp it.

A well-placed servant.

"Well, will you not answer me?"

Avers' gaze dropped from the far wall where it had migrated onto an equestrian painting by Boultbee from his late uncle's collection.

"Forgive me, aunt. Would you be so good as to repeat your question?"

Lady Goring huffed loudly. "Honestly, John! You attend me no better than Sophia when she has that excuse for a new husband of hers in tow." She smacked her fan down in her lap.

"Then count your blessings, madam, that I am without a wife—can you imagine what poor company I would be then?"

"I have no fear of such an occurrence. You are a confirmed bachelor, John. There will be no wedding for you."

Avers made no retort. When his aunt's feathers were ruffled, one had to wait until they laid back down of their own accord. After several minutes, in which Lady Goring cleared two plates of the various dishes on offer, she finally relented.

"*I said*"—both words were delivered with extra vigour—"that Lady Peregrine is due to host a masquerade ball at which the French consul is supposed to make an appearance. Something about fostering good relations in an informal manner—and I would not at all be surprised if your new friend will be there. I was due to attend with Sophia, but that minx has declined on account of going out of Town to her husband's house in the country again."

Avers' heart leapt at the opportunity. "I should be delighted, aunt."

"First you ignore me and now you interrupt me. You haven't even heard the question yet."

"But what if I promise to be a far better companion when I escort you to Lady Peregrine's ball than I have been this evening? What if I promise to be all that is charming?"

"You would be *delighted* to escort me?" she asked, picking up on his previous words, scepticism in her voice.

Avers had never before expressed delight at accompanying his aunt anywhere. It had always been an obligation accompanied by sarcastic protestations.

"Immensely so." Avers rose. "Name the time and place."

Still looking incredibly suspicious, Lady Goring gave her nephew the details, and before she could question his intent as she so clearly desired to do, he swept an overly gallant bow and took his leave.

Avers left behind him a most dissatisfied relation. Yet before him there was hope. He had discovered Mademoiselle Cadeaux's whereabouts and secured an invitation to a place she may very well be.

The faintest flicker of hope lit the darkness that had engulfed him since he had last seen her.

CHAPTER THIRTY-THREE

Emilie shifted on the sofa in the morning room of the consul's residence trying to get comfortable. She pressed the waistline of her dress for the fifth time. Her stays were laced too tight, and the maid had paid no heed when she'd asked for them to be loosened. Apparently Lord Dartois preferred tight lacing and as the maid was one procured for Emilie by the Marquis, the new servant took her instructions from him.

She threw a venomous look at the maid who sat nearby before reapplying herself to reading the book in her hand.

Her mind began wandering again almost instantly.

The middle-aged woman was not only her lady's maid. She was her guard. She had not left Emilie's side since arriving at the consul's residence. Any hope Emilie had retained that she might find an opportunity to escape once in London was doomed to disappointment.

While Dartois had kept his distance since coming to London and was more often than not out attending so-called business meetings, she was left to wile away the hours under the eagle-eyed stare of her appointed guard. The Marquis had told Emilie she would be welcome to accompany him to his meetings when she was ready.

No matter where she went within the residence of the consul—a portly little man who was deep in Dartois' pocket and of no help to Emilie—she was followed by her new shadow. The breakfast room, the library, the gardens—all of them felt suffocating because of the maid who followed. Not only did she follow, but she stuck to Emilie's side like an unwelcome fly, watching her every mood, examining the books she picked up and the embroidery she started.

What was worse, when Dartois had instructed her to shop in London for new accessories, her guard in tow, Emilie had realised how ill-equipped she was to escape.

In France she had considered leaping from the carriage or running from the Marquis' arms, and if she'd escaped, she might have been able to muddle her way through. But this was a different country, a different city. Emilie could speak English, yet the people here spoke so fast and with accents she did not recognise. Worse, the streets and buildings were as alien to her as the people. London contained strange signs she couldn't decipher, odd road networks she struggled to navigate, and no friends she could call on. Even the direction of the docks, to where she might run and secure a passage home, was unknown to her.

Her only ally, the Duke of Tremaine, could help her no longer. He had tried, he had tried his utmost, but he had... She pushed from her mind those awful images of him falling, wounded on the dockside. The very idea he might have succumbed to his injuries was too much to bear.

But she had not lost hope.

Not yet.

She would focus on what was in her control. She would not succumb to the initial terror she had felt upon arriving here. Emilie Cadeaux had never allowed life to simply happen to her and she would not now.

On her second day in England she had counted out the money she had. Then she had taken stock of the belongings she had managed to bring with her. Finally, she had done the same with the luggage that had followed them on from Paris.

The coins she had were few, but she might sell some of her clothes and jewels to shore up her funds. Most of those items had been gifts from the Comte de Vergelles and it was therefore unlikely that Dartois would countenance her continuing to wear them. Now she only needed to find a way to sell them.

"Abigail?" Emilie asked, looking up from the book she had not been reading and speaking to the maid who sat too close beside her.

"Yes, Miss Cadeaux?"

"Do you know where I might sell some clothes I no longer need?" Emilie carried on quickly, giving her reasons for the seemingly out of the blue question, before the maid could get suspicious. "My clothes from his Lordship will be arriving from the dressmaker soon, and I already have a selection of millinery and shawls from our trip the other day. Soon I will have more clothes than I know what to do with, so it seems sensible to get rid of some, though they're far too good a quality to give away."

"You wish to sell them, not hand them on?" the maid asked, clearly hoping she would have been the recipient of some of Mademoiselle Cadeaux's dresses as many maids were of their mistress' cast-offs.

"Yes, I think so. They're really quite pretty and by some of the best dressmakers in Paris."

"As you wish, Mademoiselle." There was a blankness in the maid's face. Either she was short on wit, or she was being purposefully unhelpful.

"Yes, I do wish it," said Emilie. "Can you find somewhere to sell them for me?"

"I can certainly—"

At that moment the door opened, and though Emilie had been doing a credible job of making the conversation seem as inconsequential as she wanted it to appear, she coloured a little when she realised it was Dartois who was entering the room.

"Mademoiselle Cadeaux," he said, coming in and bowing.

He had been like this since coming to London. All courtesy and gentlemanliness. No hint of the knife he had held at her throat in Cherbourg. If anything it made Emilie more on edge. He played the part of villain and the part of gentleman with such ease—and switched between them without pause—she couldn't tell which was the truth. Nor could she be sure whether it would be the former or the latter she would encounter whenever she entered his presence.

"We are to attend Lord Peregrine's masquerade ball this evening," he announced.

"We are?"

"We are." He raised his chin and stared down his nose at her in a measuring way. "I have friends attending that we would do well to meet. Friends interested in what I can offer them."

He had stopped hiding his intentions from Emilie since taking her from Paris. He seemed convinced, for some reason unknown to her, that she would come around to his way of thinking and would partner with him in his illicit endeavours. Every time he made these assumptions and spoke this freely, she remained silent and the satisfied look on his face grew. He believed, thanks to her lack of protest, that he was winning her over.

"The new dresses I bade you order on our first day in London should arrive shortly. I paid double for the woman to have them ready in time. And you will find a matching mask has been provided as well."

Emilie thanked God for Dartois' words. They would go a long way to convince the maid of her story about needing to sell clothes. Hopefully it wouldn't be long before Emilie could increase her savings by those sales and then she could devise a plan for escape.

"Very well, my Lord," Emilie said, rising to leave. "I'll get ready."

On her way to the door, she passed the Marquis and her skin prickled. A few more steps and she would be free from his presence for a time. But before she could escape, her tormentor reached out, grasping her arm and making her jump in the process.

His touch did not feel the same as when he had threatened her on the dock in Cherbourg. Somehow that made it worse. Now his touch was intimate, almost tender, and the sensation made her sick to her stomach. Not for the first time since he had taken her from the Comte's possession, he leant in and breathed in her scent, his face mere inches from her own.

Emilie recoiled from him, turning her head away, her expression one of distaste.

"I grow impatient, Emilie," he murmured against her cheek, his breath hot on her skin.

It was the first time he had used her Christian name. The action felt like a violation. It took everything within her not to yank her arm from his grasp and run to the door.

But she knew, she felt it in her gut, that had she done so, she would have sent him over the edge. This man was unpredictable. There was no telling how far his temper would flare, nor how much he would scorch those nearby. She must not react. She must bide her time—if she wished to survive.

Inhaling slowly through her nose she willed the nausea to subside and waited for the fear to ebb. In and out. In and out.

"Forgive me, my Lord," she murmured, her fear transforming quickly into anger at having to placate this brute.

He did not remove his grip from her arm and his stare did not abate. She racked her brains for something more to say, something which might help her to escape from this moment. Glancing around her, Emilie realised with sudden panic that the maid had disappeared from the room.

"You are forgiven," Dartois said at last, his tone thick with desire. "Be ready for seven o'clock."

Then he released her.

Emilie left. The sick feeling followed her, as did the imprint of his fingers on her arm, both sensations making her want to get in a copper tub and scrub herself clean. She wanted to be rid of this man, but at the moment, she could not see her way out.

CHAPTER THIRTY-FOUR

Emilie guessed there were at least two hundred people attending the Peregrines' masquerade that evening when she arrived on Dartois' arm.

All along the painted wall, candles in ornate golden scroll sconces shone out across the crowds, their light reflecting off the polished metal disks that formed the back of the clever lighting fixtures. Above them hung glittering chandeliers, hundreds of candles alight, adding to the heat of the rooms.

Lit by the myriad of candles was a series of grand portraits hung around the top of the room which Emilie took to be the ancestors of their hosts. These solemn figures from bygone ages stared down upon the multitude, the painted figures clad in silk suits with deep-fronted bodices, red heeled shoes and great cascading periwigs.

Yet for all the illumination and ancestral observants, the crowd below remained anonymous. Emilie walked through a sea of strangers in masks of all kinds. Gentlemen and ladies obscured their identities with anything from simple eye coverings to theatrical creations and, as was the purpose, the mystery provoked a feverish glee.

Some, Emilie knew, would enjoy their identity being a secret for the night and give nothing away, using the opportunity to say things they'd otherwise keep to themselves, or flirt with someone they desired. Others would be too easily recognised, and yet others would have no patience for such games and within moments introduce themselves or pull up their masks to reveal their identities.

Emilie remained behind her mask, happy for the protection it provided in this unknown environment. Despite the amusement palpable in the gathering, she found Lord and Lady Peregrine's event far more austere than what she was used to.

Aside from the gilt candleholders and crystal chandeliers, the decor was simpler, with muted tones and neoclassical decoration. The people were equally as different. Aside from their masks, they were far more staid than their French counterparts. Despite wearing a new gown from an English dressmaker, Emilie felt out of place with her bright silk and rouged face.

The mask Dartois had chosen for her covered only her eyes, and so the powder, rouge and patch she wore were on display. She noticed several women staring openly at her, clearly not recognising her from their usual Societal circles, and she saw the judgement in their eyes.

Emilie and Dartois moved from one reception room into another, the crowds only growing, and Emilie's discomfort with it. She knew her place in Paris. She was considered a mistress, but that was accepted. Here she was... what? An alien.

The idea of escaping into the city with the funds from selling her old clothes suddenly felt stupid. How could she manage it when everything about her was so different?

Her breathing grew shallow, her palms slick inside her

gloves, her heartbeat speeding. What if she couldn't escape? What if giving in to Dartois was all she could do?

The sound of the crowd grew louder. Someone laughed in her ear, the noise piercing. Another hailed Dartois, and the Marquis walked off through the masses to greet them.

Emilie was left alone, the people swirling around her. The thought of giving into Dartois caused bile to rise in her throat. Nausea followed close behind. The feeling swelled. She was going to vomit. People pressed in around her. She was going to vomit right here in Lord and Lady Peregrine's ballroom. She was going to—

"Good evening, Mademoiselle Cadeaux."

That voice.

Her brow furrowed and her eyes welled with tears.

That familiar voice.

She almost whispered his name, her eyes darting up from the floor and meeting those unmistakable hooded brown eyes behind a black mask.

The Duke of Tremaine.

How? How was he here? How had he survived that shot? She didn't care. He *was* here.

"Your Grace." Her voice was barely audible above the crowds.

"I trust I find you well?" he asked, those eyes of his, which had so often displayed bored indifference, were now full of earnest concern.

Emilie swallowed, blinking back the tears, then turned away to suck in a breath, trying her hardest to calm the emotions which stormed within her. "I thought you were..." She trailed off, unable to finish that horrible sentence.

In the melee of the crowds, the Duke reached out and touched her arm, his gaze containing such gentleness. She wanted to grab hold of that hand, to hold it to her chest, to cry with relief that all she had feared was not true.

"I am—I am well," she finally replied. "But how are you here?"

"I might ask you the same question," Tremaine said, his tone gentler than his words.

"I thought you were... " She raised a hand, touching his shoulder lightly and then dropping it again before anyone noticed.

"I was—a souvenir from the Marquis. But only winged. I have the generosity of your fellow countrywoman to thank for my salvation."

Emilie wanted to hear everything, but the jostle of the crowd reminded her they were not alone, and they did not have much time.

"I am only angry at myself for putting you in such a position with my arrogance. I thought I knew the state of play, but I was wrong. Mademoiselle Cadeaux—Emilie—I am so very sorry." His voice cracked over those last words and suddenly the crowd around them melted away from consciousness and it was just them alone.

That was the first time he had used her Christian name. She hadn't realised he even knew it. It sounded so right on his lips, it was spoken with such kindness and care.

"I am only thankful for your quick wit in leaving me that note hidden in your letters. Once I found your apartments it was the only reason I was able to find out where you were at all."

She remembered scrawling that letter. The interruption. Hoping she had said enough. Hiding it quickly among the letters she had piled up to send and the horrible feeling of having to leave—

"Lutin!" she blurted out, her eyes dropping to the floor, hoping the small shadow might magically appear.

"He's all right." Again the Duke touched her arm lightly, the connection soothing. "He's safe and well."

"Oh." She felt the tears welling in her eyes again. "Leaving him was the most dreadful thing. To think of him an ocean away is just—"

"Then I may bring some comfort. I brought him with me to England. He is with my valet at present."

Emilie's eyes widened in surprise and then a delighted smile took over her lips.

"It was a mutual dislike at first," the Duke explained. "Your petit diable did the unmentionable in one of my best pairs of dancing pumps. I'm pleased to report, though, since that bumpy start, they've become quite civil—friendly even. I believe Lutin prefers his company to mine now. Traitor."

His words flowed light-heartedly, but she could see the humour did not fully touch his eyes. The funning was for her. He was trying to calm her. When he removed his hand from her arm again, she felt the loss acutely.

"I am so happy," she whispered. A tear finally escaped her rapid blinking and traced through her powder.

Tremaine drew a handkerchief from his pocket and passed it discreetly to her.

"Please," he said in a low tone, "do not worry—not about Lutin, nor about... I shall not see you harmed."

She could not speak. The lump that had formed in her throat at his arrival would not move and it had grown. His words—those kind and caring words—they undid her.

"Tell me you are well?"

It was a question and yet it was spoken as a demand. As though he could bear no other response than a positive one.

"At least physically," he said by way of concession. "Has he—"

She could see Tremaine was not able to finish the question. The implication hung between them, all manner of endings to that question horribly present.

Again she remained silent, not through choice, but

because the care shining from his eyes was something she had never expected, nor could she fully understand it. This man had taken a bullet trying to save her. He had gone down with it, and yet here he was, coming for her again. The emotions such thoughts evoked were so strong she could barely control them. Even if she had wanted to, she could not have spoken, for how could someone respond to such kindness?

"Bonsoir, Your Grace."

Dartois' greeting came from behind her. She saw the Duke's whole frame tense. His jaw clenched, and his hands formed fists at his side. Catching his gaze again, she willed him with her eyes not to react.

"Or," said Dartois, coming around to stand between them, "is it Lord Avers? I confess I have never been good with names. But then, I do not know many *gentlemen* who go by a different name in Paris to that which they bear in London."

What was he talking about? Emilie looked at Dartois and then at the Duke. The former appeared as though he had won some verbal game while the latter continued in stony silence. Avers? Who was this Avers? Was he really the Duke of Tremaine? Had he been lying about his identity as well as his purpose in Paris?

"Ah, I think you know my beautiful companion?" Dartois stretched out an arm to the woman who stood behind him who had, until that moment, been obscured from their view. "Her Grace, the Duchess of Gravesend."

"My Lord, how delightful it is to see you in London again. We were quite lost without you." The woman stood at Dartois' side, tall and slender, with fair colouring and fine features, a beautiful dress of pale pink silk hugged an enviable figure and a diamond necklace glittered on her neck.

Her effect on Tremaine—or Avers—or whatever he was known by, was acute.

Emilie saw him jolt at her appearance. His composure, beneath the mask, faltered and then fractured completely. As it broke, she saw deep shock marked in his eyes and open mouth, and her heart ached for the man before her. This confident English Lord, who had been so sardonic and aloof and yet displayed such kindness and care towards her, suddenly appeared vulnerable. Everything within her desired to reach out and smooth away the hurt with a gentle caress.

"Your Grace," Avers said between gritted teeth.

His voice sounded alien to Emilie, formal and rigid.

"May I congratulate you on your recent marriage to the Duke," Avers said politely. "He is a fortunate man."

Whatever effect this woman had on Lord Avers, it did not appear mutual. She remained unaffected and bestowed a condescending smile across the party.

"You're too kind."

"I do not think he is, Your Grace," Dartois said. "Not fortunate but clever. Any man who allowed you to slip through their fingers was a fool indeed."

The Duchess laughed, the sound light and musical—and practised.

"My companion, Mademoiselle Cadeaux," Dartois said, finally presenting Emilie.

The young Duchess only gave the briefest incline of her head, and her pretty lips pursed slightly. Her Grace knew exactly what sort of woman was being presented to her. Despite this, Emilie curtseyed low. When she rose, Avers was still staring at the woman.

Dartois began saying something about the Duke of Gravesend's vast estates and the Duchess glowed with pride while Avers listened. Emilie watched him, the fractures in his composure slowly closing over and the shock now only visible in his eyes. She saw a muscle bulging at the corner of his jaw where he clenched his teeth. For this woman to have such an effect on him, she had to be...

A deep ache started in Emilie's chest. This was the woman he loved. The one who'd broken his heart. And to still have such an effect on him could only mean his love for her had not died.

CHAPTER THIRTY-FIVE

Avers recognised the dark pleasure in Dartois' eyes at the situation he had conjured up. How the Marquis had found out about his connection with Miss Curshaw—that is, Her Grace the Duchess of Gravesend—he wasn't sure. Yet it felt as though Avers' appearance here tonight had not surprised him. In fact, it felt as though Dartois had been ready and waiting with the Duchess as his trump card.

"The Duke has skill indeed," the Marquis said. "Not only to catch you, Your Grace, but to keep you."

Yes, Dartois knew about Avers' relationship with Miss Curshaw and he was purposefully needling him.

Then again, most of London had known when Avers had left. That was part of his reason for leaving. That and the pain. Pain which, over the months, had healed, but the shock of being confronted by the Duchess had brought the memories of that suffering back to mind.

And Dartois was like a cat with a bird. Repeatedly dragging the conversation back to places where he could pin it down and inflict the most damage on his English adversary.

"My husband has been friends with Dartois for some time

—but you have yet to tell me why we are so fortunate as to have you back in London with us," said the Duchess. "I cannot fathom why you would choose to leave Paris. It is so beautiful and full of such Society. I long to go."

Now the initial shock was wearing off, Avers found the discomfort easier to manage. In fact, he was seeing in the Duchess of Gravesend things he had been blind to before. The falseness to her laugh which never met her eyes. The over-flattery she used when speaking to others that carried with it a note of insincerity. And the way she had greeted Emilie—Avers' indignation had yet to disappear completely. Had the Duchess always been like this?

"Have you enjoyed your trip, Lord Avers?"

Drawn back to the present, he rested his hooded gaze upon Her Grace, realising how cool his feelings towards this woman had become. "It provided a much-needed respite."

"London was proving to be too much for you? Sometimes one must escape one's own life, n'est pas?" Dartois taunted.

"London is a large city," Emilie cut in. "I could understand wanting to get away."

The Duchess scoffed.

Ignoring Her Grace's impolite response, Avers turned to look at Emilie and saw in her eyes an understanding of the situation. She was trying to turn the conversation.

Then, Dartois' hand came up to her elbow and Avers saw his fingers tighten around her in warning.

"And sometimes," Avers said, drawing the attention back to himself, "that respite provides much needed perspective. With perspective, one can see things for what they are, rather than what one had assumed or desired them to be. Where beauty has beguiled, the truth can shine through, and suddenly something so very appealing is seen for what it is. I find London is not at all what I remembered or yearned for. No, my feelings are quite changed." He kept his gaze on the

Duchess, resting it on her until a faint colour appeared in her cheeks.

"I am here on business," said Dartois, reclaiming power over the conversation.

"Business—is that what you call it?" Avers asked. He would not allow this man to continue to have the upper hand. There was no need for pretence anymore.

"Ah." Dartois chuckled and leaned into the Duchess. "He is speaking of my friend the Comte de Vergelles. The poor man was recently apprehended on false charges of possessing stolen papers of some kind. The man's innocent, but I'm afraid Lord Avers never liked him. Jealous of what another man possessed. It seems there is a pattern of behaviour here, n'est pas?" The Marquis flashed him a wicked smile. "And now he implies I have something to do with this fantastical plot. What an imagination he has! I am beginning to think he does not like me."

"How awful," the Duchess exclaimed, glancing between the two gentlemen, as if unsure how to react, before turning her blue-eyed gaze wide upon Avers. "Surely not, my Lord?"

"I'm afraid Lord Dartois has me at a disadvantage," Avers replied, plucking at the cuff of his jacket to appear uncaring. "I was involved in no such dealings in Paris. He must be thinking of someone else."

"Ah," Dartois said, playing along. "Perhaps I am mistaking you for someone else, just as you are mistaking me for a common criminal. It is best, therefore, that we accept we were not what we first believed and part ways amicably."

"How mysteriously you talk," the Duchess exclaimed, fanning herself in an agitated manner, clearly unable to follow the conversation and finding her lack of a role within it unacceptable.

"Pardon, Your Grace. We men do not know how to behave when there are beautiful women present. Allow me to take you in for supper. Lord Avers—" He held out a hand, staring challengingly at him. "No hard feelings?"

Avers debated whether to take the offered hand. Was this some kind of game he could not follow? Reluctantly he shook it and Dartois leant in to him, saying in a low voice, "Bon chance in your future endeavours, my Lord. You were a wholly unworthy opponent."

Avers pursed his lips to hold back the unhelpful words that begged to be let loose, and drew back, glad to regain his hand.

"Now you will excuse us," Dartois said, offering an arm to each of the ladies. "We are expected at our host's table."

Avers watched Emilie take the man's arm and the trio walked away from him through the crowds. He stared after them, his mind trying to work out what to do next, and then he caught sight of Emilie looking briefly over her shoulder.

On one side of Dartois walked Avers' past and on the other walked his future. When his eyes caught Emilie's and they locked for a moment, his resolve strengthened. He'd found her. Now he had to save her.

CHAPTER THIRTY-SIX

In the mid-morning two days later, Avers sat half-clothed at his dressing table, pressing his snuffbox to his lips and thinking.

"I apologise, my Lord, but the water is running slowly today so we must wait a little longer before adequate can be drawn and heated for your bath," said his valet, entering his master's bedchamber and breaking his reverie.

Like many of the wealthy residences, Avers' house paid a small fee to pipe water off the main wooden conduit directly to the house. With the growth of the city and the system's reliance on gravity, however, there were days when the pressure ran low.

As his valet passed by the bed, Lutin, who was curled up on the covers, growled softly at the intruder without bothering to raise his head.

"I've ordered two of the footmen to fetch water from the well so you are not kept waiting, my Lord."

"Hmm?" Avers looked over at his valet just as the servant was glaring at the growling dog.

He had been lost in thought, trying to find a way out of

the coil Emilie was in, that he barely took in what Simmonds was saying. Putting down his snuffbox, he raked a hand through his hair, feeling the knots and realising it needed a good wash. Perhaps the bath might loosen some kind of plan from his mind as well as the dirt from his head.

"I suspect they'll get caught up nattering at the well," Simmonds continued, still on the same theme. "Can't trust them to be quick about it, these youngsters." Avers' valet, came around the bed to lay out his master's clothes and pick up the discarded nightcap. "Beg pardon, my Lord, not that I wish to speak ill of them, but they lack a sense of urgency. Always wanting to find out the goings on. One of them—I shall not name them, my Lord—had the nerve to tell me he had heard about this and that from my Lord Worth's residence. I shan't repeat it. But being as they are particular friends of yours, I boxed his ears! Doesn't matter to me that he's a young man and not a boy. Need to learn their place."

Simmonds' words washed over Avers. He'd leant back in his chair again, lost in thought. This time his mind could not help but wander towards the new Duchess of Gravesend. It was obvious that Dartois had known what he was doing. He must have heard of Avers' attendance at the masquerade after he worked out his true identity, and purposely brought the Duchess across his path to throw him off.

He had been—momentarily.

In truth, he'd been surprised by the strength of his emotions when meeting the Duchess again. The woman had not been in his mind for weeks. When he had first left for Paris several months ago he had believed she would forever haunt him, just as she had done in the months before. But with all the events that had transpired as he played the fake Duke of Tremaine, she had fallen completely out of his thoughts.

He could have said it was the distraction of adventure, or the presence of the dark-eyed and worthy Mademoiselle

Cadeaux in his life, but he wasn't sure those were the reasons. They played their part, to be certain, but he knew when his feelings and attitude towards his old amour had changed.

It had been when he had chosen to forgive her, just as Mademoiselle Cadeaux had urged him to do. It was not an instant change, and in reality, the situation had not altered, but he had. The love which he had harboured for her—an emotion which had seemed so eternal three months ago—had died. In choosing to forgive her, those feelings and the hold they had over him, had been dealt a death blow. He'd mourned them and the future he had imagined with her. And beyond the grief lay hope—a knowledge that the Almighty's plan for him went beyond that period of his life

Despite the shock of seeing her again, he realised now the depth of emotions he had felt for her were no longer a part of him. They felt like a phantom of something that had been and no longer was. A scar that showed what had transpired, ceasing to cause raw pain, just minor twinges every now and again. As it had at the Peregrines' ball.

That final act of forgiveness had freed him. And then there was Emilie.

Emilie

The thought of her evoked such deep emotion within him he almost sprang from his chair. She was like no one he had ever met before. Her quiet resolve, her strength against poor odds, and her sense of what was right.

Emilie.

He could not—he would not—leave her to her fate.

"They had best not delay." Simmonds was still going on about the errant footmen. "I shouldn't care what gossip was being spoken about at the well. Just so long as they don't divulge the goings on of this house."

Such inconsequential complaints when Emilie's future hung in the balance. Servants always gossiped, and such a place of congregation was bound to see tidbits passed from one to another, and thence across London. It must be worse in Paris where the population relied on public fountains and the service of water bearers who held no allegiance to the houses where they delivered the essential commodity.

Aunt Goring should purposely send one of her servants to her local well even if she had no need of the water—that was if she did not already do so. Such a perfect way to…

Spy.

Individuals coming and going from houses largely unnoticed.

Persons whose presence was not considered.

People with access to establishments and… papers.

Avers leapt up from his chair and began pacing. Water bearers would not have been considered and vetted like the full-time staff in Wakeford's Paris offices. In fact, they probably weren't even there when the questioning had taken place. They would be in and out in the morning before anyone of consequence had arrived. It was the perfect access.

Hadn't the Comte mentioned something about the water bearers when Avers had met them at the Café Procope in Paris? Had the noble really been so brazen as to boast about their secret lines of communication in such a fashion?

Avers was so lost in his thoughts that he almost collided with his valet as he re-entered his room carrying a tray with the day's letters.

If Dartois intended to sell the papers here in London he would have to be discreet. Would he use the same means of communication here in England as he had in France? Was that the way to catch him—to watch the consul's residence and try to intercept whatever water bearers came and went and bribe them to expose the man?

He sat back down at his dressing table and tossed off the remainder of the cold coffee he had been served half an hour since. Unthinking, he began to leaf through the letters Simmonds had left on the silver salver on his table while his mind continued to think up possible ways forward.

That hand—Avers recognised it. The letter was from Wakeford.

Tearing open the wafer he quickly scanned the contents. Relief broke out across his face. Wakeford was in London. He begged Avers' presence at his offices this morning.

Standing up so quickly he sent his chair flying backwards into the wall, Avers strode to the bed and began to yank on the carefully laid out jacket. He thrust his legs quickly into the matching breeches, fastening the buttons at the knees, and turned to check himself in the mirror. He waved a hand of dismissal at the visage before him, horrified but uncaring of the missing cravat, but deciding he could not go out with his hair in such disarray.

Raking his fingers through it savagely, he fastened it quickly with a ribbon and turned towards the door.

"I'm going out—never mind the bath, Simmonds," he threw over his shoulder, reaching for the door handle.

"My Lord!" said his valet, appearing with a towel over one arm and a sponge in the other hand from the adjoining room. A scandalised gasp escaped the faithful retainer when he took in the sight of his master thus attired. "You *cannot* leave the house in such a state."

"And yet, I must perform the impossible," Avers quipped, not in the least concerned over his servant's perturbation.

"My Lord, just think of my—that is your—reputation!" cried Simmonds. "I beg of you to at least let me dress your hair and find a fresh cravat. What will be said of you?"

Avers was on the brink of ignoring the strictures and striding out the door when he thought better of it. There was no need to attract talk by gallivanting around London half-dressed. That was not the modus operandi for such a delicate situation.

Not only that, but Simmonds had inadvertently cracked this case, so the least Avers could do was submit to his valet's ministrations. A short time later, presenting an unmentionable appearance to the public, he rose to leave. Simmonds still tried to do more, offering his master a mouche, but that was where Avers drew the line—there was no need for powder and patch in his mission.

Picking up his hat and cane he strode from the room, bellowing for his footman to call a chair. Before half an hour was up, he was at Wakeford's London offices, bursting through the door to find his friend and tell him the whole.

CHAPTER THIRTY-SEVEN

"Shut the door behind you," Wakeford commanded, unperturbed by Avers' abrupt entrance into his office.

"When did you arrive in England?" Avers asked, doing as he was bid.

"With last evening's tide. I was quick, though not as quick as you," Wakeford replied. "This is Lancelot." He gestured to the person standing beside him, a man in his early thirties, fair hair, athletic build.

Avers nodded to the stranger.

"He's assisting our investigations on the Marquis in London."

"Dartois is staying at the French consul's residence," Avers said. "He has Mademoiselle Cadeaux with him against her will."

"Against her will—how do you know she's not complicit?" Lancelot asked, missing a warning look from Wakeford.

Avers bridled at the man's question, struggling to hold his temper. "Because I saw her at Lord and Lady Peregrine's masquerade two days since and she told me as much. Wakeford may not have told you, but it's thanks to her help we found the papers at all, and that we knew Dartois was fleeing across the Channel with them."

"He mentioned her aid, but her travelling with the Marquis appeared—" Lancelot stopped, seeing the warning light in Avers' eyes. "I understand your concern over the woman, but our main focus is—"

"*My* main focus is her safety. She's an innocent caught up in this mess and thanks to our bungling she's at risk of... of..."

Avers didn't want to say out loud what he feared. Somehow, it felt as though, if he said it, the worst may come to pass. Dartois might take advantage of Mademoiselle Cadeaux. He might even kill her.

Avers squashed down the fears and concentrated on the hope brought by his revelation about the water bearers. "There's something I need to tell you, Wakeford."

"Innocent?" Lancelot interjected, brow furrowing. "Isn't she a—"

"Don't!" said Wakeford quickly. "The man's in love with her."

Surprise took over Lancelot's expression and any words he had intended to say were stalled.

Avers, too, was rendered speechless at this blunt statement. He hadn't admitted that fact yet—even to himself.

After taking a moment to master his feelings, he broke the silence, speaking slowly and deliberately. "I've come to tell you that I may have surmised how the Comte and Marquis were able to evade your Cabinet Noir, Wakeford."

"We were intercepting all the Comte's letters in Paris," Wakeford explained for Lancelot's sake. "But we found no proof of his illicit activities and assume he must have had another way of passing information." Wakeford turned back to Avers. "Well?"

"Water bearers."

Wakeford echoed his words, eyes narrowing to work out what it meant.

"Don't you see? Paris relies on them and they aren't permanent members of staff within a household. They pass all over the city unnoticed, even into your offices Wakeford. You wouldn't have questioned them like you did your staff because they wouldn't have been there at the time."

"The buckets—" said Lancelot, catching on to Avers' theory, "—we've come across similar before with the smugglers in Sussex and the West Country. They build secret compartments into the barrels or lids to hide contraband. It would be an easy way to steal papers and pass messages undetected."

"My thoughts exactly," said Avers, heartbeat quickening as the puzzle pieces came together.

Lancelot nodded, rubbing his chin as he thought. "If they were using it in Paris it's a good bet that he'll continue to use that method here, even with the piped water to the consul's residence. We should alert the watch we've set on the Marquis' movements to keep an eye out for water bearers."

"Agreed." Wakeford snatched up a quill from the ink stand, dipped it, and began scrawling a note.

"Tell your men, if they intercept one of them, to check the lid. It'll likely be hollow to store letters."

Wakeford added Lancelot's suggestion to the note, folded it, attached a wafer and rang the bell. Avers moved aside as another of Wakeford's men opened the office door. His friend handed over the note with instructions for it to be delivered to the men watching the Marquis. Once the man had gone, Wakeford addressed the room.

"Now we wait."

It was two days before the theory was proven.

Impatient for an update, Avers returned uninvited to Wakeford's office early on the morning of the second day.

"Come." Wakeford's voice emanated through the closed door.

Avers entered. "Any news?" he said without ceremony, closing the door behind him.

Both Wakeford and Lancelot were standing over the former's desk and staring at a letter laid out on it.

Wakeford looked up, seeming not to have heard Avers' question. "Did my note already reach you?" he said, brows raised.

"Note? No—I've come for news."

Wakeford pointed at the letter on the table and Avers came to stand shoulder to shoulder with the two men to see what so fascinated them.

The unfolded paper contained lines of script—unsurprisingly—but instead of communicating knowledge they appeared to be written in gibberish.

"A cypher," Lancelot explained.

"From the Marquis?"

Wakeford and Lancelot nodded in unison.

"It's already been copied out and sent to Lancelot's codebreakers," said Wakeford, grinning at the turning tide of their situation. "We're waiting on them to break it."

"How long will that take?"

It had been two days already. Two days in which anything could have happened to Mademoiselle Cadeaux. Avers had walked past the consul's residence multiple times in those two days, at a discreet distance, in the hope he might ascertain how she fared, but he had seen no sign of her.

Lancelot shrugged, though his expression remained serious. "It depends. If it's simple it could only be hours. If it's more sophisticated maybe days."

Days? Mademoiselle Cadeaux might not have days.

"We're hoping that whatever the letter says, it'll not only incriminate the Comte and Dartois, but also shed light on who they're using as their go-between here in London for the sale of the papers. They must have come here because they have contacts and that's Lancelot's department."

Avers reined back his rising frustration. These men were entirely focused on the Comte and Dartois and the innocent woman caught up in all this was being forgotten.

"We might not have days," he said.

Wakeford's grin slipped. "I know this is not ideal with Mademoiselle Cadeaux still under the Marquis' protection—"

"Protection?" Avers scoffed, failing to stop himself. "We *have* to ensure her safety." His entire body was framed by the tension he felt.

"We're doing all we can," Wakeford said, trying to sooth his friend's frayed nerves. "As soon as we have something we'll take action."

Avers' shoulders dropped a little. They all knew what was at stake. For Wakeford and Lancelot it was the papers. For Avers it was... the love of his life.

"This is my department now," said Lancelot. "We know what we're doing, and we'll take what you've said into account."

The man's words were less than comforting, but there was nothing more to be said. It was all hypothetical until that cypher was cracked.

It was under fourteen hours later that Avers was recalled to Wakeford's office. Lancelot's men had broken the code. The contents revealed a proposed meeting at St Saviour's docks for the papers to be exchanged for a pre-agreed sum.

An hour later, Wakeford, Lancelot and their men were at the docks waiting to catch their man. And Avers—much to Lancelot's chagrin—was there to save Emilie.

CHAPTER THIRTY-EIGHT

The dim interior of the carriage in which Emilie travelled with Dartois was lit intermittently by torches or link boys that they passed. It was about nine o'clock in the evening when Dartois had requested her to accompany him out. Emilie had assumed they were attending a rout or card party.

When the maid laid out a day dress, stout leather walking boots and a cloak for her to wear, Emilie assumed differently. Now she was in the carriage she surmised they were travelling east. From the small, dark view outside the window, she could see they were passing through a less salubrious part of Town, the dirt and shabby buildings only weakly lit by the half-moon.

She didn't ask their destination. The Marquis was in an odd humour. She could sense the tension rolling off him from the opposite carriage seat and she had no wish to provoke him. After more than half an hour, they finally drew to a halt and the steps were let down. As soon as the door opened, a briny smell assailed Emilie's nostrils, and she realised they must be at the docks.

What was his purpose in bringing her here? Had Dartois

grown tired of her lack of interest in him and his plan? Did she know too much and now she was a liability?

She withdrew her gaze from the opposite window, her eyes darting quickly to the open door, where she saw Dartois climbing down.

There had been several times in their journey here when her heart had raced at the possibility that she was travelling to her end. The Duke of Tremaine—or Avers as she knew him now—had not been in contact since Lord and Lady Peregrine's ball. The blaze of hope that had lit her heart had flickered, dimmed, and almost extinguished.

Rising from her seat on seeing the Marquis beckon her, she allowed him to hand her down from the carriage to the grubby dockside. She stared around, taking in crates, lumber, nets and boats. A grimy, stinking melee of industry. She had assumed Dartois was giving instructions to the coachman and finding whoever they were meeting here, but on glancing back at him, she was startled to realise he was silently staring at her.

Without warning he stepped forward and took her by the shoulders, pulled her towards him and covered her mouth with his. There was no tenderness in the kiss. It was hard, fast and spoke of his possession. She tried to pull back, the surprise making it automatic, but his fingers tightened on her arms, pinching the skin.

When he finally released her, he was breathing heavily, his hands still clamped around her arms.

"I grow impatient," he gasped against her cheek.

The words made her blood run cold. Everything within her revolted at his touch, his closeness, his very presence. She wanted to jerk free from his hold, escape from his control, and keep running until she could not be found by him or anyone who knew her.

What would Lord Avers think of her now? None of this was her fault but she could not help feeling dirty. Perhaps he hadn't come for her because of the Duchess of Gravesend. He had been struck by her appearance at the Peregrines' ball, but Emilie could have sworn his Lordship had been eschewing any feelings for his old love before this. Maybe she'd been wrong. Maybe any perspective he had gained in France had been lost now he was back in London, in his own world, where his past feelings loomed large. What Emilie had believed was born between them in Paris, in the dangers of spy rings and stolen papers, may have been nothing at all. Like smoke—here one moment and blown away the next.

Emilie was as alone in the world now as she had always been.

"Come," Dartois commanded, partially releasing her so they could walk together along the dockside.

She had a choice now. She knew she did. Either she gave in to her fate as Dartois' coerced mistress, or she fought—she forged her own path and faced the risks such a choice would entail. Those risks were growing smaller in her mind as the bile rose in her throat at Dartois' attentions. Soon the fear would be small enough for her to act.

Rolling her shoulders back, she tried to still her shaking, and blinked hard three times. She had to pull herself together. She had to. Focusing on putting one step in front of the other, her heels clipped along the flagstones, passing by piles of cargo and fishing nets hung out to dry. Several boats of different sizes were moored on the piers and even at this hour there were men working, carrying cargo on and off vessels, securing the loads on the decks of the ships.

Lanterns hung at intervals down the walkways and here and there they had companions shining on the ships' decks, pushing back the approaching night, and fighting against the mist rising off the river.

Dartois' fingers tightened around her elbow, and he picked

up the pace. She pulled back. Was he taking her out of England?

He chuckled, letting her go and speaking as if to a child. "As you wish. I shouldn't have thought a woman of your nature would grow nervous after a mere kiss."

Curse him.

She bit back the retort on the tip of her tongue.

"But you must hurry—I have an appointment to keep, and those papers won't sell themselves."

Dartois took one of the lanterns lining the walkway and held it aloft to light their path.

"This way."

He gestured down one of the piers and directed the warm glow of the lantern in the way he wished for them to go. She moved forwards reluctantly, with the Marquis following behind, his presence hemming her in.

After twenty yards Dartois bade her stop next to a ship. Emilie didn't recognise it as the one which had brought her to England.

The Marquis let out a long, low whistle and two men appeared on the deck, swaggering down the gangway to the waiting couple.

Rapid greetings were exchanged in French.

"Any trouble?" Dartois asked, when the pleasantries were dealt with.

"Non," said the first. "As soon as we received the keg, we set sail and made port in Guernsey. We waited a week as you instructed. They did not find the documents in the hollowed-out lid of the brandy keg. We arrived here without incident this afternoon."

"That's not true," said the second man, much gruffer and unfriendlier in his tone than his companion. "The customs officer."

"We took care of that," snapped the first.

"As long as you have my cargo," Dartois said smoothly, holding out his hand, "I really do not care what problems you had or what you did about them."

The two men exchanged looks and the second huffed while the first withdrew a leather portfolio from inside his coat. Emilie watched as he held out the packet to Dartois.

The stolen papers. A small, seemingly inconsequential portfolio. A tiny thing that was causing so much havoc.

She resisted the urge to snatch it from the men and throw it into the water. Let the sea do its work on those lines of ink that had upset so many lives already.

But why resist? Why not just do it?

There was nothing to lose. Not anymore.

Her courage flared. She reached out and snatched the papers as Dartois was about to take hold of them.

Just before she could throw them into the water, accompanied by a chorus of expletives from her captor, a command rang out.

"Stand where you are!"

The two Frenchmen, Emilie and Dartois swung round. A group of officials were advancing towards them, lanterns and muskets raised.

"In the name of the King! Stand where you are! You are suspected of—"

A loud rapport sounded. Emilie screamed. The accompanying flash of fire was quickly followed by the tell-tale smell of sulphur, which emanated from the pistol in Dartois' hand. Soldiers and officials scattered for cover, their mouthpiece slain where he stood.

The Marquis grabbed Emilie, dropped his spent pistol and pulled out a fresh one from his greatcoat.

Behind them the two Frenchmen had run aboard their boat and were already weighing anchor to escape on the tide.

The gangway loosened, kicked off by the gruff sailor, and fell with a splash into the water below.

"Emilie!"

Her eyes flashed towards the officials who were approaching again and she saw Avers among them. She yanked against Dartois' hold, clutching the papers to her chest. Her captor swore, his pull becoming stronger, and then she felt the cold muzzle of his pistol against her neck.

"Stay back, Avers."

"Let her go, Dartois. Your game is up," Avers said. He took a step closer, a calming hand raised.

Emilie felt an overwhelming desire to run to him. To the safety of those arms. But Dartois' grip on her was now vicelike. She was his last bargaining chip.

"The game is up?" Dartois laughed harshly. "It has barely begun."

"Let her go," Avers repeated.

"I thought you loved that Duchess of yours."

Avers stepped forward again and Dartois mirrored the movement, moving back, keeping them just out of reach.

"But perhaps, like me, you are tempted by something you have yet to taste."

Dartois turned his face in towards her cheek and she felt his breath against her. He inhaled. The action made her shiver in revulsion.

"The Comte was the same. There's something about a conquest, is there not?" Dartois asked, his voice taunting, yanking Emilie further back with him. "And this woman has eluded us all."

She glanced down, feeling the press of the gun muzzle against her, and seeing how close they were to the edge of the dock. Her wooden boot slipped on the wet stone and she jerked, losing purchase, and scrambling to get away from the edge as Dartois' grip tightened.

"Please, Dartois," she pleaded.

"Please, please," he mimicked. "You would rather this pathetic Englishman than your fellow countryman?"

"She would rather be free," said Avers.

Emilie's eyes found his. They were earnest, filled with so much concern for her that her heart squeezed.

"Free!" Dartois sneered. "We are never any of us free! She will always be a common tavern brat. You will always be the one who failed to save her."

Dartois pressed the muzzle into Emilie's neck with fresh fervour causing her to cough and choke. His finger tightened around the trigger.

"No!" Avers shouted, reaching out to stop him.

This was it.

This was the end.

Emilie closed her eyes against the fear. Breath ragged. Heart racing. Waiting for the sound of the gun…

Instead, she heard a high, indignant bark break through the night air. Then another. And another. She knew that bark. Avers lurched forward, something barrelling into his legs, and then Emilie saw her Lutin, yanking the servant who held him forward until they dropped the lead completely.

Bark. Bark. Bark. Lutin shot around Avers' legs, lead trailing, hurtling towards his mistress at lightning speed.

"Infernal vermin!" Dartois cursed, removing his pistol from Emilie's neck and levelling it at the incoming dog.

"No!" Emilie cried, dropping the leather portfolio and grabbing Dartois' gun with both hands. She thrust upwards with all her might, pointing the muzzle skywards just as he pulled the trigger, and another ear-splitting rapport rang out. This time it was so close to Emilie's ear that she was half-deafened. She staggered backwards.

Lutin, after a brief startle, was undeterred. He continued

his charge towards the couple and, upon reaching them, fastened his jaws around one of Dartois' legs.

The Marquis yelped, yanking his leg away, and releasing Emilie as he stumbled backwards. The empty gun fell from his shocked hands, clipping the side of the dock and dropping into the water. Two stumbling steps later, the Marquis de Dartois followed suit, Lutin only releasing his leg moments before the Frenchman crashed into the dark, dirty waters of the Thames.

CHAPTER THIRTY-NINE

"Emilie!" Avers cried, reaching her seconds after the Marquis fell over the side of the dock.

Lutin, who had been half-buried in his mistress' skirts, turned on the approaching English Lord and gave him a cursory growl.

"Now, now, you little devil," Avers said gently. "I am just come to make sure your mistress is safe."

Apparently the canine understood him, for Lutin stood down from his guard dog duties, and resumed bundling himself into his mistress in joyful reunion.

Avers, confident the dog would not now bite him, took Emilie by the elbows and found her shaking uncontrollably.

"It's all right, Emilie. You're safe."

She nodded, her eyes darting to the waters, as if she expected her captor to rise out of the grimy depths and take her hostage again. An overwhelming desire flooded through Avers and this time he did not fight it. Drawing her into his arms, he wrapped himself around her, pressing her tightly to himself until her shaking slowly ebbed away.

Splashing sounded.

Emilie flinched.

"It's all right," Avers murmured in her ear. "It's only Wakeford's men. They're pulling Dartois from the water and placing him under arrest."

Emilie buried her head into his chest in response, drawing a ragged breath.

"You're safe now."

He felt her shudder against him, her body tense, and then finally begin to relax. How he had longed for this moment. To feel her secure against him. To know she was no longer in the Comte or Dartois' clutches. Over the last few days he had feared this might never happen. Now here she was, guarded in his arms, and all he had to do was resist the urge to cover her forehead, her cheeks, her lips with kisses.

"Excellent work, John." Wakeford came up beside them just as Dartois was heaved out of the river by two of his men. They dumped the Frenchman, a great sodden mess of clothes and limbs, on the side of the quay.

"He's hit his head on something," said one of the men, examining Dartois' scalp and then placing an ear above the unconscious man's mouth. "But he's breathing."

As if on cue, Dartois wrenched upwards, coughing up water and rolling over onto his side.

"Lord Dartois, you're under arrest by order of the King for acts against the Crown," Wakeford said, coming to stand over the man who shot him a venomous look.

Suddenly, Dartois, who had appeared such an ominous and unknowable figure, was now merely a man. Soaking wet and caught out on St Saviour's dock.

Avers felt Emilie move within his arms and immediately loosened his grip. Her head came up from where it had been resting against his chest and she pulled herself free so she was standing beside him. But Avers did not wholly relinquish his grip from around her waist—not when Dartois was conscious and so nearby.

"Here, Wakeford," Avers said, spying the leather portfolio on the ground and bending to pick it up. "I believe this is what Mademoiselle Cadeaux was retrieving for you when she was kidnapped against her will." He handed the packet to his friend.

Wakeford looked between Avers and Emilie, his stare hard upon them both, as he took the portfolio. He examined the papers and then, satisfied they were those that had been stolen, he looked up again, with a relieved smile on his face.

"A nice tidy story we have then, John. Take him away," he commanded the men standing over Dartois. They hauled the man to his feet and dragged him off down the quay to a waiting carriage.

Wakeford turned back to shake Avers warmly by the hand. "I owe you my reputation and my career after all you have risked on my behalf. And you, Mademoiselle—" He turned to bow towards Emilie. "I thank you for the service you have done for my country. I see now that my friend Avers was not remiss in putting his faith in you. A lady who would risk her life for others is a woman worthy of his affection."

Avers' fingers tightened around Emilie's waist at the overtness of Wakeford's words. He glanced down and saw her colouring.

"Now," Wakeford continued, oblivious to this response to his words, "if you will excuse me—we must run down that ship and try to find out the identity of who Dartois was planning to sell the papers to." He nodded to Avers and bowed towards Emilie. "I trust you will see the lady safely home?"

"You have my word," Avers replied.

Wakeford departed, following the trail of water left by

Dartois visible in the lantern light, and the couple watched after him in a sudden stillness after such a burst of excitement.

"Let me see you," Avers said now they were alone, aside from the servant who stood a little way off waiting for them. Avers coaxed her gently around to stand before him and reached up, hands cupping her cheeks, running over her shoulders and down her arms. "Are you hurt at all? You're trembling. Are you cold?"

"N-no," she stammered, teeth chattering. "It's not th-the cold."

"The shock," Avers said with a nod, his eyes staring deeply into hers. "You are safe now, I promise. Dartois will not hurt you anymore."

She nodded dumbly, but when she felt a little movement in her skirts, she came to life. Remembering Lutin, she bent to pick him up and hold him against her.

"Your little protector." Avers smiled. "I knew you would want to see Lutin as soon as you could. Now come, I must get you out of this night air. If you will allow me, I wish to escort you to my aunt's house. You'll be safe there and we can decide where you will go after that."

He saw a flash of anxiety come into her eyes again and hastened to reassure her. "Have no fear, you will be protected with my aunt. Trust me, no one would dare cross her. You will understand when you meet her."

"What?" Her fine brows puckered. "No, I cannot stay with your aunt. I could not put her in such a position."

It was the most she had spoken since her ordeal so Avers didn't want to argue with her despite the strong feelings urging him to do so. He opted for a more gentle approach.

"Nonsense. My aunt will be delighted at such drama crossing her threshold. You have no idea how she lives for just such intrigue. Oh, do not fear. We will not tell her about your—"

"That is exactly why I cannot go there," Emilie argued, and suddenly the fear and the shock all disappeared, revealing the vehement, strong, independent woman that had both intrigued and frustrated him for weeks in Paris.

"*You*," said Avers forcefully, all jollity gone from his voice, "are a woman of worth. My aunt will be honoured to host you, and I will not leave you alone until you agree to accompany me."

"And *who* am I accompanying?" Emilie asked, looking from the small bundle of fur in her arms up into his eyes.

He felt a stab of guilt.

"John, Lord Avers, third son of my father, with very few prospects, and friend of Wakeford, whose absent cousin I bear a striking resemblance to."

"His Grace, the Duke of Tremaine?" Emilie asked.

"Exactly so."

Avers watched her dark-haired head bob as she took in the truth.

"So, you played a part in order to help your friend?"

"I did." Avers did not try to defend his actions. He had spun a tale for her to believe and now the truth was out. "Please, let me take you to my aunt," he said, the gentle tone unfamiliar in his usually sardonic mouth.

A pucker appeared between her brows as she looked at Lutin's fluffy little head in her arms and then down the dock towards a dark city.

"I have nowhere else to go." Her voice was so small Avers felt an absurdly strong desire to pull her back into his arms and squeeze her tightly against him again.

"Come with me."

She finally took his offered hand and they turned from the site of her salvation and walked towards his waiting carriage. He had persuaded her to stay with his aunt. The latter would derive immense pleasure from the arrangement, he was certain. He must ensure he kept Emilie safe from his aunt's sharp judgements and sharper tongue.

That would settle Emilie for the immediate future, but the longer-term was another matter. Avers' next task would be to persuade Emilie how much he cared about her.

CHAPTER FORTY

When Avers turned up on his aunt's doorstep with a strange woman in tow at gone midnight, it was inevitable he would face a barrage of questions from that relative. They made it to the drawing room, where candles were hastily lit by a bleary-eyed servant, when his aunt descended on them in a swathe of silk and ruffled nightclothes demanding answers. Avers, who was usually inclined to humour his aunt, gave her a curt command to stop, and told her there would be no tale-telling tonight.

"But John, this is scandalous! Who even is she?" Lady Goring's beady eyes bored into Emilie who stood in the middle of the room clutching Lutin in her arms.

"*She*," said Avers in a warning tone, "is Mademoiselle Emilie Cadeaux and under my protection. And you will treat her as such. But for now, we have had an incredibly taxing day, and I need you to take her in."

"That is all very well, but at midnight—"

"Aunt!" Avers snapped. "You are better not knowing. Please trust me on that. I will not tell you all tonight, so please desist."

The Dowager Countess opened her mouth to argue, but Avers gave her a warning look. He was so rarely serious that it had the desired effect on his relative and she gave a reluctant nod.

"I shall call on you in the morning," he said gently, turning to Emilie.

She barely nodded, glancing warily at his aunt.

"I am to play host to that little dog as well?" asked Lady Goring, pointing a finger at Lutin. "Will he not be happier in the stables overnight?"

Whether it was the mention of the stables or the finger pointing, it was unclear, but Lutin's head popped up from where it had been resting on Emilie's arm, and he began growling at Avers' aunt.

The older woman snatched her hand back, a look of abject horror on her face.

"If you will permit me, he will be happy on a blanket at the side of my bed," Emilie said, her voice small and placating.

"I—"

"Yes, aunt. You will permit that for Mademoiselle Cadeaux, will you not?" asked Avers archly.

"I will permit it," Lady Goring replied, her eyes narrowing. "And pray tell, what story am I to give the servants, John?" Her brows rose at her nephew and her beady eyes bored into him. "They have already been in here and seen you both at this unconventional hour."

"That a family friend from outside Paris has arrived to stay with you, aunt. Her parents were dear old friends of yours before they died, and you are lending her countenance while she's here in London—with her little dog," Avers added, the corner of his mouth curving.

The Dowager Countess sniffed. "Well, you clearly have a story already spun." She smoothed the various layers of silk and muslin she was wrapped in and touched a hand to her turban to ensure it was still in place. "And I am to have no more information about a stranger staying in my home?"

"No more information than that Mademoiselle Cadeaux requires shelter, and you are being so gracious as to offer it to her."

She eyed Emilie suspiciously.

"We should perhaps tell Lady Goring the truth," Emilie said, breaking her silence and looking pleadingly at Avers and then back at his aunt.

Concern coursed through Avers. They could not reveal secrets of the Crown, especially not to his aunt, of all people.

"Emilie—"

"Your nephew saved me from a cruel fate," Emilie interrupted in melodramatic accents. "There was a man in Paris..." She trailed off meaningfully and Avers saw the size of his aunt's eyes double. "A cruel man."

Was she... spinning a tale?

"He persuaded me to elope with him, but he broke his promise when he brought me to England and cast me off when I refused to become his mistress."

Avers watched as his aunt drank in every drop of the story which was so artfully close to the truth that it remained believable. He realised, as Emilie leant into the tale, that she had got the measure of his aunt far quicker than he had imagined. She knew exactly what his relative required to be satisfied.

"Your brave nephew has saved me from my fate."

"John!" Lady Goring gasped. "That is why you wished to know who had come to London? You followed this poor girl here to save her?"

If there was something his aunt enjoyed more than gossip, it was the idea of being a virtuous aid to others... and hopefully, being able to tell everyone about it.

"My dear girl," Lady Goring said, coming forward, and

beginning to place an arm around Emilie's shoulders only to retract it when Lutin started growling again.

"I'm sorry," said Emilie. "He's overwrought with everything that has happened."

"And no wonder, my dear, no wonder. He is only protecting his poor mistress. Come, we will draw you a warm bath to ward off this night chill and get you into bed. John, you may call on us in the morning."

Avers bowed as the women passed him. "Good evening, Mademoiselle Cadeaux,"

"Yes, yes, John! Now do go—the poor girl must rest."

Before his aunt could take Emilie away entirely, Avers reached out. His fingertips traced down the length of her arm and her dark eyes flicked up to catch his gaze. Her expression was one of pure gratefulness. Her lips curved into a trembling smile and tears welled in her eyes. Avers' touch grew firmer, pressing her arm, and it took everything within him to stop from pulling her into his arms and kissing away those tears.

"Be gone, John!" his aunt cried again.

He relinquished his touch and saw the veriest hint of humour appear in Emilie's eyes. She would be safe here at last. His aunt would see to that.

CHAPTER FORTY-ONE

Avers returned to his aunt's house in time for breakfast, eager not to leave Emilie to face her ladyship's questioning alone.

"Good morning," he said, upon entering the dining room and bowing to his aunt and her guest.

While Emilie looked tired, Avers was pleased to see some of the shock from yesterday's encounter was no longer present in her face.

"Well—hurry up and sit down, John. We are already eating," said Lady Goring imperiously.

He took his seat and ordered coffee from the waiting servant.

Lady Goring's eyes followed the servant out of the room, and when they were alone again she spoke. "We have already been discussing a suitable story to explain Mademoiselle Cadeaux's visit. I think it would do nicely if she was an orphan from a genteel family outside of Paris—a long-time friend of mine or something—and she has come to stay with me out of charity."

Avers resisted the urge to role his eyes at his relative managing to make herself the hero of this story.

"I sent you, John, to escort her from the Continent so she might make her entrance to London Society under my wing." Lady Goring nodded her head in satisfaction. "That will nicely wrap up your absence from England and Mademoiselle Cadeaux's appearance in London."

"Your machinations are formidable, dear aunt."

Emilie's hands were hugging a cup of steaming tea, lifting to sip it every now and then, while listening to the others. At Avers' words he saw a slight curve appear on her lips.

If Lady Goring noticed her nephew's sarcasm she was not perturbed by it. "The fact that Mademoiselle Cadeaux has already been staying at the French consul's residence in London and attended Lord and Lady Peregrine's ball is a minor inconvenience—but not insurmountable."

His gaze had been lingering on Mademoiselle Cadeaux, tracing every line and curve of her face, wishing they were alone in this room so he might kiss her. At his aunt's words he looked sharply at her.

"And just how do you know those details, dear aunt?"

"I told her," Emilie interjected, placing her teacup back down on the table. "She needed to know all the details to spin a suitable tale to protect me. I am so thankful for her help."

Her sincere words caused Lady Goring to smile, raising her chin, preening at the complimentary words.

"It is the least I can do, my child, after your ordeal."

Avers' mouth dropped open in astonishment. He had never seen his aunt take so quickly to someone and it was clear that she liked Emilie very much indeed if she was so affected by her praise.

"But we must go over your story entirely to ensure my proposed tale is watertight." Lady Goring proceeded to ferret out holes in the tale she was to spread by interrogating both of them. She came up with suitable solutions for any discrepancies and after quarter of an hour, ceased her questioning and considered all the information for several minutes before speaking again. "We must thank God that Lord and Lady Peregrine chose a masquerade for their ball. It will provide sufficient concealment of your identity to refute anyone who tries to counter our story. Good! Now all that is left to do is to send out my informants to spread the story abroad." Lady Goring rose from her chair, having managed to finish her breakfast during her devising, and rang the bell.

Avers got up impulsively and strode over to his aunt, embracing her before she could protest.

"Thank you, aunt," he said quietly at her ear, before releasing her as quickly as he had hugged her.

The older woman, for once, was lost for words. Her thin lips were parted in surprise and there was a softness in her eyes Avers had not seen before.

The expression only lasted a minute. After this, his aunt shook herself, smoothed her skirts and turned to the door just as the servant entered.

Over the next few days Lady Goring's network of spies did an admirable job of spreading the new story of Emilie's appearance in London. Perhaps for the first time they performed a virtuous act by relaying the false story around the backstairs and drawing rooms of London until no one was in any doubt who Mademoiselle Emilie Cadeaux was.

Those who had seen Emilie's face at the French consul's residence before Lord and Lady Peregrine's masquerade, such as the diplomat himself, had no interest in exposing her true story. The infamous tale of a French spy caught in London was now abroad. The last thing anyone with sense would wish to do was inadvertently connect themselves with the Marquis de Dartois by identifying Emilie.

And so, her true origins were sufficiently protected, and

for once, Avers was thankful for his aunt's vociferous gossiping.

In fact, the story of a poor friend from France was so much believed that by the following Thursday, Avers was able to take Emilie for a walk in Hyde Park, with one of his aunt's maids in tow for the sake of propriety.

The day had dawned fine, a gentle breeze clearing the skies and banishing any last vestiges of the dark happenings on St Saviour's dock four days since.

"I see my cousin Sophia's dresses fit you well," said Avers as they walked sedately down the main boulevard of the park.

There were many others taking advantage of the change in the weather. Some tipped their hats to Avers and Emilie. Others simply smiled.

"Yes," replied Emilie. "I've thanked your aunt for them. If it wasn't for your cousin's old dresses I would still be in the same clothes from..."

"I have already sent to Paris for the remainder of your things," said Avers, easily covering over the break in her speech. "We may not be able to retrieve your items from the consul's residence here in London, but at least you might have your other things. It will be easier for you to feel settled while you decide what to do if you have your own possessions around you."

She did not reply, but gave a slight bob of her head in understanding. He wished so very much to cup her cheek and coax her to look at him. To tell her that everything would be all right.

"Your petit diable is enjoying his stroll," Avers said instead, as Lutin made a lunge for a pigeon that had been pecking at the ground close by.

"I think he's felt cooped up," Emilie replied, and then added quickly, "Though your aunt has been very good about him, letting him on the sofas, and feeding him all manner of treats."

Her tone had turned to one of loving affection, and a joyful smile hovered over her lips as she watched her petite companion trotting here and there on the end of his lead.

"I instructed her cook to bake liver biscuits for the little sprite."

Emilie glanced across at him, surprised gratitude in her eyes. "You did? I thanked your aunt for her thoughtfulness."

Avers laughed. "And I expect she accepted the compliment without demure. Devil take her—she is a slippery one, that aunt of mine."

"I should not say it, for she has been very kind to me," Emilie said, looking behind them to check that the maid was out of earshot, and then whispering conspiratorially to Avers. "But she is the greatest gossip I have ever known. I find it hard to comprehend just how much information she has on every individual of consequence in Society. Even the servants."

Avers laughed without restraint, having to stop his stroll and clap a hand to his thigh. "Has it taken you four days to realise that?" he asked, wiping his eyes, a broad grin on his face.

"Non," Emilie replied, shrugging. "Only one. But I have not had the opportunity to tell you until now." She began chuckling, the sound so sweet and refreshing that it made Avers' heart ache. He pressed a hand over hers which rested on his arm, his smile becoming more tender as he looked down at her.

"You handle her very well, you know. I actually think she likes you. The way you ask open questions—she thinks herself in charge of the conversation, with no notion that you're staying relatively silent."

Emilie smiled, her eyes twinkling at him. "She may be a gossip, but she is very fond of you."

Avers only grunted at that. He didn't wish to talk about his aunt. He wished to talk about Emilie. About her future. About his...

"Have you given any thought as to what you wish to do now?"

The question asked now hung between them, and every fibre in his being tensed in anticipation of her response.

"Do?" Emilie asked, puzzlement in her voice, and then she laughed humourlessly. "You say that as if I had choices." Then, apparently aware of the bitter sound of her words, she added, "It is thanks to you I am even here—safe and well. I don't take that for granted."

"I know you don't," Avers said, drawing her to a stop so he could turn to face her. He searched her face and saw so many emotions there. They were spoken by the shape of her mouth, the expression in her eyes and the furrow of her brow—apprehension, fear—he wished to wipe that all away.

Without thinking, he brought up his gloved hand to her cheek and ran a gentle thumb across the smooth skin. He'd forgotten they were in public, that others could see this intimate action, because all he saw before him was her. Emilie. The woman who he had come to care for so very deeply. The woman whose strength and goodness had given him hope for a future he had not expected.

"But what do you want for your future?"

Her brow furrowed and he saw the shining mist of tears gathering in her eyes. He did not want to make her cry.

"What do *you* want?" she asked tentatively, flipping the question back at him, her expression one of nervous hope.

A crease appeared at the corner of his mouth, deepening as his lips curved into a private smile meant just for her.

"You," he said simply.

"Oh." Her mouth formed that perfect, silent exclamation, but instead of happiness in her eyes he saw a rise in anxiety.

"I did not mean to upset you," he said, watching with concern and guilt as tears began to spill down her cheeks. He had been a fool. He shouldn't have answered her so honestly. Perhaps he had misread her feelings and she didn't love him as he had hoped. "Forgive me. I should not be telling you I love you—that I wish to marry you—so soon after all you've been through."

"Marry me?" Emilie's voice asked in shocked accents. "I thought—the Comte—Dartois—they offered me..." She couldn't bring herself to finish that sentence and Avers didn't want her to.

He felt sick to his stomach at what she was implying. That he too was asking her to become his mistress. He was the stupidest man in England. How could he not have foreseen her assumption?

"No, Emilie," he said forcefully. "I offer you my name along with my heart if you will have me."

She made a choking sound, pulling away from him, and starting to wring her hands as her breath came in quick gasps.

"Oh, my darling," he said, still holding one of her hands, as she caught her breath.

"You cannot want me."

It came out in such a small broken voice Avers almost missed it. But as the words sunk in he felt a lance of pain straight through the middle of his chest.

"Cannot *want* you?" he asked incredulously. "Cannot *want* you?" He put his hands on either side of her face, cupping her cheeks, and staring deeply into those soft eyes of hers. "You, Emilie Cadeaux, have given me hope. You have caused me to fall in love again. You have helped me to forgive and to move on. You have shown me what strength of character, and goodness, and beauty, truly is."

Her tears came thicker and faster, coating her cheeks with wetness, making his gloves damp.

"But that is how *I* feel," he said gently—tenderly, "not you, my dear Emilie. You are free to make your own decisions. If you wish to return to Paris I will aid you in any way I can. You do not have to... to..."

"Love you?" she asked, brow creased with concern for him, her eyes now searching his face.

"Yes."

"I am not worthy of a gentleman."

"Oh, my darling." He kissed first her forehead, and then each eyelid, and then hovered over her mouth looking deeply in her eyes. "My sweet Emilie—it is *I* who feel unworthy of *you*. I thought my heart too wounded to live or find love again, but you have renewed it, and with you I see a bright, new future."

She began to smile through her tears. "So do I—" Her voice cracked, but she swallowed, determined to carry on. "With you."

The simple words were all that Avers had hoped to hear. They sent a spark of joy through him. A smile broke out across his mouth and any concern that Emilie did not return his feelings evaporated.

"My darling Emilie," he murmured, his lips now very close to hers. His gaze flicked to them, then to her eyes, and reading there an invitation, he dropped his mouth to hers. Their lips touched, warm and soft, and feelings of pleasure rolled out through his body. He lowered one hand to her waist, pressing on the small of her back, pulling her into him. Their bodies fit together so perfectly and the yearning he had felt to do this for days, weeks, months, was finally satisfied with her in his arms.

"John!"

The couple pulled reluctantly apart, but Avers wouldn't let Emilie go completely, even if they shouldn't have been kissing in such a public place. He turned with vexation to see his aunt, leaning out of her halted landaulet, peering at them with a quizzing glass.

"What *are* you doing, John? In public, no less. The scandal!"

Not content with knowing everyone else's dramas, apparently his relative was determined to create her own, her volume far louder than it needed to be. One person had already stopped to look over.

Instead of answering his aunt, Avers turned back to look down at Emilie, his arm tightening around her waist.

"Marry me, Mademoiselle Cadeaux?" he asked, leaning down to place a roguish kiss under her ear. "Please?"

"Yes," she said, letting out a sigh, and to his delight, he felt her shiver against him.

"John!" Lady Goring cried.

"Can't you see, aunt?" he called over his shoulder. "I'm getting betrothed!"

Satisfied to see the redoubtable lady suitably shocked, her jaw dropping as she thumped back down against her carriage cushions, Avers looked down at the woman in his arms.

Lutin had grown bored with their stationary position and began to pull on his lead, straining this way and that, and causing the leather strap to wrap around their legs and force Emilie and Avers closer together.

"Emilie," Avers murmured, kissing her neck, his breath tickling her skin between ministrations and causing her to shiver again. "Lady Avers." His lips curved into a satisfied smile. "Oh, yes, I like that very much," he said, drawing up to look into her eyes for a moment. "My Lady Avers." And then he lowered his face to kiss her once again.

The End

AUTHOR'S NOTE

Like most of my books, *Duke of Disguise* holds a special place in my heart. Often I write themes into my books—knowingly or unknowingly—that speak to me at different times in my life. The main theme of *Duke of Disguise* is forgiveness.

Unforgiveness is something that can end up binding us up in anger, resentment and bitterness. People unintentionally allow other's actions against them to shape their lives, sometimes for years.

Forgiveness is hard.

Yet, I often think that there is a misunderstanding of what exactly it is in our culture. Oftentimes people think that you forgive when you don't feel so angry towards the other person. When you feel 'okay' about what's happened. If that's the case, some people will never forgive, and I think one of the saddest things I hear is when someone says to me, 'I will never forgive them.'

When people do forgive, they often follow the old adage, 'forgive and forget'. So if they don't feel ready to forget about the wrong, they won't forgive yet.

As someone who believes in Jesus, I believe forgiveness is

very important—and some of the above is not quite right. There will be wrongs that people will do to us in life that will never be 'okay'. Which means, if we follow our culture's thinking, we'd never forgive. But I don't believe you have to feel okay to forgive someone.

Forgiveness is a choice.

You can choose to forgive (I have many times before), and in doing so, you're not saying, 'what you've done is okay'. What you're saying is, 'I'm not your judge, God is, and I'll defer to him.'

Neither does forgiveness require 'forgetting'. After all, if someone repeatedly hurts you, though you may choose to forgive them, to forget would be unwise. Forgetting would lead to you being treated badly again and again. If that person asks for forgiveness and changes their behaviour, then you may allow them to slowly earn back your trust. But if they do not, you put in boundaries to protect yourself from further hurt.

There's been lots of times over my life that I've needed to forgive—it's the same for all of us. And there have been lots of times I've needed to ask for forgiveness too!

While I was writing *Duke of Disguise* I was facing a really painful period in my life where someone hurt me deeply. I knew when this happened, I did not want to become bitter. I also knew that, in order to avoid that, I would have to choose to forgive them. And it wasn't a one time thing, I had to choose to forgive them over and over. I was able to do this not because of my own strength (I'm weak), but because I've been forgiven by Jesus, and in turn I have the strength to forgive.

I chose to write about this action of forgiving in *Duke of Disguise* because I really do believe that our culture has its understanding of forgiveness wrong.

My hero, Avers, has faced heartbreak. He's lost a future he imagined and the certainty of the person he thought he'd share

AUTHOR'S NOTE

it with. The pain has left him with a wound that runs deep and a hurt he can't seem to walk free from.

I wanted Avers to be challenged to forgive in the story. And I wanted him to choose to do it, to show what that looks like in the circumstances of betrayal and hurt.

I hope I've done it justice. And I hope you've been able to see the beauty of what forgiveness can do and the hope that there is beyond it.

So, along with the wit, the glitter, the danger and the drama of this romance, is a depth that I hope blessed you.

REVIEW THIS BOOK

Thank you for reading *Duke of Diguise*.

If you enjoyed it, please share your review on Amazon, BookBub or Goodreads to help other readers find my book.

GLOSSARY

Agamemnon - was a king of Mycenae who commanded the Achaeans during the Trojan War.

Cabinet Noir / Cabinet du Secretes des Postes - a government intelligence-gathering office in France that would intercept correspondence between people, open it, copy it out or read it, and then reseal the letters and send them on to their destination. The Cabinet Noir was real, running from the time of Louis XIII onwards and the idea was to do its work without the recipient knowing their correspondence had been read or interrupting the normal running and timings of the postal service.

Café Procope - this café still exists in Paris to this day. It was originally opened in 1686 by Sicilian chef Procopio Cutò and quickly became a hub of the Parisian artistic and literary community. It attracted many famous individuals from the Enlightenment who came to discuss thoughts and ideas of the day including Rousseau, Condorcet, Voltaire, Diderot, Benjamin Franklin, John Paul Jones and Thomas Jefferson.

GLOSSARY

Comédie-Française - founded in 1680, the Comédie-Française was a merger of two Parisian acting troupes and became a state theatre in France.

Comte - this is the French version of the title Count.

Cravat - usually a strip of linen that was tied around a gentleman's neck, the equivalent of a tie for the 18th century gentleman.

Caron de Beaumarchais - Pierre-Augustin Caron de Beaumarchais (1732-1799) was a French polymath, watchmaker, inventor, playwright, diplomat, spy, arms dealer and financier of the American Revolution.

Duke - the highest hereditary title in the British peerage.

Ennui - a feeling of listlessness and dissatisfaction arising from a lack of occupation or excitement.

Enlightenment - a European intellectual movement of the late 17th and 18th centuries which relooked at traditional understandings of God, nature and humanity through the new lens of reason and rational thought. The Enlightenment was a complex and often contradictory movement of intellectual thought with some streams becoming the bedrock of modern thinking around such subjects as equality both of sex and race, freedom of speech and religious toleration.

Eau de Vie – a concoction of water and brandy sold by street sellers in Paris.

Flintlock pistol - a gun that used a flint striking ignition system.

GLOSSARY

Hérisson - French for hedgehog.

Hôtel - an 18th century town house in Paris, France.

Île de la Cité - is an island in the river Seine in the centre of Paris housing legal and ecclesiastical buildings as well as the Place Dauphine.

Jardin des Tuileries - this was the gardens of the Tuileries Palace, originally built by Queen Catherine de Medici in the 16th century. It was opened to the public in 1667 and was the first royal garden to be so.

Khol - this is a traditional eye cosmetic used to outline the eye. Likely originating in Egypt, it is still used throughout the world today.

Lutin - a type of hobgoblin from French folklore, the equivalent of a brownie, elf, pixie, sprite, imp or fairy. They could be good or mischievous.

Marie-Emilie Maryon de Montanclos – a French journalist, feminist, and playwright (1736-1812). She became editor of the *Journals des Dames* in 1774 where she defended the rights of women to education and independence.

Masquerade – a ball where the attendees where masks and sometimes costumes.

Montmartre - a large hill in Paris home to the white domed church Sacré-Coeur.

On dit - a piece of gossip.

GLOSSARY

Patch - patches, or mouches (French for flies), were false beauty spots usually made from black taffeta or velvet and cut into shapes like hearts or crescents. They were worn on the face, neck or chest to hide imperfections and highlight the whiteness of the skin. They became fashionable in the late 18th century, particularly as a way to hide scars caused by smallpox.

Polite Society - during the 18th century, politeness became an ideology and the way of the higher social classes to distinguish themselves from the rising middle classes. The term Polite Society referred to that high social set.

Roquelaure - a heavy, knee length cloak popular in 18th century France.

Rout - a name for a social gathering or party.

Salon - a French cultural institution of the Enlightenment consisting of a weekly social gathering at the private house of an aristocratic lady, at which social, artistic, and scientific questions of the day were discussed.

Salonnière - a lady who hosted salons.

Simian - relating to an ape or monkey.

Snuffbox - a small decorative box to hold scented and powdered tobacco (snuff).

Smuggler – an individual who smuggled goods into a country illegally in order to avoid import and export taxes. There were extensive smuggling operations between Britain and France during the 18th century as different wars brought about increased excise duties. Smuggled goods weren't limited to alcohol such as brandy but also included other high taxed items such as lace, silk, hair powder and tea.

Sou - a low denomination of French currency in the 18th century made of copper coins.

Southern Department - a department in the English and subsequent British government from 1660 until 1782 which dealt with home and foreign affairs for Southern Europe and the British colonies.

St Saviour's Dock - is an inlet dock on the south bank of the River Thames in London.

Théâtre des Tuileries – a theatre in the Tuileries Palace also known as the Salle des Machines due to its elaborate stage machinery. It was home to the Comédie-Française acting troupe.

Tête-à-tête - a private conversation between two people.

Tragedienne - an actress who specialises and is known for playing tragic roles.

Vieille chèvre – French for old goat.

Water bearer – an individual whose occupation was to fetch water from public wells and fountains in buckets and deliver it to the residences of the wealthy.

WANT TO BE IN THE KNOW?

Be the first to know about freebies, sales and when Philippa's next book releases by signing up to her newsletter.

Sign up below:

philippajanekeyworth.com/newsletter

ALSO BY
PHILIPPA JANE KEYWORTH

LADIES OF WORTH

From the gaming hells of 18th century London to Bath's fashionable Pump Room, the Ladies of Worth series opens up a world of romance, wit and scandal to its readers. With formidable heroines and honourable heroes who match each other wit for wit you'll find yourself falling in love with the Ladies of Worth.

philippajanekeyworth.com/FMT

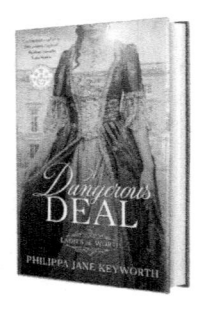

philippajanekeyworth.com/ADD

philippajanekeyworth.com/LOW

philippajanekeyworth.com/DOD

REGENCY ROMANCES

philippajanekeyworth.com/TWR

philippajanekeyworth.com/TUE

FANTASY

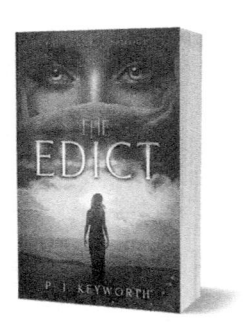

philippajanekeyworth.com/TE

ABOUT THE AUTHOR

Philippa Jane Keyworth, also known as P. J. Keyworth, writes historical romance and fantasy novels you'll want to escape into.

She loves strong heroines, challenging heroes and backdrops that read like you're watching a movie. She creates complex, believable characters you want to get to know and worlds that are as dramatic as they are beautiful.

Keyworth's historical romance novels include Regency and Georgian romances that trace the steps of indomitable heroes and heroines through historic British streets. From London's glittering ballrooms to its dark gaming hells, characters experience the hopes and joys of love while avoiding a coil or two! Travel with them through London, Bath, Cornwall and beyond and you'll find yourself falling in love.

Keyworth's fantasy series The Emrilion Trilogy follows strong love stories and epic adventure. Unveiling a world of nomadic warrior tribes and peaceful forest-dwelling folk, you can explore the hills, deserts and cities of Emrilion and the history that is woven through them. With so many different races in the same kingdom it's become a melting pot of drama and intrigue where the ultimate struggle between good and evil will bring it all to the brink of destruction.

Printed in Great Britain
by Amazon